TAL[illegible]
FR[illegible] A
SMALL
VILLAGE

Graham Warby

ISBN 9798397392181

INTRODUCTION

Have you noticed that the faster the world turns the longer we spend waiting for something to happen? It might be the endless half hour you spend at the bus stop hoping country buses are not simply a folk myth; the two hours you spend desperate to speak to insurers having been told you are number one hundred and thirteenth in the queue; the forty-eight hours you pass begging for the emergency plumber to stop the water dripping from the bedroom ceiling or the decade long wait for a roofer. Well, this book offers something to do with that idle time and it won't be the slightest bit offended if you put it down and come back to it later.

This volume has been harder to write, not least because I wasn't sat there during lockdown with nothing else to do. Don't musicians always say the second album is harder? Or is that the third? At least its existence proves once again that anyone can write.

All the stories are newbies and it's another self-published effort so the cock-ups are all mine. All proceeds will again go to the Family Holiday Association, a charity arranging holidays for kids and families who have never had one. Isn't that a wonderful idea?

Deepest thanks are again due, to brother Ian and friend Jeanie Tognola for all their encouragement, and to my wife Liz for just about everything. The best stories also reflect the influence of those lovely people in the Chipping Norton Creative Writing Group.

Can I also say how much I appreciated the help from Jane Foster whose wonderful cakes (available Freeland Village Hall, first Tuesday morning of the month) so fuel my imagination.

Contents

THE STORY OF MOOSE MUNROE

Moose Munroe was about five feet ten inches tall when he took off his thick steel capped boots, which was mostly on Saturday nights. His hands and feet were large. His nose had been broken more times than his wedding vows and pointed mostly towards his left ear. His mouth was all cut up at one corner too. The line of the scar across the upper lip and lower jaw showed through the growth of beard over his face like a crooked smile. Yeah, that had been one hell of a party all righty and he only wished he could remember at least part of it. A quietly spoken man, Moose had a habit of speaking in long rambling sentences and had trouble retaining people's attention, leastways until he sobered up some.

He was a broad, well-built man. The muscles on his huge forearms rippled and rolled like a ball of fighting Piranhas. His many jagged scars were worn as proud souvenirs of a hard life lived to the full. He stood like a prize bull and no sane man ever walked in front of Moose Munroe. No sane man ever walked behind him either as he had a temper like an outraged war god.

For Moose was a drinker. He was a drinker the way the Mississippi was a river – all over the place when in full flood. There were barmen in Kansas who would see Moose pull into town and take up tiger hunting for a quieter life.

He had a thing for women. He liked them strong willed so he could break them down one little piece at a time. Of course, he preferred it greatly if they belonged to someone else. He once broke up a senator's marriage, a long-term Hollywood romance and a war veterans return home party in one weekend. One scorching glance from those pale blue eyes could burn toast and women were soft as putty in his ursine arms.

He had guts too, and not just the large coiled protuberance bulging out of his generous belly. During the last days of the war, he took on an SS panzer unit single handed for a bet armed only with a walking stick and a hatpin. Those bad boys came in like a line of well-trained puppy dogs. Not that he took prisoners too often. They say once on expedition in Africa he took on a couple of silverback gorillas, had one for breakfast and brought the other one's teeth back as a souvenir necklace for his dog.

For most of all Moose was a hunter. The man would shoot anything that moved, simply on principle. Didn't miss much either. In the wrong mood he would even shoot redwood trees and take a cross section as a trophy. He hated big fish too. Seemed to see them as some kind of threat to navigation. There's a famous picture somewhere of ol' Moose holding up a Great White he took out with just an old pair of braces.

But you can only hunt what you can see and the biggest game in Moose's life was the elephant in the room. I had it as gospel from Moose's Ma that as a boy he would spend hours alone making daisy chains and the only times he would get into trouble was when she caught him with her playing with her make-up.

Moose's Ma was a short, skinny woman. Having Moose was something of an eye opener. She walked kind of funny afterwards and the experiment was never repeated.

The family were real poor. They had to make do with what his Ma could scrape together from her work at the stables, which was mostly second-hand straw.

His Pa was a trapper, a cold man Moose hardly knew, who would keep his damaged squirrel pelts to form the basis of the family's diet. Pa had trouble using a compass and would disappear into the forest for weeks at a time. He always said a good thrashing would solve anything, even toothache. If Moose ever upset him, maybe asking for a plaster when a bear bit him, or getting himself stuck in one of Pa's mantraps, his Pa would clear the fridge and make young Moose sleep in there all hunched up overnight. One time young Moose found a kitten stuck up a tree. He was all set to climb up and rescue the varmint when his dad called him back down. He said it had to find its own way down or stay up there and fulfil its feline destiny. I don't think Moose ever forgot that kitten. I think he was always tryin' to, but he never could. His Ma said it was the only time she ever saw Moose cry.

He had a tough time at school too, and it all changed him. He got beat up a few times and all they did was make him the pencil monitor so he didn't have to go out lunchtimes. It changed the way he put himself around. Ol Moose grew up all grizzly on the outside, but inside I guess he was still as soft and lonely as that ol' kitten.

--/--

After the War things had changed a mite. There weren't so many wild things with teeth and claws to kill, and most of 'em had learnt to run away when they saw Moose. No Nazi's either damn it. Ol Moose sure missed the Nazi's. He said once he wished they had kept a special game reserve just for hunting Nazi's. He was still drinking like a vampire after a long sleep but he was older now and the kind of woman that found a scarred, foul-mouthed drunk with a scratchy beard attractive preferred their men a little younger and just maybe a little less drunk?

About this time Moose heard about a pack of wolves had busted out of the Sierras and were headed for a nearby Seminary. Now Moose didn't give a damn about priests, you couldn't drink 'em or make his kind of love to 'em, but he sure did hate them wolves. All that running about with their tongues hanging out and howling like a bunch of devils that's sat on a hot spike. So Moose fancied facing down this wolf pack mano a mano. But he sure wasn't the only one, every mean hombre in fifty miles was headed out that way.

The Seminary was about five miles north of a little town called El Asquerosa and Moose hightailed it into town whenever he felt like a drink, which was pretty much when he woke up. There was a small bar there. It wasn't much, even the bacteria had died of food poisoning, the tables were dirtier than the underwear in the miner's laundry next door, and the drink was blended with the produce from the antifreeze factory which was the towns main employer. There was a singer there though, name of

Delores. She liked her men imaginative, solvent and at least semi-conscious. Moose often met at least one of her criteria.

On the night it kicked off Moose was looking for a game of Texas Hold'em. He couldn't play, but he liked the pictures on the cards. He'd been there about five minutes and was half way through what he wrongly believed to be his second bottle of Bourbon when his life changed forever. Into the bar walked "Chain Saw" Charlie Jackson, his sidekick Pancho "Piledriver" Pasquito in his familiar gold rhinestone boots, and Charlies little brother Freddie who carried Charlie's signature chain saw. Pancho was short and squat. He had been a cage fighter, at least 'til he chipped a nail, and he was a hard man's hard man. Charlie was tall, lean, and bad for business the way potato blight is bad for fish and chips.

Chainsaw Charlie and Moose hated not just the sight, the smell and the sound of each other, but the very idea of sharing the planet. They had once been rivals in love and it was at Mooses wedding that Chainsaw had carved Moose's face to look like a badly designed jigsaw. Moose could no more remember the experience than Chainsaw could account for waking up with only two fingers on his right hand.

Despite all this aggravation Moose somehow got into a game with Charlie and Pancho. Pretty soon he began to figure they were cheating. Every few rounds Pancho would scratch his jaw. The sound was like a match being lit and Moose noticed that sometimes he scratched with two fingers, sometimes with three, and always straight after a deal.

Moose stood up and looked straight into Pancho's eyes. Pancho stood up and returned the death stare. "Where did you pick up an ugly creep like that?" Queried Moose. Pancho glanced at his friend Charlie. "I was talking to the boots stupid! Hey Pauncho, raise those fingers once more and you'll need surgery to find them"

"Oh yeah?" Pancho raised one lone finger in Moose's face.

Well, that did it. Moose went for Pancho, who slapped him hard. Charlie grabbed Moose from behind in a vice-like grip but Moose hit him with a backwards headbutt he had picked up one night from a principal in the Bolshoi ballet. Moose put Pancho down with a straight right which was holding the bottle of "Bourbon". When he woke up, Pancho was wearing a bar stool. Charlie then pulled a knife only to realise it had been Moose's and he was holding the wrong end.

At this point young Freddie, "Fretsaw Freddie" to his friends, sitting forgotten in a corner, started the chainsaw and Moose spun round to watch his left leg bouncing off the pool table to find shelter in the far corner of the bar.

--/--

When he was finally discharged from the small potting shed behind the Seminary vegetable patch which they used as a hospital, he knew life would be different. For a start he would need a lot less shoes. The damage however was even more extensive than first feared. Two weeks later his old innamorata, Delores from El Asquerosa, announced that Moose's bedroom broomstick was now useful only as a pink doorknocker. The chainsaw had cut to the very core of Moose's being.

He poured all the savings from his stunt work into a private zoo and gathered together as many venomous, carnivorous, horned, sharp-toothed, climbing, crawling and fast-moving animals as possible, added a few cute ones for appearances sake, and began a new career as a depressed alcoholic Zoo keeper.

And that was when I first met 'ol Moose. I had been a lion tamer with Cyrus Cornballs Comedy Circus until the day I bent down in the wrong place, at the wrong time, to tie my shoes. When we met it felt like we both had a sensitive side we didn't much like to share. Moose took me on as a keeper and I like to think I never looked back. Mind you that was pretty much the mistake I made in the first place.

Moose had figured out a way to ferment popular Cola brands and built a still in back of the meat store. We'd sit out there evenings drinkin' when we finished clearing out the big Apes. Sometimes Moose would invite some of the Apes to join us. That was when he would tell me the story of his life. We never got much out of the Apes.

It happened one August morning when the sun was pressing down on us like a great solar steamroller and there wasn't a breath of air. It had been like that for weeks. The penguins had mostly boiled dry and we'd had to shave the polar bears. It just felt like something bad was about to start up. Then it did.

One of the other keepers rushed into the office and told Moose and me one of the Nile Crocodiles had broken out and somehow gotten into the bushbaby enclosure.

Moose spun round and told him we didn't have any Crocodiles called Niles. Then he caught on, grabbed a can of Crocodile repellent and rushed out of the office.

I tried to reason with him. I reminded him the Doctor had said undue stress would aggravate his sinusitis, I told him extra tension was bad for his eczema, and then I told him a one-legged man stood no chance against a hungry full-grown Crocodile.

I'll never forget the look he gave me that August morning. Just made me feel plain ashamed, and then he said "No one is ever gonna say Moose Munroe let a small furry baby animal down twice!"

He had gone before I could tell him Bushbabies were marsupials who lived in trees while Nile Crocodiles kind of crawled around on all fours.

When I reached the enclosure all I could see of Moose was his head poking out oof the Crocodiles mouth. His last words while the Crocodile gagged on him were "tell the Kitten I'm sorry." He took the Crocodile down with him of course. The vet said there were enough toxins in Mooses liver alone to deforest South East Asia.

"Yeah, that was Moose Munroe all right, most stupid man I ever met.

PUNCH AWAKENS

"But why did I have to come too?" There was nothing for Jenny here in the Garden Centre. No one to play with. It was BORING. Just a load of plants, flower pots, fencing, tools, and in this bit, old statues, hundreds of them. She was showing how bored she was by stomping along behind, trailing Mr Bunny by his loose ear. She was walking very slowly so her mum and dad would notice her, but they were picking their way ahead at such an excruciatingly slow pace she actually kept catching them up.

Then she noticed him, a little stone man in a funny costume, with a large hump in his back, wearing a funny hat and clutching a stick. He was a bit over a foot tall with a big nose and a wicked grin on his face. He was creepy, no doubt about it, but he looked as if he knew how to have fun.

"Daddy. Can we buy him please? That funny looking man. Who is he?" She clutched her dad's arm and pointed to the small figure on the low wall.

"Him. Oh, he must be Mr Punch. He used to be very popular. I don't suppose you have seen a Punch and Judy show? Well, they were puppet shows and Mr Punch there had a funny squeaky voice and was always causing trouble. He stole things, sausages mostly, and to say the least, he wasn't very nice to his wife, or to anyone else for that matter. I think that's why you don't hear much about him these days."

"Well could we buy him please. He looks like fun."

"Well, he would be a good size for the new patio, and look there's Judy, his wife, over there, we could put her at the other end of it. They would be like book ends. It wouldn't be right to have Mr Punch without Judy? I think she should be at a safe enough distance down there, don't you?" He asked his wife.

She bent down and looked at the price label hanging from Punch's stick. "That's pretty reasonable. Even the two of them won't exactly break the bank. Why not? Get them, and maybe we can have a look at the roses?"

--/--

Punch woke suddenly. It felt warmer tonight, with a good strong moon. He had no idea how old he was, but he felt the cold keenly these days, especially in his poor old back. His compulsive urge to make mischief, something he seemed to have been born with, was becoming harder and harder to put into action. He rubbed his proboscis and felt the large missing chip. It was the frost that did that, it had been fine only last year. His poor old hump was aching badly tonight as well. Perhaps if he moved around a bit? He stretched round so that his stick made contact with his stony backside and gave it a good scratch. That was a bit better. It always helped.

The truth was that he hadn't felt in good spirits since they left that place with all the statues. He had quite liked it there. There were so many people and animals he could tease and torment. He could move them all around, push the bigger ones over in the mud and hide the small ones. He particularly missed the old lady gnomes, the ones visitors called "Thatcher." He had made their lives a misery by tipping flowerpots over their heads. They hated that. For some reason they were too stiff to move their arms about and had to wait for the staff to discover their plight and retrieve the situation while cursing the visitors they held responsible.

One time he had actually gone a bit too far and rather frightened himself. There was a model heron standing stiffly with its long beak up in the air as if it owned the place. Now one thing that really annoyed Punch was pretentiousness, although that wasn't a word he would have recognised. He felt the heron wouldn't be standing so high and mighty if he gave it a great thwack on its skinny legs. He could imagine it hopping about making a loud squawking noise. Whack!

He was wrong about the squawking noise but right about the bird not standing so proudly. His other victims had been moulded from concrete but the heron had slim wooden legs. The one he hit snapped, and down came the rest of him breaking the other one as well. When the staff found out the next day, they muttered about something called vandalism and talked for the first time about calling in the police. Punch had vague but very unpleasant memories of policemen, and of a place called jail. It was three days before he resumed his pranks.

And now there was just this little garden! Still, the show must go on. Time for a caper or two.

At the other end of the patio Judy was still snoring soundly and, as ever, clutching that ridiculous baby. He couldn't remember ever not having to listen to it bawling its eyes out and making that horrible racket. It must have been born that way. Would it never grow up? Normally he would stride over there and wake them both up with one good whack of his stick. Tee hee, that would shake them up all right! Then the baby would cry and the fun could begin. Except it wasn't so much fun really, not any more. No one was laughing nowadays, and he couldn't be sure why he still did it. He just did. Tonight, though he felt like finding doing something different to do.

Who could he torment? Oh yes, Nome was as ever presiding pompously over the small pond, standing under his big red hat, proudly clutching that stupid fat fish. Who on earth slept standing up clutching a fish? In a rare moment of self-awareness Punch then reflected that he himself slept standing up clutching a stick which he could see might be regarded as equally peculiar. On second thoughts though, who ever heard of anyone using a fish as a weapon? No, sticks were different!

He moved quickly on fired by a sudden inspiration. He skipped over to the vegetable patch, looked around and with effort tugged out a sizeable parsnip. Then, tip toeing quietly over to Nome, he gently teased the fish from his sleeping grasp and replaced it with the parsnip. If Nome ever woke up tonight, he would be mortified to think he had somehow lost it.

"Thath's a cwuel thing to do Mithta Punch!" Squealed a high-pitched voice behind him.

Punch threw up his arm in alarm and dropped the fish into the pond with a loud plop. He spun round. Of course, it was that annoying shrubbery nymph, soppy Sylvia. There she was dancing balletically and half naked around the Azalea clutching her urn and singing to herself about moonbeams.

Punch, irritated by her rebuke now pranced awkwardly towards her in crude mimicry of her delicate movements. "I thee thumbody wanths a nice thtwong thmack fwm my thtick! He mewed hopping from foot to foot. As he approached within thwacking distance Sylvia stopped dancing and froze, her urn held in her right hand above her head, eyes wide in sudden fear and expectation. "Pleath don't hurt me Mithter Punch, you have a nathty temper. I have theen all the nathty beatingth you give Mitheth Punch and I haven't thed a thing! But thtealing thingth fwom Nome when heth athleep, honethtly, thatth the limit!"

Punch clutched his stick closely to him and decided on a different line of attack. He stretched out his free arm and pinched her exposed right nipple hard. "And thath none of your buthineth little girl!"

"Owww!" Sylvia yelped and ran sobbing behind the Azalea, "that really hurths!"

For a split-second Punch felt something unusual. Humiliating soppy Sylvia hadn't made him as happy as he had expected. What was wrong with him these days? He felt maybe he hadn't enjoyed making her cry? He had known she was never going to hit back and besides; this delicate scantily clad innocent made him feel funny somehow in a way that Judy didn't.

He chose as ever not to pursue the thought but to bury it down deep inside himself. Punch is as Punch does tee hee! It was his job to provoke and persecute. What had happened to his trademark wheezy squeak lately? When had he lost it?

He recognised the risk of floating off into another reverie. It happened more and more these days. Why did everyone in the garden have to be holding something? Nome had his fish, soppy Sylvia had her urn, he had his stick and Judy had the baby. Even the mole in the pansy patch who never woke up was clutching a garden hoe? Maybe their makers had realised they would be bored to distraction in this stupid place without something to fiddle with.

The truth was that Punch missed something. He missed his… sausages. It came to him as a revelation. He could, he really could remember having sausages, big juicy ones…he could remember losing them… and battles with a creature…a big fierce creature, a worthy adversary…a crocodile. Now there was someone who just loved being whacked, someone who fought back ferociously time after time. They had had some wonderful battles and people loved watching them. Where was crocodile now when he needed a friend to thwack? He couldn't remember having seen any crocodiles in the statue place either.

He felt a big ache in his chest, a terrible sense of sadness, and the loss of something he couldn't ever get back. At these scattered recollections of his old life something wet fell out of his right eye and ran down his cheek. It often did nowadays. He rubbed it off with his left hand. He had no memory of ever having had a mother but he surely must have done? Didn't everybody have a mother? Even Mr Punch? Whoever she was, he was sure she would have disapproved of the wet stuff. Even Judy didn't do that.

Actually, Judy had cried her eyes out the first time she woke in this strange garden instead of the familiar statue place, and just that once he had dropped his comforting stick, put both arms around her and given her a hug and a pat on the back. Then he had come to his senses and hit her hard across the legs. People didn't expect sentiment from Mr Punch, especially not Judy. The cuddle had given him one of his funny feelings and he didn't know what to do with it. Hitting her made it go away.

As he gazed at her now wondering how long they had been together, why they had teamed up in the first place, and what it might have been like before the baby, Judy was dreaming. It was a strange but very real dream. She and Punch were on a small stage. There were a lot of children below them shouting, pointing and jumping up and down. She and Punch kept rushing on and off the stage. There was laughing. Punch was making that strange squeaking sound and lashing out at everything and everyone around him, including her and the baby. Poor baby. It didn't even have a name. Nobody had thought to give it a name. There was a policeman and a fierce creature that kept snapping at people, but in the dream she felt strangely happy. She felt she belonged, that she was needed and had a place in important events.

For a moment she woke up, the dream still fresh in her memory. Here she was in this lonely little garden. No children around except baby, and no laughter anywhere. She had never liked the bashings of course, that wasn't very nice at all, and she had always had to do her best to protect the baby. She couldn't remember when they had started or what started them. She realised they had always made the children laugh and that the laughter only made Punch worse. Was that why he did it and why he wouldn't stop? It couldn't have been could it, because he was still doing it now, just not as often.

She had a feeling there might once have been a younger, happier Punch but she couldn't quite remember and couldn't be sure. Punch was a fool to himself, she had always been able to see that, but she had never thought of leaving him. She couldn't imagine Mr Punch on his own? He wouldn't be Punch on his own, would he? She wasn't even sure she could leave him if she tried. There was another question somewhere inside her she kept trying to ignore. It was eating at her, had been for ages. Judy didn't want to be awake. She liked dreaming. But was it Mr Punch's baby? Was that why he was so angry? If it wasn't Mr Punch's baby, whose baby was it? She dozed off again.

Punch meanwhile was ready for more trouble. The nasty thinking mood had passed. There was a stone bird by the side of the bird table. Perhaps if he threw stones at it, he could knock it off its perch this time. How would Bird like to wander round with a chip out of its nose, beak, whatever? He could imagine it trying to suck up water from the bird table and the water squirting out again through the side of its nose. People would laugh at that.

Suddenly however there came a long low sound like a deep but happy moan booming out across the garden. "OOOHHMM" It was Buddha up there on the rockery. Punch had strange feelings about him too. What annoyed him most about the big golden statue was that the ridiculous creature never moved. He just sat there with his legs sticking out, feet tucked under his knees, and arms by his sides, hands open on top of his knees as if they should be holding something, his eyes permanently shut and mouth fixed in a look of rapture. He appeared to be deep in a sublime trance, yet still managed somehow to be aware of everything that happened in the garden around him. In truth, Punch was rather frightened of him. There had been Buddha's at the garden centre, some standing and some lying stretched out on the ground. They had all exuded this strange air of quiet untroubled authority and never once, until now, had Punch plucked up the courage to whack one. This made him angry with himself. It was surely his job to trouble authority?

This garden Buddha now exclaimed "if you do not do something about all that repressed anger Mr Punch, I fear you will be reborn as a wasp. You would attain some degree of peace and contentment if you could acknowledge your inner turmoil and make even occasional efforts to befriend people. It is said that the tree that survives the storm is the tree that bends in the wind."

That did it. Repressed anger was just what Mr Punch was all about. He had never asked himself why he was so angry, he just was. That golden goon up there was interfering with his unwanted advice and asking for trouble. Well tonight, he was going to get it, Lord of the rockery or not! But get what? Punch surveyed the garden at length before fixing his attention back on the pond. "Oh yes! Perfect. A nice new hat for Mr Buddha, who wouldn't be able to take it off again without breaking out of that ridiculous smug position at last".

As he approached it the pond reeked of slimy smelly weed which floated across the surface like an old green wig. Buddha would be unable to help himself. Punch had never seen him move and it was even entirely possible that he wasn't capable of movement at all. Imagine him having to sit there for ever with a big stinking lump of pond weed over his silly face. "Oh yes, oh yes!" Extending his stick, Punch scooped up as much weed as possible and carried it carefully over to the rockery. For a moment he considered the crumbling red brick garden wall at the top of the garden immediately behind Buddha. The wall was old, possibly older even than Punch himself and like him, crumbling and flaking in an undignified way. It had slowly bowed forward into the garden over the years so that the top was slightly closer to Buddha than the bottom. Was it safe to climb?

"Honi soit qui mal y pense Mr Punch," intoned the immobile Buddha.

The funny words meant nothing to Punch who had already resolved to risk the ascent. He had to pick his way up the overhang from brick to brick with both hands without of course being able to drop his stick. This took great care for Punch had never been much of a contortionist, and the stretching involved made his hump throb and ache more than ever. Having at length reached a position directly above the statue he excitedly extended his stick, the reeking weed dripping from the end of it. He was about to deposit all of the stinking slimy mass over Buddhas head when he felt his gripping hand slipping as the ancient mortar powdered and the small brick he was clinging to parted company with its ancient fellows.

There was a brief moment of blind panic, and then he fell silently onto the rockery. His head made contact with a large rock. It split from his body and rolled down onto the garden path.

“Told you so” thought the Buddha.

--/--

Jenny woke early, even her subconscious was apparently aware that this was the first day of half term. She peeped sleepily out through her pink and pale blue unicorn curtains at the garden to check the weather and gasped. She leapt off the bed and ran into mummy and daddy’s room without remembering to knock. “Mummy, Daddy, come and look at the garden. Mr Punch has fallen into the rockery and his head has come off!”

Daddy groaned and turned over, submerging deep beneath the duvet. Mummy however sleepily re-assured her: “It must be the mad woman from No 17 again, people round here have had trouble with her before. I’ll phone the police. If she is back collecting garden ornaments again, they will probably have to take her away. Don’t worry darling, Daddy will get another from the garden centre, they were only about £10 each. I’ll take the pieces down to the tip”

GHOSTS?

The three academics were gathered outside the University's Faculty for World Cultural Affairs. It was late on a chilly November day and they stood huddled quite close together continuing a dispute which had raged earlier that day in the common room.

Grainger had believed in ghosts since he was a child. His father had been Irish, born in Cork County, and swore that as a child he knew several people in his village who claimed to have had encounters with them.

"The priest for a start saw them regularly in the churchyard. The woman who lived next door to him claimed she had spoken in the High Street one cold afternoon in February, to an old lady she knew for certain had been carried off with a fever the previous year. A boy in fathers' class had actually watched a boy from a more junior class, who had drowned some years earlier, rise from the small lake by the road out of the village, hold out his hand to him and beckon him to join him. Mind you, father admitted that lad was a lying bastard and was probably trying to wind him up."

"I find", and here Browning paused typically, for effect, "that those who claim to have seen ghosts invariably have some strong personal reason for making that claim".

Grainger interjected "You're saying they are not merely disinterested bystanders?"

Browning glared reproachfully at the interruption and continued. "Attention seeking is the obvious motive for such a fabrication, or perhaps they seek favour with some valued other. Then again there are those who simply relish the ghoulish atmosphere they can conjure up. The claim has even been made for acquisitive purposes, to keep others away from a particular spot or to deter them from pressing a claim to ownership of otherwise valuable property. In the eighteenth century it was a common local code to cover smuggling activity, as in "the headless horseman will be out on the moors tonight". Meaning don't go up there tonight if you don't want to see us at work".

"A shallow oversimplification of a phenomenon found all over the world for thousands of years" tutted Grainger. "Homer tells of ghosts, Celtic history is littered with them, they have them in China, in South America, and India Look here, even Aborigines talk of spirits – and they have surely just about the most isolated culture in the world? Who would they have been trying to impress, and as far as I know, they don't even go in for owning property never mind trying to swindle people out of it?"

"A most virtuous people no doubt, but also one of the most primitive" gloated Browning scenting the gaining of a valuable debating point. "I should hate to base my understanding of mathematics on anything I heard from an aborigine. Have either of you ever seen a spectre? Perhaps a headless horseman or a black monk scampering guiltily around a ruined cloister?"

They shook their heads. Grainger had already admitted that his belief was rooted in family history, popular culture and perhaps a certain plausibility.

Cavendish spoke out for the first time in the debate. "Well, I would love to believe in them, and I do know a number of people who have had spooky experiences.

I suppose the nearest I have ever come to one personally would be the time about twenty years back when my brother and I were being shown an old school which had been used as a hospital during the Civil War. We were in York at the time and had been told that the besieging parliamentarian army had launched an attack one Sunday morning while the Royalists were at prayer, selecting the hospital in the knowledge that it would be poorly defended. Apparently on certain occasions you could still hear the cries of the wounded begging for mercy. I can't claim I heard any such thing myself but I commented to my brother that I could well imagine such a thing in such a place at such a time. I distinctly heard him express a word or two of agreement, but when I turned round, he was at least twenty feet away."

"My case entirely" guffawed Browning. "You heard no more and no less than what you expected to hear. Too easily influenced old friend, always have been".

A note of irritation now entered Grainger's voice "well, as an academic you can hardly disprove something purely by claiming that you personally lack the evidence can you. I could as easily argue the non-existence of tigers on the grounds that I had never been to India or to a Zoo?"

"Ah but its not just **my** lack of evidence, is it?" Wasn't it Houdini who swore to his friend, it may even have been written into in his will, that if there was an afterlife, he would manifest himself to the unfortunate fellow at a certain time and place? If Houdini couldn't wangle himself a spot of haunting surely neither can anyone else?". He raised his jaw scenting victory in the air.

"If there are no ghosts why do the catholic church employ exorcists?"

"Demons and ghosts are not the same thing, and anyway exorcists are surely primarily a kind of psychotherapist?"

"Well then, premonitions. So many examples exist of people who were warned by a spirit of some forthcoming disaster and took highly appropriate avoiding action. It happened with intending passengers on the Titanic and it happens in regard to flights and train services with so many instances of people saying they "listened" and avoided tragedy."

"Wise after the event. Probably couldn't swim and got cold feet anyway," Browning laughed at his own dreadful joke, "or couldn't face up to their own secret fear of flying."

"I suppose" muttered Cavendish "it's true to say that many of us would prefer there to be ghosts. They would make the world a more interesting place, they would be valuable evidence of some kind of life after death, and they would bring us closer to our predecessors. They are also of course, an absolute commercial goldmine. Look at Shakespeare, couldn't keep himself away from them. Hamlet, Macbeth, Richard the Third, ghosts were best sellers in Tudor times. Found them all over the place."

"Cultural constructs in tune with changing times" intoned Browning smugly. "That's the reason one finds so many rustic ghosts in a Victorian Britain that was fast levelling the countryside in the wake of the Industrial Revolution."

"Look, it's getting chilly and dark out here, why don't we go up to my room for a glass of something warming before supper?" queried Grainger.

They entered the buildings imposing foyer. Under its tall, modern and fiercely lit domed ceiling it was cluttered with small groups in eager conversation with the occasional individual striding purposefully across the marbled floor. They crossed to the stairway and Cavendish pressed the button to summon the lift.

--/--

Grainger however proved unwilling to let the ghosting debate lie.

"Have you really never felt yourself to be in some unhallowed place, irrationally terrified, and desperate to be off before you witnessed something otherworldly?"

"Well once I suppose!", Browning replied. Another pause for effect. "Immediately before Brighton played Burnley. It did end up as a nil nil draw as well come to that".

"Oh, ha, ha" sulked Grainger. "Help me with this Cavendish, you must have had that "someone standing on my grave" feeling some time or another?"

"Oh, several times I'm sure, but I'm afraid I have never encountered an actual manifestation during the experience" the doctor apologised.

"Well, this very building is said to be haunted for a start! Some poor guy jumped or fell to his death about ten years ago, they were never entirely sure which it was. He is supposed to have roamed the place ever since warning its occupants of their imminent demise. You see Browning, its not always a case of ghosts haunting isolated backward rural locations. Not always ruined manor houses or windswept crossroads."

"He'd probably been asked to take an anthropology seminar at short notice" snorted Browning. I know I'd jump."

"I'd forgotten about him" said Cavendish thumping the lift button a second time. Didn't old Castle meet him last winter?"

"Well, there was a ruined location if ever there was" chuckled Browning. I don't think anyone would have given good odds of him making it to the Easter Semester? Some Friday nights they say he drank the faculty bar dry almost single handed."

"A tragic loss" insisted Cavendish. "Ah, here we are.

The lift door opened to reveal an elderly attendant in a shabby uniform.

"Third floor please" Cavendish continued, "assuming Grainger's offer is still on?"

"Certainly, dear boy" affirmed the portly professor. "I'll even stand that old philistine behind you a couple of glasses to show I haven't taken any offence. Mind you, he hasn't shaken my faith one bit. You're still on the fence I suppose?"

"Well short of an actual personal encounter, I can't see any reason to move beyond a willingness to believe I'm afraid"

"Look here, for goodness' sake, are we going up, down or standing here for eternity?" Cavendish addressed the attendant who at second glance seemed to be considerably younger than he first appeared.

"Oh, I don't think that has been quite decided yet, do you"? The lift attendants' eyes seemed almost to glow as the overhead light dimmed. As the three colleagues stared at him in concern and astonishment, these seemed to grow, and a strange unpleasant grin lit the sides of his mouth.

Cavendish noticed for the first time the absence of floor numbers in the panel at the side of the door.

I KNOW YOU

"O.K., I'm here now. You said you needed to talk urgently. I've got to say you look terrible, your eyes look hollow, you obviously haven't shaved, and I'm guessing you haven't slept properly for a while? Let me get you a coffee before we start."

Dan, the older of the two queued patiently, ordered two americano's and brought the scalding polystyrene cups back to his brother's table. He was early thirties, overweight and slightly balding, an accountant known as the "Mr Safe and Sound" of the family. At times like these he was just the person Greg needed to have around.

"O.K. What the hell has happened?"

"It…it was two days ago, in Bisborough, on the High Street. I saw this girl Helen…"

"Well done you. I say, its about time you found someone to replace Janet…"

"No, you don't understand. She wasn't there, she couldn't have been, I invented her."

"You what? What on earth are you talking about…"

"I wrote about her. Last month. In a new story I have been planning for some time. There's this boy, Max. He's a struggling artist. His stuff doesn't sell and he's in a bad place. Then he meets her, Helen, at the market where he has been trying to sell his stuff. She is on the veg stall next to his. She makes him laugh, for the first time in ages. He invites her for a drink after the market closes, and she says yes..."

"You're trying to tell me you just saw someone who didn't exist? Someone you made up in your story? Well, I'd say the explanation is simple, wouldn't you? Since she doesn't exist, you didn't in fact see her. You saw someone who looks like the person you were describing in your story? Unless you invented someone with two heads there are bound to be lots of people looking a lot like the people you make up. If anything, its surely the other way round, you see someone you think you would like to write about and then build the character of your fictional person around the person you actually saw? I don't see why there shouldn't be an interchange between them either? You get a half-formed idea in your head about a possible character, see someone looking vaguely similar and then flesh out your original idea based on that actual person?

"No", Greg was insistent. "Typical of you to find a rational, tidy explanation, but I actually saw her. That's not how I work. You know that. I have to have an exact idea of the people I write about, their age, background, appearance, personality, the lot, before I put pen to paper, otherwise I can't develop their story. I can't work out their motivation. Helen is twenty-four. She has lived in Bisborough all her life and helps her parents Tony and Sheila out on their vegetable stall because she has just been fired from a local supermarket job, she was too good for. She's bright but has no idea what she wants to do with her life. That's where Max is going to come in. He has the ambition and the talent, but doesn't believe in himself."

"Oh, she becomes a kind of muse I suppose?"

"Yes, that's it exactly, but he can't make it as a painter. His stuff doesn't sell. He plays guitar pretty well and they make plans to join a band and ...then there's an... she... well, it doesn't matter, I haven't finished the book yet, I haven't quite figured out what happens at the end, there are several possibilities."

"Look. Go. Home. Put your feet up and write nothing for a day or to. Go out somewhere tonight for gods' sake. Enjoy yourself. Its not as if you have to live on the earnings from your next book, is it? Not with a best seller on your C.V. No one could say you're not good at this kind of thing, you're very good, but you push yourself way too hard. Just ease up for a bit, that's all. Late twenties and still living on your own? Do you not sometimes wonder if you are getting a bit too intense for your own good?"

"I know what I saw Dan. She was wearing an old denim jacket, grey tee shirt and jeans with a battered old pair of red shoes. She has hazel eyes and a round face with pageboy haircut and small round white earrings. That's exactly what she's wearing when we first meet her in chapter three. If I could paint, I could paint her exact picture now. There's no way she could be anyone else. What's happening to me?"

Dan had a client appointment in fifteen minutes. It was time to be firm.

"Look Greg, listen to yourself. What you are suggesting is ridiculous. You know it is. Thank heavens you chose to confide in me. Come to that, thank God you are not writing a period costume drama! Go home please, and do not think about this any more for a few days until you can see the funny side. There has to be one once you quit obsessing over this imaginary girl. And please, don't say a word to anyone else. Promise?"

Greg promised nothing, but realising he was wasting his time he gave up, offered to pay for the coffees and giving his brother an affectionate slap of thanks on the back, walked out of the café.

--/--

It was market day. Greg had tried hard for the best part of a week to stop himself from going into Bisborough, but the urge to check was too strong to resist. If the impossible had happened and he had somehow conjured someone who didn't exist into existence then both she and Max could be there at the market. If not, as he now realised had to be the case, he could get over this and get on with his story in relative peace.

He was late leaving as though something inside him was trying to hold him back. Sainsbury's car park was busy too and he had trouble finding a space. By the time he finally jostled his way into the town centre the market square had long since filled up with bargain hunters. The market was set in a large old medieval square now covered with scores of brightly coloured stalls like a giant patchwork quilt. He walked around for a couple of minutes but it was too crowded with people considering last minute purchases to see clearly and the light rain didn't help matters. Soon though the traders' vans were beginning to move back onto the selling areas to clear their goods away. He couldn't see either Helen or Max. At least he assumed he would be able to see Max if he could still find Helen. He would be wearing his thick blue pullover with the jagged holes in the sleeves and a pair of old brown cord trousers as was his habit …and then suddenly there they were, both of them. Helen was sideways on to him, wearing the same denim outfit as before and helping pack crates with the remaining vegetables. Max was facing him, smiling shyly to himself and loading his work into the back of a grey transit van. He was skinny. Greg hadn't realised how skinny he had made him until he saw him standing there. "Yeah, and maybe he would really have to come up with someone a little more distinctive and colourful for at least one of them" he realised.

They must have still been a good fifty yards away as he pressed through the crowd towards them. "What could he possibly say when he reached them?" But that wasn't important. What was important was that they had to exist. They had to be there. They just had to say something. Anything.

A stout middle-aged man in a grey raincoat leaning on a walking stick stopped him and asked for a time check. Greg lifted his wrist only to realise he had come out without his watch. He apologised to the man and stepped carefully round him. To his horror he had lost them. Helen was gone, so was Max, and so was the van. Now he remembered, in the book they **drove** off for a drink…or had he just that second invented that part? No, he was certain, but he hadn't given the pub they went to a name so he couldn't follow them. Idiot!

He felt sick. He was trembling with shock, and a kind of self-disgust. Both of them. He had seen both of them this time, and had stupidly let them go. How could he let that happen? He walked round and round the fast-emptying marketplace although he knew they would not be there, could not be there. Now he might never know for sure who they were…except of course he was certain he knew who they were.

He spent the next hour or so wandering round the centre of Bisborough in the vague hope he might just run into them somewhere, but to no avail.

He went back in most days that next week at different times, but still no sightings. He tried the banks, the supermarkets, the major pubs, nothing. After a while the immediacy of the near encounter left him and he began to wonder again if Dan was right and he had imagined both incidents after all. What could he do? Who could he discuss it with who wouldn't laugh at him? His own brother was barely tolerant the last time they had spoken.

He went back to the work on his p.c. and read the work on his latest book back to himself again and again trying to find some specific reference point, some definite time or specific event or landmark at which he could wait for Helen or Max to appear. Then he had the idea. What if he rewrote Helens pages? What if he created a new incident, one in which he could participate? Perhaps she could meet a friend for coffee in a specific cafe at a stated time and date. He could be there to see her and speak to her. This time he would bring a camera.

It took a major redrafting effort and several weeks work to integrate the coffee meeting properly into the plot he had mapped out earlier but eventually he was satisfied with what he had. For the first time the book was unequivocally set in the present, literally this month. Now she couldn't hide from him in the crowds.

--/--

He arrived at "Bean Time" about four that afternoon, ordered tea and a doughnut, realising it was the first thing he had touched that day, and settled down to wait. It was busy for a Tuesday, mostly with female shoppers going into Bisborough for a few specific items and maybe using the excuse to meet up with old friends? Still, he knew it wasn't busy to the extent that he could possibly miss her. He had parked himself straight opposite the front door so that was impossible. He had removed his camera case and sat with the camera gripped on his lap in his right hand, finger waiting on the button. Time seemed to hang like the last day of a school year or perhaps the wait for a particularly worrying doctor's appointment. The café began to empty again. Then five o clock came and a large lady in a blue smock he took to be the proprietor came over to his table and asked him politely to leave so she could close up. He could see he seemed to be making her nervous. Helen had not appeared and neither had her friend April as prescribed in the book.

He drove reluctantly home and reread the chapter involving the café meeting looking for an omission, an oversight or some ambiguity which might explain her absence but it was all spelt out clearly. Helen and friend were to have been in "Bean Time" that very afternoon.

So, it was all in his head after all!

Except that he knew, just knew, it wasn't. How else could he explain their absences? He could think of just one thing. Whatever had happened had only happened with the first draft. He could perhaps summon people into being but not re-order their lives. Once in existence perhaps he couldn't ever re-write them.

--/--

It was several miserable weeks before he could face going into the town again. He wasn't sure whether he was more afraid of seeing Helen or Max again or of their not being there. It was simply a dilemma he would rather not face at all. He now gazed at his reflection in the supermarket window. His brother would be telling him that he looked more neglected than ever. He certainly hadn't been eating much of late and had started recycling the least tatty of his clothing. Yeah, no question he needed to get a grip…except that all of a sudden, through the grimy shop window, wasn't that Helen, at the checkout on the other side of the store, still in her perennial denim uniform.

He rushed to the entrance and ran across the store gathering furious looks and utterances from the other shoppers as he went. It wasn't easy as Saturday was peak shopping day, and when he got to the far side, he realised he was not one hundred percent sure which queue she had been in.

"What an idiot! Why hadn't he waited for her outside the shop? If he hadn't been in such a panic, it was the obvious course of action. As it was, she was gone. He fought his way out and scanned the high street but knew it was hopeless. She could have gone in either direction or simply entered a shop. When he started checking the shops one by one, she could be out of a different one and on her way home again before he emerged. He had to recognise he was feeling some kind of depression. It felt like every time he even began to put this insanity behind him something happened to trigger it off again. He had to ring Dan again, even at the expense of the inevitable telling off. There was no one else he could possibly speak to.

"Look, I know you think I'm going mad but I saw her again, Helen. Just now, in the supermarket. I've seen her boyfriend Max as well actually. I saw them both together at the market some time back but I keep missing them. I can't begin to get them out of my head when they keep turning up in the street. You'll say it's impossible but I know what I know and I know what I'm seeing. Help me please. Its tearing me apart. Am I going crazy or something?"

Dan stared at the pile of paperwork in front of him. How typical of someone like Dan to require his assistance just when it was least convenient. Still, there was a tone in his brothers voice he found worrying so he put his pen down and gave his brothers conundrum careful thought. His brother's sanity had never been in the slightest question until now, only his leftfield outlook on life, but it was the obvious explanation. He sighed deeply and began to work through the possibilities.

"O.K. Have you been taking something…?"

"You mean drugs, don't you? Nothing except the occasional paracetamol I swear".

"Have you had these kinds of delusional episodes before with other stories? I mean how many other books have you written?"

"Two, both published, and no, it's never happened before".

"Then I doubt it has suddenly become part of your creative process? I fear you have no alternative but to see medical help? A psychiatrist I imagine. There is nothing I can do for you; you must see that? If you could only catch up with these poor people every once in a while, you could arrange for me to talk it through with them and maybe I could establish why, in your head at least, they won't let you alone…"

His ear rang with the sound of the phone slamming loudly down.

--/--

There were some things Greg was not going to compromise on. He could cut Bisborough out of his activities pretty easily in the interests of a quiet life free of disturbing fantasies, because, let's face it, he didn't have trouble with imaginary people in Oxford or Cheltenham – nor in London for that matter which, if he was going seriously screwy, would surely offer far greater temptation. He had however been going to the same family-based Optician for years now and wasn't going to run off to someone else just to avoid…avoid what he still wasn't sure. He would just go straight into town, park and head straight for the Opticians, then home again.

He was nervous just parking the car. This was ridiculous, even his palms were sweating. Whoever these people were, either real or fictional, they meant him no harm…in fact quite the opposite. That of course was what was so frightening!

He saw her even before he reached the Opticians. Helen was standing outside by the roadside and he knew she was waiting for Max just as she was in the book. He tried shouting her name as he swerved past the shoppers and the short man with middle eastern appearance who offered him a “Big Issue”. She looked briefly his way but then turned back to stare across the road and he knew she only had eyes for one person.

She was maybe three feet away from him now, still waiting and he could feel himself hyperventilating. It was now or never. No way he could miss her this time. He moved in front of her to block her view across the street and grabbed her firmly by both shoulders. Suddenly he had no idea what to say. Anything, just make her speak…

“Helen. We haven’t met but it’s me, Greg. I know you. Do you know who I am?”

“Of course, I do.”

“Oh, thank God. Look, you can’t be here, not now. Please, I’m begging you, go to your parent’s house or somewhere. Anywhere but this spot.”

“I can’t visit them, you never said where they live!” Her familiar hazel eyes bored into his, and it hurt.

“Please, get out of my way, I’m waiting for my boyfriend. You know I am”

Again, his chest tightened and he felt almost unable to speak, pushing the words out desperately. “You can’t meet him, can't you see, in the book you get killed. You see him and rush suddenly out across the road. A bus ploughs into you!"

"Get out of my way please, I can see Max…"

Greg pushed her hard back into the middle of the pavement, the force taking him out into the road. He never saw the red bus that he knew was going to hit him with fatal force.

--/--

Dan was in the mortuary having made the necessary identification. The staff had provided him with a cup of tea of extraordinary strength. The police Inspector opposite him was speaking.

"So, he had no reason you know of to take his life, and no enemies you can identify. It has to be just one of those horrible accidents which take place almost daily. I am so sorry sir.

Dan had no intention of alluding to his brothers' bizarre fantasies. It would do neither him, his family or their parents any good now. He hardly heard the Inspectors next words.

"One more thing sir. We had a witness who saw the whole thing from across the street, an old lady. She seems certain that when the incident occurred your brother was talking loudly, possibly even arguing, with a young lady. She was in her twenties, thin, hair cut in a bob and wearing denims. I don't suppose you have any idea who that might have been? Only we have been unable to trace her."

WEDNESDAY'S LETTERS

Olivia Green sat at the old living room table and made herself comfortable. She liked to get everything in its right place before she started writing. Paper, envelopes, pen and spare pen, something to lean on and of course a fresh pot of tea, milk, cup, saucer, and a plate of bourbon biscuits.

She wrote now about once a month on average. There was a time when she had devoted part of every Wednesday afternoon to "dealing with correspondence". It was a habit she had inherited from her mother, though in her day of course there would have been an inkwell and blotter as well. In truth though there were not as many letters that needed writing these days. People had drifted away, or died, and no one seemed to bother with writing the way they used to. It was all these word processors and this new technology. Postcards for example were a dead art form now, though she still kept most of those the children had sent in the first years after they left home. They never wrote now either, though to be fair they still came over to see her from time to time.

She always liked to save up her correspondence until there were enough letters that needed writing for her to make the effort to get properly into the mood for it. A nice sunny day streaming through the window behind her helped considerably. She decided she would start with cousin Barbara.

19 Pancho Villa Gardens

Banbury

Oxon

OX4 2HW

31 March 2021

Dear Barbara,

I just wanted to slip this letter in with the card to express my deep sorrow and condolences at the tragic loss of my dear cousin and your husband Ray. I know he suffered for some weeks after the accident before passing, but of course it could have been so much worse as I understand he never recovered consciousness and so wouldn't have known he was dying. That must have been a great comfort to you. It must also have helped to know it was clear he had jumped a red light, so it couldn't have been anyone else's fault.

His brother David tells me the car was written off as well which must be a great inconvenience, although as I remember the Sierra was quite old and you were probably planning on replacing it anyway? Will you go for one of those new electric cars? They sound like great fun, and so good for the environment although they say you can't get very far in them before they need recharging.

The house must seem so big and empty now you are on your own, and so quiet. As I remember Ray used to snore terribly and had that awful habit of singing to himself all the time (not while he was asleep obviously!). Heaven only knows what he had to be so happy about? At least you will be able to get a decent night's sleep now and have more time for yourself. When my friend Doris lost her husband she moved to a nice bungalow on the south coast, near Hastings, I think. Will you be staying on in the old place or starting again somewhere new? It's a great chance to make a new start you know, maybe meet someone new and less irritating? You are still quite young and anyway, I am told many men prefer an older woman, though of course you will need to do something about that waistline of yours. I think there are specialist shops that can help with that kind of thing. Or you could take up a new hobby, perhaps crosswords, or line dancing?

I've been well enough considering. I got over that nasty cold that just wouldn't shift last Christmas and I have had the bathroom redecorated in beige. Very restful. I got invited to the vicars do next month, though now I have to find someone to take me over there as its quite a long way on foot at my age. It's a shame really you haven't still got the Sierra. Do let me know if you replace it before then.

Was it a bit of a shock to read in the papers that the woman found in the car with him wasn't wearing any knickers, or did you know about the affair? David tells me he was always bragging about her, so I feel sure you must have known. He tells me they discussed moving in together but felt in the end that with all the fuss and expense of a divorce it wasn't really worth it. David met her a number of times and tells me she was quite a looker, and very funny. It sounds as though you would have liked her, although of course she was considerably younger than you.

It's a funny thing sex, isn't it? My Ralf went right off sex when I turned forty. He started going for long walks instead, at least until he got that nasty infection in his thingamabob. He went right off walking after that. I don't know about you but I find I am much better off without some man making demands on me and I think you may have a lot to look forward to living on your own in future. Maybe you should get a cat? I might be able to help there.

I must sign off now, that awful religious woman from the church group is driving over this morning to see if I need anything. She does go on a bit so I usually hide in the loo until she wanders off again.

It was so sunny when I started this letter, but it looks like rain at the moment, so miserable, although of course it would do wonders for the lawn. Of course, I suppose I will need to find someone else to mow it now!

Oh, while I'm on, don't forget cousin Jessica's birthday two weeks on Thursday. I know she hates it when she feels people are forgetting her. I think you can get like that living on your own?

Much love,

Olivia

p.s. Write soon!

There, all done. She wouldn't want Barbara feeling no one was thinking of her. Mind you, that Ray was a terror. He was always offering to help with the lawn and then phoning at the last minute to say he couldn't come over. Perhaps the exhaust on the Sierra was rattling and needed taking to the garage, or there was a glazier coming to fix a broken window, or he had to nip into the office to deal with something urgent.

Somewhere at the back of her mind a light went on and suppress it as she tried, she couldn't help wondering for the first time whether this might all have had something to do with the woman with no knickers?

She wished she had been born with more of a gift for words. Face to face especially she tended to stumble over expressing herself and often got muddled up about what she was trying to say. At least with the written word she could take her time. She could try and think things through, relax, and try to say just what was on her mind, though sometimes Terry said she then said far too much!

Time to reward herself with a cup of tea from the little metal teapot. She had to be careful with this because the lid had a habit of falling off into the cup and splashing everything all over the table. She really ought to get a new one, but somehow that metal pot was part of her writing ritual and she couldn't bear to think of parting with it. It was a comfort of sorts to have your things growing old at the same rate as you were.

After the next letter she decided she would reward herself with a chocolate bourbon.

Now strictly speaking Prue was the daughter of her old friend Hermione who hadn't replied to her letters for some years now, so she probably should have cut her off in retaliation, but Prue was a pretty little thing when she had come to visit as a child and Olivia had always had a soft spot for her. Beatrice down the road had told Olivia the news of Prue's father's death and if, after that first unanswered letter, she could no longer console Hermione, at least she could comfort her daughter.

19 Pancho Villa Gardens

Banbury

Oxon

OX4 2HW

31 March 2021

Dear Prue,

I have suddenly realised I hadn't written to you since you lost your father last month. I was so sorry to hear about that. As you know, Ralf and I knew your mum and dad for ages and there was a time when we were very close. At least, as you were adopted, he wasn't your real father, so it could all have been so much worse for you. You will be all alone in the world now, apart from your mother of course, but you must face the challenges this will bring with courage. At a time like this you must wish you had found someone to marry who could look after you instead of having to share a house with that awful Madeleine person? I know there is a lot more of that kind of thing these days, it's maybe something to do with that global warming or all the hot spicy foreign food people have taken to eating now? At the end of the day though I don't think it's what your parents brought you up to expect and now might be a 0good time to pull your socks up?

Do you know whether your mother is planning to get rid of that little table they had in the snug, or for the old coat stand? If so, could I possibly declare an interest? I would ask her myself but as you know she has been a bit off with me since Dans death, I don't know why. Those things bring back such happy memories of all the times Ralf and I spent with him and Madelaine. I wouldn't want anything else as I don't honestly think I would have room for it.

I've been well considering. I got over that nasty cold that just wouldn't shift last Christmas, the one doctor thought might be flu, and I have had the bathroom redecorated in beige. I find it very restful.

Don't be afraid to ring me if there is anything at all I can do to be of any assistance, although not during the week please as I have a lot of commitments nowadays what with U3A and WI.

Much love,

Olivia

p.s. I really <u>*don't*</u> *like the idea of you sharing with that Madeleine. If you do get her to leave perhaps you could get a nice cat. Not one of those big fluffy ones that leaves a mess on the furniture, just a nice black and white one to curl up with? Rosie next door had kittens and Anita is looking to find homes for them all.*

Olivia signed off the letter and stared vacantly at the living room wall in front of her. Perhaps she really should join the U3A or re-join the W.I.? Oh well, time for that chocolate bourbon. An old song from her childhood had wandered into her head, perhaps Dean Martin or Perry Como. People didn't do ballads any more, they seemed to have gone the same way as postcards. Now she remembered the holidays she and Ralf had spent with Dan and Hermione. Those were the days. Nobody had much money but that hadn't seemed to matter at the time. They had met at a holiday camp in Norfolk and all got on so well together. Maybe Hermione was a bit distant with her even in those days, but Ralf had always been able to make Hermione laugh and it turned out they had a shared interest in bird watching. Well north Norfolk was perfect for that kind of thing.

She sighed deeply. It was time to turn her attention to her children. Not her favourite task as they were so stubborn and, what was the word...intransy something. Her mother had been just the same. She had always found she could trace most of their irritating traits back to her mother.

19 Pancho Villa Gardens

Banbury

Oxon

OX4 2HW

31 March 2021

Dear Terry,

It was so nice to see you last month and just a shame you were not able to sort out my little heating problem. I know you are an accountant not a plumber but I did hope they might have taught you something more useful at school than just all those numbers. Never mind. I won't mention it again, but I still don't agree that it was an unreasonable thing to ask of you. I'm sure your father never needed a ladder to get into the loft!

I haven't had the chance to tell you before but Barbara lost her husband Ray in a car accident recently. He jumped a red light and the car was hit by a large lorry. A terrible business and I feel so sorry for her. Apparently, there was a woman in the car with him he had been having an affair with and I am not entirely sure Barbara knew about it! The papers say she was found without any knickers on. Honestly, if that was me, I would have died of embarrassment.

On reflection, I don't think you have ever met Barbara, her Ray was on my side of the family but even we were never very close although since your father passed, he has been coming over to help with the lawn.

And Terry, no, I haven't been across the road to see the old lady who moved into No 20 last October because the weather has been very severe this winter and the road looks treacherous. There is a lot more traffic about than there was when we moved in and you have to be so careful.

I think it's cruel of you to suggest I can't be bothered to make friends round here. You know U3A and WI don't provide regular transport. I am a poor old lady and I do think perhaps a caring community should be making some efforts to help <u>*me*</u> *out. On that point, no, I do not want one of those damn cats from next door thank you very much, I can't stand the things. What I want is to get into that lovely new home we discussed, the one near you. There would be lots of people to be friends with there.*

Actually, somebody has offered to help at last. I met a very nice man when I looked in at the Book Café last week. He was absolutely charming and very interested in me and my little problems. He is apparently a financial consultant of some kind and we got to talking about my investments. He says he thinks he can help me with them so I was wondering if you could bring them all up to date in some kind of table and post it to me. He is coming round here for coffee next week so I would be grateful if you could see to it by then.

Do you know when you will be coming over here again, only apart from U3A and WI, I have to confirm an appointment with my hairdresser. I am managing to cope with the new cleaner by the way. She's Polish or something, or at least from somewhere in eastern Europe, or maybe it's the Middle East? She's got a funny name, and a very familiar way about her. Her English could do with a bit of brushing up and she smells terribly of garlic. She seems very cheerful although she tends to talk mainly about the weather. She comes on Thursdays so maybe you could avoid coming then?

See you soon, and do be careful driving in all this heavy rain they are predicting.

Yours mum.

p.s. Actually I think you may have met the cleaner?

There, one child down and one to go. Her daughter Theresa had to be handled carefully. At Terry's last Christmas she had invited Olivia over for this year, but Olivia had since met a nice lady at St Thomas's who had said she would be welcome to join them over next Christmas period. They lived in a very nice detached house in Vicarage Road with a huge garden, near the vicar and one of the foremost conservative counsellors. There were two young children and her husband was apparently a successful businessman who travelled widely abroad on business. He himself would not be around next year as he had got himself into some kind of difficulties over his tax affairs which would need sorting out. Christmas was never the same without children and besides, Theresa lived in Manchester and had suggested Olivia could travel over by train. She couldn't remember the last time she had travelled by train and didn't like the idea of sitting there surrounded by strangers.

She was about to start the letter when she heard the slap of the letter box on the front door. Second post! With a trill of "just a minute, I'm coming" aimed at no one in particular she pulled herself to her feet and hobbled off into the hall.

There was nothing much there, only planting or clothes catalogues and adverts for Care Homes. They were originally Terry's idea. He had once said she should try one, said she would meet lots of new people. She had said, "no, I will only meet lots of old people", and there was nothing much worse than watching other people grow old. Lately though she had realised it could be a means to an end. When she pressed him about the home that had opened near him, however, Terry seemed to have suddenly gone off the idea. It was so very quiet now without Ralf. Apart from his music he always seemed to have been on the phone to someone or other, or helping a neighbour out with a problem. She often had no idea who they were. He had been so helpful to that young widow Mrs Glanville when she had that problem with her central heating that took so long to fix. She had been so proud of him. No, it was just a quiet bungalow in a quiet cul de sac in a small traditional village. Mother would have thoroughly approved. Most of her life seemed to have been spent seeking mothers' approval, but she couldn't remember ever getting it?

Back in the living room, she settled back down into the chair and stared across at the bookcase. Every book there was on history, art or travel and they had all been Ralf's purchases. She had never been very good with books, and couldn't remember ever having bought one that wasn't about cookery. Even those she bought mainly to look at the pictures and to fill the shelf in the kitchen. She should probably clear Ralf's books out, but an empty bookcase would look as sad as the empty drinks' cabinet nearby. She sighed and thought again about the letter to Theresa. When this was done, she could pack everything away, settle down to a nice Quiz programme followed by a good Australian soap and the prospect of a comforting microwave dinner, probably shepherd's pie.

19 Pancho Villa Gardens

Banbury

Oxon

OX4 2HW

31 March 2021

Dear Theresa,

I thought I would write to thank you for the lovely flowers you sent me for Mother's Day. It's such a shame they don't last very long these days, isn't it? I don't know what they do with them but it seems you have no sooner trimmed them and put them in water than they start to wilt. Perhaps you bought them in a sale, or in a supermarket? It's never quite the same thing as getting things from a proper florist.

Now about next Christmas.

She put the pen down and thought for a moment. Terry had insisted the Vicarage Road husband had been caught with a suitcase full of cash in a motorboat off the coast of Belgium but she refused to believe a bad man could have such a lovely wife or live in such a nice area with such a big stripy lawn. The papers always got everything mixed up, everyone knew that. No, she was going and that was that.

I am afraid I don't feel I am going to be able to accept your offer. I have thought about it long and hard but frankly dear I am amazed that any daughter of mine could seriously ask her old mum to struggle up to Manchester on her own at any time, never mind at Christmas. I know Simon had to sell the car after he was made redundant but I still feel some other arrangement could have been made regarding my transport, perhaps a kind neighbour? Incidentally what was Simon thinking of letting himself be made redundant during a recession? Your father would have turned in his grave (if we hadn't had him cremated) at the idea of me spending Christmas here on my own, but I shall muddle through somehow.

Best not to let either of them hear any more about the Vicarage Road family. She would ring them first thing Christmas day so they didn't know she was out somewhere, or maybe later on saying she had popped next door to see the kittens and been out when they rang?

Please don't bother to ask Terry to help out, I haven't forgotten the trouble I had at his house last year over the children's presents. I am perfectly well aware that Jemima doesn't like pink and I didn't need reminding, but I don't think its good for children to always get what they want, and besides it was the only colour they had at the church sale. As for the shenanigans over Barry's chess set, I apologised at the time for the missing pieces and I think it was in bad taste for Terry to go on about it in front of the whole family on Christmas day. Sometimes I wonder what I did to deserve a family like this. No, I shall be quite happy here with my own company thank you very much.

Olivia didn't like to finish on a sour note but couldn't really think of anything else to say. Then she remembered the weather.

Hasn't it been awful lately, the weather I mean. I have hardly been able to get out this week and am become dependent on that odd woman from the church driving me everywhere. I do sometimes wonder whether I ought to invite her in for coffee, but I am sure she would be busy with her other good causes.

By the way, I have had the bathroom redecorated in beige and find it very restful.

The garden is looking very sad at present and after Rays death I don't have anyone to help me with it. I suppose I shall just have to wait for one of Terry's visits?

Speak soon,

Mum

The arthritis in Olivia's right wrist was aching badly as she struggled to push her epistles into their envelopes. That was more than enough for today. Was it quiz time yet? She gazed across at the brass carriage clock on the mantlepiece but it had stopped again. She would have to ask Terry to fix it on his next visit.

THURSDAY'S VISITS

Olivia liked to keep things tidy. She always had, even as a girl, when the importance of establishing and maintaining good habits had been repeatedly drilled into her by her mother. She dealt with correspondence on Wednesdays and, as far as possible, she dealt with callers on Thursdays. Today was Thursday.

The Podiatrist when he came was always the first, scheduled for 9.00am on the second Thursday of every month. Olivia had never warmed to Mr Norman who had cold podgy hands and little conversation. She intensely disliked the process of having her poor little feet literally pawed over by an "expert" who muttered to himself as he worked about ingrowing this and corns that while she gazed silently down at the few straggling hairs on his bald bobbing pate and tried to think about something nice. Somehow strands of seaweed on a tide receding down a sandy beach came all too readily to mind.

It was undignified, no doubt about it, but she felt the benefits of his ministrations immediately. Since Ralf died Olivia had acquired a trove of about twenty pairs of outdoor shoes from various catalogues. Few of them fitted and she had started with the Podiatrist in the hope that he could somehow magically re-engineer her feet into a few more. This had not proved possible but she still quietly blessed her maker when the time came to spoon herself back into an old pair of battered slippers.

Happily, however today was the eighth of April and Olivia had had time for a leisurely cup of instant coffee before her encounter with "the cleaner".

She was supposed to arrive at 10.30am but it seemed to Olivia that she was almost invariably late. She had some ridiculous name with too many Z's in it. She had it written down somewhere but never used it because she did not entirely trust it. "The cleaner" seemed cheerful enough, though she spent an awful lot of time talking about the weather, which usually wasn't. Olivia had been told where she hailed from but had forgotten and now feared increasingly that uttering her name out loud, assuming she could ever remember it, might launch her visitor into some disconcerting Islamic rant.

The lady was short and very heavily built, perhaps in her early fifties with thick curly black hair, extravagant eyebrows, and a way of talking to herself while she worked which to Olivia was a clear sign of a lack of commitment. As she had complained to her daughter Theresa, the woman didn't use the hoover properly (she used the nozzle), didn't clean under the beds or furniture, and stank of garlic. Olivia tested her calibre regularly by dropping crumbs on doormats or under dining chairs and once atomised a small crisp around her reclining armchair. The pass rate in her opinion was borderline but she would never have dared to raise her disquiet openly – besides what could she say?

Worse than this however the woman clearly presumed to some degree of friendship, though heaven only knew on what premise. Olivia still thought of her as "the new cleaner" as she wasn't "the old cleaner", though she had been around now for nearly six months. When they met in the hall or doorway, she would ask after Olivia's health and bring her host up to date with the sordid intricacies of her son's latest sexual intrigues. While she had never previously shown the slightest interest in such matters Olivia felt a disquieting curiosity about these which she made only token efforts not to indulge, especially as her visitors limited English meant much was left to the imagination. "He put it where it not supposed to go. She love it!" Somehow, however this exotic intruder could never be induced to show much interest in her new cactus or in the progress of Rosie the cats' kittens, and to be fair, neither could Olivia.

Her worst crime to date however was the affair of the pottery mouse. This beloved if cross-eyed artefact, implausibly yellow with the hind legs of a kangaroo, had been made for Olivia by Terry in his early schooldays. Ever since then it had taken pride of place on the living room mantlepiece. Until that was the day Olivia found it smashed to pieces on the hearth. This was back in the days when Olivia had actually had a role in the WI, before she fell out with the new committee. She could never have proved the breakage was "the cleaner's" responsibility since she had hosted a small WI meeting the previous evening. It was however surely unthinkable that one of her closest friends could have been so careless, or so heartless, as not to mention the accident when it occurred? She had left the fragments back on the mantlepiece for a fortnight in the hope of shaming the woman into a confession, but without success. In the absence of a confession this merely served as further proof that she didn't dust properly!

Olivia's own big mistake, in her opinion, had been the time she had returned early from a church party high on sherry and offered "the cleaner", who in those early days came in the late afternoon, a drop of gin. It had been December and the offer was made as a gesture of seasonal goodwill. Now however this generous act had somehow morphed into the convention that the pair would regularly share a large G & T at the end of her shift. "The cleaner" would somehow squeeze her generous backside into Olivia's favourite reclining armchair, close her eyes and slowly savour her drink while Olivia sat opposite impatient to be rid of her.

Today she would have to be gone, come what may, by 12.00am because this was the day Olivia had her hair done by Suzie in the kitchen.

Suzie (who was invariably on time and in pink) would sweep in on a cloud of cheap hair spray and pungent perfume, go quietly through her setting up procedures, decline Olivia's kind offer of tea or coffee and set too. She would bring priceless intelligence from the furthest flung reaches of the village, tales of infidelity, neighbourly disputation, disreputable behaviour on the part of sundry pets, news of new jobs and redundancies, patio extensions, loft conversions and best of all, ill health.

There was little that so stimulated Olivia's curiosity as much as episodes of serious ill health, especially in people she hardly knew. There was surely no moral conflict involved in considering the health of strangers? She was free to speculate shamelessly on their prospects of recovery or the consequences of their possible deterioration. She was able to interrogate her witness on the prospects of contagion or the possibility that she herself might fall victim to some not dissimilar misfortune.

Death of course, whether coming as a bolt from the blue or at the end of a long and painfully protracted illness, was even more cheering. She, Olivia was still here! She was still in the land of the living, whilst old Mrs Somebody else had thrown in the towel and passed on. This was surely irrefutable proof of the sterling quality of her genes and the steadfast way she had maintained herself, regardless of how many years the deceased had had on her.

Suzie's monthly visits stood therefore at the very pinnacle of Olivia's social calendar. Even her invitation to one of the vicar's "Do's" had been disregarded in the not too far distant past. Terry and Theresa were never allowed to intrude on her sacred audiences, and "men" were never to be allowed on the premises to conduct their noisy rescue missions on any part of the crumbling fabric of her property. Even when Ralf had still been alive, he was expected to be elsewhere, anywhere, on the second Thursday morning of the month and was not allowed back until at least after two, although that seemed never to have been a bone of contention.

--/--

Pink Suzie had gone. Olivia opened a few windows and used the hairdryer to expel Suzie's cloying scent from the dining room. She tidied away the discarded carton of microwaved lamb hotpot, rinsed the empty tin of pineapple chunks that Suzie had helped her to open and finished the warm vinegar and honey she took for her arthritis.

It was nearly time for another of the day's features, the 2.00pm visit from the church visitor to play Scrabble.

She had at first greatly preferred this one, Mrs Walpole over her previous visitor, Mrs Lancaster. Mrs Lancaster, steered in her direction by the lady who often ferried Olivia to and from village activities, had used a lot of very long and obscure words. She didn't seem to notice that Olivia had no idea what they meant and had clearly never heard them applied in everyday life. If she had, it certainly hadn't embarrassed her the way Olivia felt it should have done! She had intimated to Anita next door that she suspected Mrs Lancaster of palming tiles to use when it suited her. Maybe she scooped up a few vowels, or perhaps the "Q" or "Z" when putting the tiles in the bag?

How else to explain the ease with which she deployed this extraordinary vocabulary. No one who could trot out words like zygote, oblate, or cedilla should be allowed to play Scrabble! It wasn't fair! Mind you, Mrs Lancaster had insisted that a cedilla was a kind of speech mark and Olivia knew for sure it was a Spanish dance. Perhaps Mrs Lancaster was not as bright as she thought she was?

Olivia had tried entrapping her with sudden unannounced offers of tea and chocolate bourbons in the hope that she would shame herself by dropping the concealed tiles while accepting refreshment. It had never worked.

She had it was true, exhibited a consistent interest in Olivia's welfare which had given her the chance to pass on some of Suzie's juiciest titbits. She had also been able to pass on her concern about what's-her-name the cleaner's excessive drinking (it wouldn't do for her to have too wide a choice of cleaning opportunities in the village? Anyway, surely Muslims were not allowed to drink? At least not before dark?)

Last month however the new one, Mrs Walpole, about sixty, tall, slender, elegant, with knees that clicked when she sat down, had produced a laminated sheet from her bag claiming it contained a list of all the two letter words allowed for use in Scrabble. This had floored Olivia. Admittedly her visitor intended it to be for their shared use, but it still felt somehow like raising the stakes. It would never be Olivia bringing Qi" or "Zo" to the table, would it? There was also surely a thin line between being helpful when Olivia was stuck for a word, and taking over before she had really given up. Mrs "Two Letter Word" Walpole did not it appeared know where to draw the line!

It seemed as though even Scrabble was no longer what it had been when she had played on Sunday afternoons with her mother. In those days nearly all the words on the table seemed to be in household use, related to one's holidays or to the weather. The truth was that words were in short supply in her parents' house after her sister died. She had sometimes wondered whether the reason her father spent so long in the garden was that he was hoping to find them all. Perhaps this was the reason she had such difficulty now in expressing herself clearly. It seemed she either said too little or too much, and rarely exactly what she was trying to say.

Those difficult childhood days were long gone. The tiles had worn to the colour of old bone and much of the lettering had faded. She had no intention of investing now in a new set.

--/--

All the way through Scrabble Olivia's mind had been focused on her next visitor. Mrs Walpole had won by a landslide and frankly, today, Olivia was glad to see the back of her. One of the problems with relying on church folk for entertainment was that none of them, not Mrs Lancaster, Mrs Walpole or "her driver" as she thought of her, ever had the slightest morsel of gossip. She had far higher hopes of the Vicarage Road lady and at 4.00pm she was expecting the man from the Book Café who had so generously offered to help her sort out her finances. Such a charming man.

She wasn't rich, at least not in her own mind, although Ralf's death had brought her a degree of financial security which she knew many would envy. The man, Mark (he didn't offer his second name), had not been at the Café long. He told her she was lucky to meet him as he was only in the village, on business, for a few weeks. More than the others there, he seemed to take a genuine interest in her and in her health and circumstances. Before long they were discussing the current economic situation. She explained that she didn't follow it much, having never been good with numbers and that she had personally relied in the past on assistance from her son Terry, who "is an accountant you know".

Mark had revealed that he was a financial adviser by trade. When she told him Terry wasn't giving as much attention to her money matters as she felt they deserved, he had kindly offered to come round to help sort out her financial affairs, provided she could gather the paperwork together beforehand. She had then asked Terry to send her a table of all her accounts from his copies, hoping to present Mark with a tidy schedule of notice periods, expiry dates, interest rates etc for his attention. Terry had let her down and she had received nothing from him! Instead, he had phoned back insisting that she deferred their meeting until he was able to attend. She had rung

Mark who regretfully informed her that he would have to fly to Ireland the next day and couldn't postpone. She therefore had to face Mark in a state of complete unpreparedness. This was highly embarrassing as she didn't want her new friend to think she wasn't grateful for his offer of help or that she was going to be wasting his time. It was typical of Terry!

The situation called for the best tea set. Unfortunately, this had been squirreled away at the back of a top shelf in the kitchen since long before Ralf's passing, and Olivia was a little dizzy on chairs these days. Then she remembered the old blue rose pattern China set she had inherited from her mother. It was possible she had never used this, but she knew it was stashed away in a cupboard in the spare room, so as soon as she had ushered Mrs Walpole through the front door, she had dug it out and given it a thorough cleaning.

She prepared a plate of buttered current buns, another of her favourite chocolate bourbons and a fresh pot of tea and settled down to wait for her new friend...

--/--

Mark, in his thirties perhaps, tall with broad shoulders and lovely eyebrows, had arrived promptly. He had treated her to his best, slightly crooked, smile and looked keenly through her tangled paperwork. Their meeting, laced with complements on the antique tea set and the new beige bathroom, had been over more quickly than she had anticipated. It concluded with her signing a cheque for an initial deposit of £2000 to open a new capital account that Mark assured her was an exclusive product only available through selected advisors.

She had only just sat back to review her busy day when the doorbell rang. This was a worry, she was not expecting any more callers and it was now 5.00pm, time for her favourite TV quiz show.

It was Terry.

"Hello mum. Am I still in time? I was hoping to get here earlier but the traffic was impossible. Is that Mark character still here? I'm guessing you decided to see him anyway? Please don't tell me he's gone already?"

"Oh darling. What a nice surprise Come inside and sit down. Why didn't you tell me you were coming?"

"Why do you think?" He's gone, hasn't he? How much did you give him?"

"I don't know what you mean Terry. Mark is a very kind man who has generously devoted his time this afternoon to helping a poor old lady with her money."

"Helping himself **to** her money you mean? Come on, how much did he take you for?"

Olivia opted first for character assassination.

"Why must you always be so nasty about people Terry? Why can't you just accept them for what they are?" pleaded Olivia. "You were just the same about that poor man who came round wanting to sell me one of his paintings, and you said horrible things about the Vicarage Road husband. You're always so suspicious." An uncomfortable feeling was however creeping over her and she had an unwelcome feeling she was blushing.

"And a very good thing it was that I was here when the painting man appeared. The story about the Vicarage Road guy was in the papers. I showed you! You gave this Mark money, didn't you? Don't you realise he saw you coming? Probably you and a lot of other old ladies at the Book Café. He's a con man. It sticks out a mile! Did he show you any authenticating credentials? Who is he supposed to work for?"

"Mark is self-employed dear. I don't see what is so wrong with that!"

"Oh mum" Terry slumped into the nearest armchair staring in horror at the piles of financial paperwork around him. "So was the husband from Vicarage Road! What the hell are we going to do with you?"

Olivia next opted for righteous indignation.

"I keep telling you I can't cope here on my own any more. I get lonely, you know I do. I just need a bit of company now and then. Why do you keep refusing to talk to the people in that nice new home near you?"

Terry sighed and paused before replying. "Because you have absolutely no intention of staying there, have you? We have had this conversation so many times before. You are just about the least "institutional" person I know. The very idea of anyone managing to keep you shut away in a home with its own set of rules, norms and expectations is ridiculous. You won't like the food; you won't like the people and you won't even be happy with the way they look after the garden. You won't like the staff, the cleaners, the décor or the meal times. You probably won't even approve of the place settings or the way they put your clothes away. The only home in which you have ever shown the slightest interest is that one. I'm not stupid mum. Your long-term intention is to force me to take you into our place where you can perch like an old crow in our best armchair and snipe at the way Betty and I run our family. I'm sorry, I didn't mean to put it as bluntly as that but we have been having the same conversation for months. The penny has dropped and I am just not buying it."

"I don't know how you can say such an awful thing! I don't judge people!"

"You don't see it do you? You really do not realise? Honestly, the only people with less capacity for self-reflection than you are vampires!"

There was a heavy and prolonged silence before Olivia gathered up the tea things and took them through to the kitchen.

Terry waited several minutes before following her.

"I'm sorry I said all that, I really am, but...and I didn't mean the bits about the old crow or the vampires, but you can be **really** difficult to live with. You know Theresa says the same thing. Now how much did you give him?"

Olivia now opted for distraction.

"I had that awful cleaner round again this morning. Honestly Terry, the woman drinks like a fish and she only does half a job. I'm sure she is one of those refugees, one of those who sneaked in because of that war."

"Zuzka is Czech. Anita told you that, and she said she cleans for the vicar as well. She does for lot of people round here. She is apparently very popular. Frankly mum you are lucky to have her." He hesitated. "...and Anita says Zuzka only accepts a drink because she doesn't like the idea of you drinking on your own, and neither do I."

"But I don't dear."

"No, because you get her to join in! Do you have a drink every morning?"

"Of course, not dear, well, not every day. Oh well, if she looks after the vicar, I suppose I had better bear with her."

Olivia had been persuaded in early childhood that vicars were gifted with special divine powers on, if not before, confirmation in the same way that policemen were born incorruptible and headmasters were infallible in their judgements.

"And I am not letting you change the subject. How... much... did... you... give... him?"

Olivia, in desperation, attempted flattery.

"Look dear, I know you only have my best interests at heart, and I do appreciate all your efforts, really, I do. No mother could wish for a more devoted son, although you could perhaps help out with the lawn now Ray has gone, but you must allow me to manage my own affairs?"

"Really? (Olivia knew immediately she had made a fatal mistake) I suppose that's why you asked me when dad died, to sort your money out for you? I suppose that is why you asked me to make all those changes and just signed on the dotted lines? Did you give him cash, cheque or credit transfer?"

"Cheque dear, you know I'm not very happy with those transfer things."

"How much?"

Olivia conceded defeat.

"£2000. While you're here do you think you could possibly fix the toilet seat? It's a bit wobbly.""

FRIDAY'S APPOINTMENTS

Friday was going out day. Olivia worked her way through her usual porridge and toast and just had time for coffee before going out to the Day Centre – for coffee. The driver picked her up shortly before 10.00am. He was a chubby red-bearded man who reminded her of Father Christmas and she felt they could have been good friends if it wasn't for that Mrs Wise who he picked up just before her. That woman couldn't have shut her mouth if the bus suddenly filled with wasps! Olivia put on her blue overcoat and collected her umbrella, opening the door just as he approached the house and contenting herself with a gracious smile.

"And how are we this morning Mrs G?" he beamed as he helped her in, and off they went.

--/--

The Day Centre was never quite as warm as she would have kept it and felt slightly damp. That couldn't be good for the biscuits? Or the old people come to that? At some point it had served as a Primary School and it somehow retained that rather formal, functional feel. It was peppermint green, not like someone's nice cosy house and the chairs were not the most comfortable ones she had known. In her opinion, they were not really the kind of thing they should be offering to a poor old lady.

On arrival, Mrs Hardiman, one of the organisers escorted her across the room to where a small lady of very advanced years was curled up in an old brown armchair.

"I'm sure you must know Mrs Hardaker pretty well? She has been living just across the road from you at Number 20 for about six months now, but this is the first time she has been well enough to join us. I'll just get the coffee and leave you two to chat. O.K.?"

Olivia made a rapid appraisal of the interloper. So, this was the new neighbour Terry was so keen to pal her up with? She didn't look much? She had tiny gnarled hands, was covered by a thick grey shawl and had a small head with a rigid array of stiff permed curls like a field newly covered in silage bales. No, she saw nothing to like in the competition, and someone of her obviously considerable age was going to be competition for attention. They always were.

The organiser returned with a tray of coffee and biscuits and left them again. "Custard creams" sniffed Olivia to herself.

"Hello," said the small head. "I have been hoping we would meet for such a long time. You live just across the road from me."

Was this a veiled accusation or just a superfluous observation?

"I do, yes."

"I see you had a visitor yesterday, several in fact?"

What was this? Was Olivia under surveillance now? "Yes, I did."

"You have Zuzka, same as me. She's lovely, isn't she? So cheerful."

"Yes, I suppose she is," said Olivia thinking "if you like that kind of thing." She couldn't help herself. "Perhaps a little too cheerful sometimes!"

"Oh, but she does ever such a good job! And you had that pink lady. Does she come to help with your bath?"

Olivia bristled visibly. "It's not carers uniform you know. I keep myself clean and I do not require the services of a carer! She's actually a hair dresser."

"Ooh. Perhaps you could point her in my direction, it would be more convenient than coming over here."

Olivia had no intention of sharing her primary source of juicy snippets of village gossip with anyone. "She is very popular, I'm not sure she would be able to fit you in, but I'll let her know you're interested."

"And that gentleman visitor? Was he family?"

Really the woman had no shame. It was absolutely none of her business. It was almost as though Olivia had been caught out conducting an illicit affair. It was also not an appointment of which she particularly wished to be reminded, least of all by a nosy neighbour. There would be enough “disclosure” to come later in the day.

“Family yes. I’m sorry, you’ll have to excuse me, I left some washing on the line and its beginning to look like rain.”

With this Olivia, who was perfectly capable of scuttling the five-minute walk to and from the Day Centre strode across to the toilets and let herself out by the back door.

--/--

At 2.00pm Olivia made her way down the cutting at the end of the road and across the high street into the Book Café where she regularly assisted on Friday afternoons. She had thought hard about this appointment. Guilty or not, Mark was not going to be there, he had said he was going to be in Ireland that day, so there was little risk that the nature of yesterday’s meeting would come up in casual conversation. On the other hand, just being there made her feel awkward and uncomfortable, seedy perhaps? In the end she had decided there was a lot to be said for keeping up appearances and the man was after all innocent until proven guilty. That was the law.

As she opened the door, its dark blue paint peeling genteelly in the wind, the old-fashioned bell jingled in the depths of the shop where she could discern three people huddled round a kettle sipping tea from chipped yellow mugs.

There was Mrs Winters the co-ordinator, a rather solemn dark-haired lady in her forties, Dolly Jennings doyenne of the Bowls Club (and pink Suzie's auntie) who spoke rather loudly and had an unfortunate habit of spitting when she spoke, and Mr Carpenter the human skeleton, a charming elderly man. If Mrs Winters hadn't already told her that he was in the early stages of Alzheimer's, Olivia was certain she would have reached her own conclusions.

She had hardly closed the door when Mrs Jennings fairly leapt at her. "Have you heard? About Mark? He's a crook! He's been arrested!" she spluttered as Olivia tried her level best to dodge the spittle.

"This morning. He was arrested this morning. He tried to take money from Mrs Johnson but her daughter Dawn is a policewoman. My niece Suzie, the hairdresser says he has been trying it on with lots of ladies in the village."

Olivia experienced a sudden flood tide of mixed emotions. On the one hand Terry's suspicions appeared justified and she had been taken in by a cheap charlatan, but on the other she was not apparently the only one. Her credulity it seemed was not unusual. She felt vindicated in placing such trust in this plausible stranger.

"Well, I didn't like to say anything before, but I always felt there was something a little too much about the way he came on to people." Olivia confided. "He turned up here posing as a customer and seems to have stayed hanging around to no obvious purpose."

"That's interesting" suggested Mrs Winters, "I always thought the two of you got on so well?"

"Well, we did, I suppose. But I always had my doubts honestly, I did!"

Mrs Winters looked unconvinced. "But wasn't he coming round to see you about money?" she continued in a sceptical tone.

"Well yes" confessed Olivia changing tack. "Yes, he did, yesterday as a matter of fact, but Terry and I smelt a rat when he couldn't produce any plausible credentials. Terry reported him to the police on my behalf, and we are due round there late this afternoon to give a statement. In fact, I just popped in to say I was going to have to leave early today."

Mrs Winters nodded slightly in the manner of a prosecuting counsel unconvinced by a defence witness's testimony.

"Well, I found him charming" offered Mr Carpenter. "We had all sort of little chats about...well, all sorts of things I imagine." His face suggested he was trying desperately to remember something about these encounters but couldn't quite nail it down.

"I hope **you** didn't give him any money?" asked Mrs Winters.

"So do I" muttered the old gentleman ruefully.

"Well, I think it's disgusting Tricking his way into the confidence of a bunch of poor old pensioners. I hope they throw away the key. Tea love?" Mrs Jennings had already half-filled Olivia's cup.

Discretely wiping her cheek Olivia cautioned the assembly with her observation that Mark would not yet have been tried, never mind convicted, and that they should not be rushing to premature conclusions. It seemed however that the topic was not to be so readily filed for future reference.

"They say he's been done for it before!" confided Mrs Jennings turning her enthusiasm, to Olivia's relief, in Mrs Winters direction.

"And how about you Dolly?" asked Mrs Winters "Did he take anything from you?"

Mrs Jennings crumpled visibly in reply. "I was a fool. He was so nice....."

"There, there Mrs Ehm Mrs Ehm. There, there old thing," offered Mr Carpenter giving the sobbing woman a hug and a gentle pat on the back. "All in it together old thing. No harm done."

"No harm? I'm down three thousand quid!" confessed Mrs Jennings. "My Dan isn't talking to me."

Olivia had been wondering how news of Marks arrest had reached Dolly Jenkins so promptly and concluded that Dawn Johnson's mother must have been another of

Suzie's clients. She lived about three doors down from Dolly. She was going to have to watch herself carefully with the exuberant pink one for a few months to come if her financial indiscretion was to remain a family secret.

"Well, if you will excuse me, I really have to meet Terry at the police station."

--/--

It was a small intimate station, scheduled for closure in the wake of a forthcoming amalgamation. In the steamy humidity of the small overheated interview room were Terry, Olivia, Constable Dawn Johnson and Sergeant Dan Griffiths.

Sergeant Griffiths seemed obsessed with the exact wording of the exchange between Mark and Olivia which had immediately preceded the writing of the cheque Terry had arranged to have stopped at first light that day.

"But was it his idea or did you volunteer the deposit? Did he actually ask you for the money?"

"Oh, I don't know" pleaded Olivia. "I have to admit now that its pretty obvious what he was there for. Isn't that enough? If I'd known anyone would have wanted the actual words we used, I would have asked him to record the meeting. I thought it was just a nice confidential chat between friends."

"A friend you hardly knew?" said Terry. "A friend we now know as Miroslav Pavlovic, a thrice convicted conman?"

Olivia stared hopelessly at the floor knowing exactly how other people felt when they said they just wanted it to open up and swallow them whole.

"This kind of white-collar crime is on the increase" stated Dawn Johnson (smugly in Olivia's view). "We are keen to get to grips with it before it gets any worse."

"Well, it's a bit late for that" Olivia chipped in with something of her old spirit.

Both police looked at her with something a little like distain.

"I'm sorry."

"Unfortunately, I don't think we are going to be able to nail him for yesterday afternoon" sighed the Sergeant. "Don't worry Mrs Green, you weren't the only one. We have plenty of other charges to choose between, and at least it means you won't have to go to court."

"I suppose not" reflected Olivia who had actually been very keen on the idea and who had already chosen a suitable outfit.

"He's been at it in all the local villages lately, and he is after all a kind of professional."

Terry looked across at his mother. She was impossible, hopeless. She could hurt people terribly. She was gullible, pompous, a snob, a hypocrite, probably a racist, and certainly manipulative, but she was also shy, frail and vulnerable. She was in many ways a just typical elderly middle Englander. There probably were millions not unlike her, all just as impossible. Thinking back to the stash of hidden letters he had unearthed after his father's death he was still amazed their marriage had lasted as long as it had, but again there were probably far too many out there just like him. It was a good thing for her he couldn't help but love her.

Before she had arrived, he had discussed vulnerable adult status with the police. Should he involve social services on the grounds of the evidence that she was vulnerable in the future to others like Mark. Their advice was that she had probably learnt her lesson and that he should just watch her closely from now on.

Let it go for now.

--/--

Olivia had begged and begged Terry not to mention the "Mark" incident to Theresa. Did she have to know? After all, Theresa wasn't the one that helped her with her investments. In the end she had worn him down, and now here she was back at Wednesday's letter desk, pen in hand facing a pot of freshly brewed tea and a plate of inviting chocolate bourbons.

She had SO much to write about this week. Cousin Barbara and that old gossip cousin David would need to know about the key role she had played in bringing an international swindler to justice. She really hadn't done badly for a poor old lady. Young Prue would want full details and so would Doris. She hadn't actually written to Doris for ages, but this was just the opportunity she needed. Tomorrow she could look forward to swapping details of the case with pink Suzie or she could pop down to Beatrice's. And why after all shouldn't she give Theresa her version of events as long as Terry was going to keep mum? She might even consider going over the road and giving old Mrs Hardaker a little of her time seeing as she was now using the Day Centre.

TO THE POND

The two men rode slowly along the country track, the shorter man always in front, making a point. They passed empty houses, not ruined or burnt out, but merely abandoned. Their gardens and fields were waist deep in sour thistle, brambles and nettles but the little stone walls around them were still in good condition. The war had not so much ended as slowly fizzled out and there had been a gradual reduction in the rural population, especially in these northern royalist parts. Only the stubborn, the stupid and those without choice still tilled the land, which was perfect for the line of work in which the two were highly regarded specialists.

There had been not a hint of breeze all morning. Breathing was almost unpleasant with the stale scorched air singeing the lungs. The grass around them was dead with only the weeds seeming to flourish. It had been like this for weeks.

The two reached a small deserted village by a crossroads. Here they found a simple country church. It too looked lifeless and unused, its only parishioners a couple of mangy black dogs scratching at a fresh grave at the edge of the graveyard. So, there were still people around here somewhere.

The lead rider doffed his tall hat to the dogs, they were after all clearly survivors, and indicated to his colleague that they should take the right hand turning onto the river path. Here they rode more carefully over the uneven ground serenaded by the sound of the river, greatly reduced in volume now but still busy, until they reached the village they were looking for. Here they passed a group of children busily playing with a blindfold...

"North, East, South, West, show me the boy who loves me best". The blindfold was removed to peals of laughter and a chase game ensued.

The shorter man, clearly from his appearance and manner the more senior, watched the children closely as he rode past and on reaching a small limestone manor house pulled out a worn notebook and pencilled an entry before dismounting. The far taller, broader, man behind him was Henry, an elemental giant in black who rarely spoke and then never in more than a whisper. He now took both horses and walked them off towards the village centre in search of lodging for men and horses while the shorter man rapped firmly on the manor door.

--/--

The door was opened by a maidservant and, as they were expected, they were shown straight through.

Sir John Harrington was an old man, his white hair thin on top but his cool blue eyes as piercing and clear as ever they had been when he was a youth. He was plainly exasperated by his visitor.

"But there **are** no witches".

Atonement Watkins, Witchfinder, sat himself opposite, by the empty fireplace. He was portly with poor greasy skin and looked as though the foul nature of his work had insinuated its way into him. Watkins had a terrible reputation. A thin voice as sharp as a scythe, cold grey eyes as searching as a raven's and a long pale gaunt face. He looked as ungovernable as the fells around them. He had rooted out some thirty alleged evildoers this past year alone. For now, he took his time sipping his wine, put the goblet back on the rough oak table and said slowly, quietly and deliberately "the late kings father believed there were witches. He believed he was the victim of a great witch conspiracy some years ago. They tried to drown him. He wrote about it ... in... his... book. Are you perhaps suggesting we have been so effective we have wiped out this foul sisterhood? Sadly, I doubt it?" He returned Sir Johns piercing stare.

Sir Johns children, a lively brood, had enjoyed a surprisingly liberal upbringing for these wild upland parts and had been raised to play with the village children in the meadows along the river. "This man is perhaps suggesting my children have played with the children of witches" he thought. "Certainly, he proposes that they have grown up with witches around them. He presents a real danger, if not to my own family, then to my community and yet there is nothing I can do to prevent his vile practices."

Watkins coughed theatrically "Need I add that Parliament also believes in witches which is why I am here?"

"Then surely there is far more scope for devilry in all these filthy new towns where no one knows their neighbour than in these beautiful parts where good god-fearing folk have lived in the same small communities for generations?"

"You clearly think so, but Parliament seems more concerned with the goings on in these isolated, backward and - formerly royalist places. Now why do you think that might be Sir John?"

Sir John sighed and spoke again "well what exactly are your requirements?"

"A room to interview witnesses, a small, preferably dark room to hold suspects and a small room for ...interrogation. My interest here is in Martha and Mary Goodhew. I have heard stories about their activities. We will be staying in the Inn. I wouldn't want to put you to any trouble!"

Sir John rose to indicate the meeting was over and added without looking at his visitor, "I'll make the necessary arrangements."

In the hall, having showed the Witchfinder from the house, he called a servant to him, gave him his instructions and as he turned to leave, called him back and added "inform Mary Goodhew and her aunt Martha that they should expect to be called to answer his questions and should on no account leave the village"

He went then up the creaking stairs and knocked enquiringly on his wife's door. She responded encouraging him to enter where he found her dressing her hair in the mirror. "How did it go?"

"He clearly means to find witches from among our number and has singled out the Goodhew's. I do not see how I can stop him."

"Well then, he carries the authority of the Parliament. Mind yourself John. Do not attempt to stand in his way. Accept what must be done and see him on his way as soon as possible."

"But it is he who brings evil into our village damn him! I never thought to see times like these."

--/--

Had Mary Goodhew been of more comely appearance she would, beyond doubt, have been married with a brood of healthy children before now. Instead, the tall overweight girl in her mid-twenties with the cast in her right eye and the lively sense of humour had found employment in the Red Cow. It was from there that Atonement Watkins asked that she be brought to the manor.

"Your pardon sir, but I see no harm in it? 'Tis but a harmless jest."

"Harmless?" Watkins let the word hang in the air like a bad smell. "I understand you sell small crosses of rowan wood bound with red thread to protect against the plague."

"Why then sir I do but protect against the devil?"

"The plague is part of the Apocalypse brought by God to punish the wrongs of man. You defy Gods will!"

"She laughed again. "But they don't work sir. It would surely take more than a piece of stick and ribbon to protect against the plague? If I am guilty of anything Sir, I am surely guilty of taking money from foolish country folk to feed myself. I am alone sir; I have no protector."

"Oh, but you do! I put it to your witch that your protector is none other than Beelzebub Lord of Flies. There are other charges. I understand your aunt Martha has fled the village?"

Mary hesitated for the first time. "I am not accountable for my aunts' actions sire. I am also unaware that she has done anything to be afraid of."

"I have been told there has been no rain to speak of these past months? I understand the crops hereabouts have failed in the light of this drought. Had your people not lived by the side of this river you would likely all have starved? There are those who hold that this can only be the work of the Devil."

"Then surely, they are fool's sir?"

"I wonder. How long has your aunt lived with you here in the inn? A little over a year I am told? This out of the way community must have few visitors? Why did she come here? What had she done that made it necessary for her to leave her last village? Was it perhaps your Aunt Martha who caused the drought? There are those who say that it was."

"There may be those she has offended, she has a sharp tongue, but my aunt must speak for herself – if you find her."

Watkins seemed to find this amusing but continued "Yes, of course, but let us return to your own sins. You made love potions and sold these even beyond the village!".

"They don't work either sir unless they give a bashful person a little bit more courage. I see no harm in that?"

"Even now you see no harm in the devil's work!" Watkins reached behind him for a small wooden box. "These will find you out!".

The box was old and worn. It radiated evil.

"We shall seek out the devil's mark. My man Henry will prick you. He will seek the Devils mark and we will find the place where he is fond to suckle on your blood."

He leaned forward and whispered into her ear "You know, when I found Henry, he was working in a Bradford slaughterhouse. He enjoyed that work almost as much as he enjoys working for me"

He smirked and opened the box in her face to reveal over a dozen slim iron pins about three inches in length.

"We will prick you all over and when we find a place dead of all sensation, we shall have you as a witch!"

--/--

"She was also guilty of Catoptromancy. We found a scrying mirror in her room."

Sir John and Atonement Watkins were back in the parlour at the manor.

"So, the girl owned a mirror? What young woman does not own a mirror? Why should that come as any surprise?"

"She is not of comely appearance; I do not see vanity as the likely root of her behaviour!"

Watkins paused and stared closely into Sir Johns eyes. "Despite my strict instruction you warned her aunt Martha Goodhew to leave the village."

Sir John sighed deeply. "I had her told that she would be required for questioning and should **not** leave the village, that's hardly the same thing?"

"It's exactly the same thing, and it had the effect I believe you intended?" Watkins sneered. "She fled, but to no effect. We are not amateurs Sir John. We have our methods and one of them is to advertise the names of our suspects when we enter a village. When they run, we have evidence the magistrates will accept that they must have had something to fear. I had Henry watch her and she is at this moment in your barn awaiting our questions." He leaned back and grinned triumphantly.

"And doubtless if they stay you would argue that only a woman who believed she had the Devil behind her would dare face you?"

"That would surely be the logical conclusion? Where does it come from John Harrington, this easy air of defiant authority? Centuries ago, some forgotten ancestor was given the land you farm today and the unlettered peasants of the time simply accepted him as their lord and master. From that day to this the Harrington word has been law around here." He laughed again. "What a wonderful life!" His eyes suddenly blazed. "I was born and raised in Bradford. You know what the royalists did to Bradford? My authority comes from my own gifts, my own powers, ... and of course from Parliament."

Sir John nodded "For now. And its Sir John to you."

Watkins paused dramatically before continuing and raised his index finger. "As I first entered the village, I noted children playing along the riverside. They were using a blindfold and seeking to divine the future. Were your children perhaps among their number?"

Sir John rose suddenly and moved to the window. "For the love of God man, it's just a game they play. Anyone in the village...all of the village children..." He realised where his words were leading Watkins and saying no more, turned to face him.

"Very well then. I shall be ready for my presentation to your magistrates by Thursday morning. I shall expect them to be here and that the necessary arrangements will have been made for the burnings by then."

"Before they have even heard your evidence? I'm sorry, even before you have gathered all your evidence?" He paused but was lost for words. "Oh, very well. I will make the necessary arrangements."

--/--

By the time Henry had packed their possessions and followed his master out onto the York Road their work there was done and the last globules of fat were skipping over the last fragments of burnt wood. The searing heat around him however continued.

--/--

Mother Bellingham had lived by her village all her life. Certainly no one could remember her not being there because as far as anyone could reckon, she was its oldest inhabitant. Time was she had also been seen as one of the most important, handing out herbal cures, potions and poultices. Some had seen the reassuring and calming influence she could bring to a crisis on a farm or within a family as an even more important function, but those days were over now.

Since the war nothing was ever held to have happened by chance. In times of fear and shortage everything had to have a ready explanation. If a lamb was stillborn or cows gave no milk, folk looked for a supernatural cause. If a child drowned playing by the river it stood to reason, she had been pulled under by old Jennie Greenteeth the Water Hag!

Mother Bellingham with her bent back, distant milky blue eyes, twisted hands and untidy turban of iron-grey hair, lived in a shallow cave, strictly a fissure, in a scarp slope on Cold Fell. The reassuring smoke rising from her fire could still be seen down in the village, but now few would take the short walk to seek her intervention, and none of them openly. She had never charged for her work, but was happy to accept milk, honey, a roughly woven blanket or a basket of vegetables all of which she could more or less do without, but her heart was troubled. As she worked below her cave gathering the few shrunken ramsons that had struggled into life in the shadow by the stream she thought of the witchfinder she knew had recently taken residence in the village. She had felt almost excluded from the village of late and now felt vulnerable as never before. Atonement Watkins and his man Henry were said to be in a foul mood. Three sisters in their last village had escaped them. They were clearly aware that their success rested in part on the fear they generated and that this would not survive repeated setbacks. They were said to be bent on revenge.

Jane Furnell had warned her. "Best run." Mistress Hanson had let rats into her corn store and told the Witchfinder Mother Bellingham had threatened her with starvation when she hadn't paid for posies placed under her pillow to ensure fertility. It was that or face her husband's strap for her foolishness. Farmer Judd told of seeing dancing by moonlight on his return from the "Green Man", though everyone knew him for a drunkard. But she could not run. She could barely walk and was bonded to these hillsides as surely as their sturdy sheep.

…And here they came, four of them, as though her broken frame could offer any resistance.

--/--

She was held in a broken-down barn by the side of the church for two days while Watkins tried to trick her with his questions, and when that failed, to break her will, he deployed hot irons, but she had always had to be tougher than most. So, when even this failed, he turned to Henry and purred. "Enough of this. We'll duck her. If she lives, we burn her, if she drowns, she's innocent - but there's no comeback." He raised thick black eyebrows quizzically.

Henry growled his reply "six feet left in the middle. It's enough".

"One last question" continued Watkins, "why do they call you mother? You have no children."

Mother Bellingham struggled to speak through bleeding lips, "I am mother to my community. I watch over them as a mother does her children. I comfort and heal. I have given my life to them."

Watkins laughed. "Well, your work here has certainly cost you your life if that is what you mean!"

Mother Bellingham stared deeply into his eyes and whispered, "you represent a new kind of evil. Cheats and liars cannot prosper in a small village like this. Those without means cannot cheat and liars are seen by all for what they are. You're town born from some dark grubby place where you can hide your true nature, but it's not hidden here."

"Oh, is that so? Well then. It's a guinea either way for us. Richer pickings await down Scarborough way, I hear word of an entire coven awaiting our attentions." He ducked through the sagging doorway out into the heat and addressed the small but expectant crowd "To the Pond! Test the witch!"

"Test the Witch. Test the Witch. "To the pond with the Witch" they bayed as she was half dragged and half carried by Henry and two of the village elders some fifty yards to the duckpond. A posse of local children threw stones and a couple of the younger women, one who had given birth at Mother Bellingham's hands, to a child with nine fingers, and one who had never conceived at all, came close and spat in her face. "Witch! You'll burn for your sins soon enough!"

As rough hands pulled her onto the ducking stool Mother Bellingham whispered softly into the cool air above her "Tis time to leave Grimalkin. Master will take care of me whether I drown or burn, though I'd sooner not burn for their pleasure. I'll see you soon enough."

Under the thick lengths of tousled hair her imp gave her leathery scalp one last suck of acknowledgement and, transforming into a small brown moth was away unseen into the fading light of early evening.

As Henry spun the stool out into the pond Mother Bellingham screeched her curse into the smirking face of Atonement Watkins. "From this day hence, Hellfire will burn in your brow whenever you come to the presence of water. You will die in torment, and pay in full for the lives you have ruined. Your man Henry will die by iron. There will be much blood."

Watkins looked at his servant, remembered the clumsy way he sharpened his knives and laughed lightly. He was utterly convinced in his head and in his heart that there were no such things as witches. The popular belief in their presence was however an extremely lucrative source of income for a man with his skills. He was really very good at this game. He knew he could turn children against their own mothers if necessary. Today had however been a long day. He felt weary now, and he was developing a murderous headache.

TROUBLE IN PARADISE

"What, but that's impossible. You can't be talking about our Dreadlor?"

"Yes"

"Dreadlor, the Terrible, Keeper of the Silver Sword and Holder of the Sacred Spear?"

"That one!"

"The God of War, Carnage and Devastation?"

"The very same"

"Says he's done what…says he's become a… pacifist?"

"That's what he told me."

"Well, you had better sit down and tell me very gently how that happened. You, a stool for messenger Cefaboko at once" said Uno switching his attention and clicking his fingers at a passing minion.

Uno, Father of the Gods was a huge man (his mother was reputed to have been half giant), with a waist long thick grey beard and a booming voice that could topple mountains when he was having a good day. He was draped over an enormous couch wearing a brilliant white toga like outfit showing off his oak-like thighs. Revealing togas had been quite the thing since the recent social call by Vulcan the roman fire god.

Cefaboko, Messenger of the Gods sat down, poured himself a goblet of ambrosia and proceeded cautiously, to explain how the God of War, Carnage and Devastation had come to declare himself a pacifist.

"You remember Smitus the Terminator, hero of the last war against the Hittites? He who stood alone against thirty men armed only with a broken stick…"

"I do. About the only hero we had as I remember. We were absolute rubbish."

"Well, anyway, after we surrendered, he joined the siege of Term great city of the …"

"I know perfectly well who lived in Term thank you!"…"and endured untold hardship, suffering great wounds in daily combat against great odds for ten hard years" …

" Yes, you told me all that at the time…"

…"and after the sacking of Term he swore a solemn vow over the dead Termite kings head to go on a quest to find and recover the great golden tooth of Denticus which once was ours".

…"and?"

"He found it."

"He found it?"

"Yes".

"Considering I employ you as a messenger, no, **the** Messenger, getting information out of you is like sometimes like trying to get a funny story out of Grumpious the Mirthless".

"Well Boss, if you will please only let me finish, as you know, the golden tooth is said to bestow great wisdom on whoever possesses it, and it seems that as soon as he acquired it he had what you might call a "Road to Damascus" moment. He said he had seen and wrought great slaughter and destruction over the years in battles, sieges and on his travels, and now found it all utterly pointless. In fact, he said warfare was unnecessary and disgusting! He has applied to become a high priest of Barbie, Goddess of Wisdom."

"Not one of my finest appointments that one, let's just hope he takes his tooth with him. Oh, and by the way we don't use the phrase "Road to Damascus" round here thank you very much. Smitus has long been considered one of our greatest fighters. What did Dreadlor do about it? I mean he must have realised it was the job of the God of War etc to talk him out of it?"

"He invited him over for a little chat. They were together for two days fed only on the raw flesh of the wild boar and the blood of savage wolves killed and prepared by Dreadlor's personal bodyguards. When they emerged Dreadlor announced that he too was now a pacifist. Oh, by the way he sent you this box."

"Open it!"

Cefaboko did as he was commanded and opened the large heavy box. Inside was a big sharp looking shiny sword and a broken spear.

“I think”, Uno boomed “we have a problem!”.

--/--

Uno was reclining on his enormous couch sharing an amphora of ambrosia with his wife Diaphronite. She had been an early advocate for the adoption of short tunics amongst the gods and goddesses. This was unsurprising as they suited her voluptuous figure and long sculpted legs to perfection. The legs in question were currently wrapped around him like a pair of sinuous snakes tightening their hold.

“I tried dear heart; I really did” complained Uno. “I got Cefaboko to send Dreadlor to me straight away. I reminded him of his past triumphs, praised his martial talents and his great slaying abilities but he said he didn’t want to go around slaughtering the ungodly, wielding the Silver Sword or brandishing the Sacred Spear in battle against our enemies any more. Frankly I don’t think that canning we took from the Hittites did much for his confidence. I reminded him that everyone loses to the Hittites and he shouldn’t be taking it personally. I told him Smitus was a fool who had been hit on the head far too often, but he pointed out that as the current proud owner of a golden Tooth of Wisdom, he was probably the least foolish person in the country right now. I couldn’t argue with that! He wants out. Either a new role or to be cast down to earth to take his chances as a mortal. Honestly, you never hear about Jupiter having problems like this? Any ideas?"

"Poor darling, let me sooth your brow. Let me oil your body. A few hours in the company of myself and perhaps a couple of my loveliest priestesses and you will feel so much better!"

"For heaven's sake Diaphronite, can you never think about anything but sex?" exclaimed Uno to his lovely wife.

"Darling, that's my job remember? Goddess of Love and Carnal Passion. If you want other ideas from me, you should have given me Barbie's job."

"I'm sorry dear, you're quite right but frankly I don't expect much help from that quarter. That's not our only problem either. Cefaboko now tells me Plentia, Goddess of Abundance seems inadvertently to have conjured up a famine, a great big hungry one. He tells me our people "lie in great numbers in woods and fields with swollen bellies close unto death, crying out to the Gods for bread to sustain their wretched lives". He says in effect that folk are beginning to lose faith in her. Apparently, she is finding it almost impossible to recruit new nymphs for her sacred temple precincts these days, and offerings during the sacred rites have gone right down recently. I'm going over to see her tomorrow first thing. By the way, did you have any particular priestesses in mind for the next few hours? I'm in no particular hurry to be off."

--/--

He found Plentia in one of her favourite forest groves weeping under a large oak tree attended by a group of nymphs and dryads. She was pink cheeked, with long curly hair and as generously proportioned, as befitted the Goddess of Plenty. She was comforting herself with a large bowl of juicy olives.

“Honestly Boss I think it’s a bit rich to be blaming me” she sobbed. "A girl can only do so much. We tried rites and incantations, inspected entrails and commissioned omens, invoked blessings and sacrifices (I mean, I’m practically out of goats) but I can’t make corn grow when the fields are plagued with mice can I?”

“Well, what idiot sent mice? Where do they come from?”

“Loki sends them. You know, the Norse God of Mischief.”

“Yes, he’s a pest, but he’s not one of ours, is he? He shouldn’t be bothering our farmers?”

“Try telling that to the mice! Look, it’s not written in Tablets of Stone! “Norse gods mind your own business”? Our people live alongside Norse folk for hundreds of miles in the northlands and if the mice get into their fields, they don’t stop short at ours either. I don’t understand why he wants to see his own people starving but Cefaboko says it’s something to do with sibling rivalry?”

"So I understand, yes, although technically he's not one of the family. Look please don't say "Tablets of Stone", it's another of those dreadful modern monotheistic cliches I'm trying to stamp out."

"And another thing" Plentia continued without appearing to draw breath, "nothing much is going to grow when its constantly raining, especially these great continuous cloudbursts. Half the farms seem to be flooded these days. I don't know what prompted you to appoint Nari as God of Thunder and Lightning, I really don't. He's overzealous! That's what he is, he's showing off, out of control."

"Well, I always found him perfectly satisfactory as a Demigod," said Uno. "Most promising I thought. Best of the bunch and well deserving of promotion. I was aware that a lot of people thought we should have a Storm god, especially up there in the north! It's that damn Thor that's the problem there, a real crowd pleaser," he grinned "or should I say cloud pleaser?"

Plentia looked at him in disgust.

"Its not you Nari is trying to impress though, is it?"

"I'm sorry, what do you mean?"

"Oh, come on. You surely must have noticed?"

"Absolutely no idea what you're talking about bluffed Uno, who actually had a nasty suspicion he knew all too well what was coming.

"Its Diaphronite he's trying to impress. They are all at it. Eric won't write anything but love songs these days and apparently even Cefaboko keeps sending her little notes. Please don't tell them I said anything? You won't will you?"

"Eric is another of my mistakes" murmured Uno. "What use is a God of Music who can't read the stuff? I knew it was a mistake appointing a left hander, all the prophecies said so. Cefaboko however is someone I really thought I could trust. I don't much like the little gossip, and half the things he tells me turn out not to be true, but he is pretty diligent in his job and there isn't much happens round here he doesn't get to hear about. Thing is, he is supposed to tell me everything, not run about writing secret love notes to my wife. I need to give all this careful thought. I think I'm going to have a word with brother Nick.

--/--

Visiting brother Nick wasn't easy as he was God of the Underworld. It wasn't a journey Uno had made before, and having reached the end of the world soon enough, he had to wait impatiently for the small craft being punted gently in his direction across a flat expanse of dark water. Uno had always harboured a deep mistrust of water and assiduously avoided travelling by boat whenever possible. On this occasion the vessel was steered by a small hunched individual dressed in shabby rags and sculking under a huge hat. This was Puntor the Ferryman who had for many years controlled the only access route to the Hereafter.

On docking, the boat's owner extended his slim floppy wrist for Uno to take and guided him onto the craft. "You may of course skip the usual payment Boss, seeing as you are who you are. It is a unique privilege to have you aboard my modest craft. May a humble boatman ask what brings the Lord of All aboard this simple vessel?" he purred unctuously.

Do I know you?" queried Uno "Only I am pretty sure I'd remember a creep like you. Oh, and incidentally you're damned right we'll be skipping payment. It appears I don't have any change about me this afternoon" he added sarcastically.

"Of course, I have never had the good fortune to be invited into your actual divine presence Sire, but I do naturally recognise you from your many statues" trilled the boatman.

"Oh, this I suppose?" said Uno tugging his great fibrous beard. "Good God, this damned thing leaks! The boat idiot, not the beard! Look my toga is ruined. I should have you torn apart by vultures. I would for sure if I thought anyone else would do this miserable job."

He glanced fearfully at the glowering sky and muttered to himself "Not now Nari or there will be serious trouble!"

"Oh, great Lord, I fear this modest craft was never built for one with such a magnificent physique" his host mewed obsequiously. “And I fear the dead care little where they put their feet”.

“All the same, a few cushions wouldn’t go amiss!”

“Certainly Sire”, responded the boatman in a tone which clearly implied he had no intention of doing anything about it any time soon, “I’ll see what I can do.”.

They were sullenly silent for the rest of the passage.

--/--

When he finally arrived at the Great Palace of the Dead his younger brother Nick was lounging half naked on a blood red throne sipping ambrosia at the back of an echoing cavern. He was watching several of his demons poking a bunch of naked sobbing humans with glowing pokers. Others hung from chains dangling from the ceiling while barely visible smoke-like ghosts writhed sinuously around them. The air was dark and humid.

“Oh, hello Boss” said Nick, surprised into sitting bolt upright in his seat. “What brought you down here? Please don’t get the wrong idea. It’s not always like this but Wednesdays is our day for torturing newly arrived moneylenders and tax gatherers. You should have told me you were dropping in. I would have recommended Mondays. That’s “Warrior Day” and we have a great party. Free booze and it lasts all day. Everyone gets absolutely blotto and then I hand them over to the Vestals – the vino saves the Vestals a lot of graft actually. Half of the heroes have passed out by that stage.

"Gosh! I absolutely cannot remember the last time you came to visit! I don't suppose there's a problem is there? I know we had a bit of a glut a while back. Too many warriors expecting to be royally feasted after the Hittite War. Couldn't you and Dreadlor arrange a nice little war against someone who hasn't heard of chariots? Perhaps the Zorrians, or maybe the Grontians, I'm told they are a pushover. Apparently, they still use stone axes? Ooops, sorry, forgot. It was bad news about Dreadlor wasn't it! Who would have thought he of all people would have gone off bloodshed? Still, it will give us a bit of peace down here. Mind you I had the warrior problem solved already. Had a little word with a contact and arranged to borrow a number of Valkyrie from Odin to cope with the rush."

"Really?" queried Uno raising one of his magnificent shrublike eyebrows. What was in it for Odin? You can't tell me the Norse Gods do a favour for anyone unless there is something big in it for them?"

Nothing much to it really. I had a word with our other brother. You do remember him, don't you? Now him you really don't visit? Anyway, he agreed that whenever Odin's people fancied a sortie against the Saxons, he would send them a nice little following wind to get them over the North Sea. They only have to ask. Very welcome that apparently".

Nick looked at his brother expecting praise for this useful initiative but all he could see in his stern and lordly demeanour was… what… was it guilt!"

"I did actually offer to drop in once, and you know what he did?"

"No"

"He sent a Tsunami! I got the message"

"You don't even talk to him nowadays, do you? I know he doesn't talk to you, that it's mutual, but is that so very surprising after what you did to him?"

"What exactly did I do to him?" snarled Uno. I gave him the sea. That's most of the planet that is. Healthy fish-based diet, travel, and he can take his pick of all those lovely mermaids and mermen whenever he fancies. What's not to like about being God of the Sea?

"Oh really, come on? It's not the job, is it? He loves the job; I know he does. You know perfectly well what you did to him?

"I suppose you mean the name, don't you?" rumbled Uno.

"I most certainly do. What kind of a name for a god is "Salti" for goodness's sake? Other sea gods get called things like Poseidon or Neptune. Adult names with heft and authority and you call your own brother "Salti".

"Don't go quoting Zeus to me! His record on women's rights is about as bad as it can get! Imagine, disguising himself as a swan and forcing himself on young women. That kind of thing that brings godhead into serious disrepute!

"I'm rubbish with names you know that, and I can't swim. I have absolutely no affinity with the sea, that's why I wanted my brother in charge, someone I could trust. It's a big job!"

"Certainly is, and from what I hear he does it very well. Shipwrecks are down, fish catches are up and journeys seem to be taking half the time. Don't you think you should nip down there once in a while and give him a pat on the back, maybe show a bit of appreciation?"

Uno sighed. "Oh, dear, oh dear. You just don't get it do you Nick? You see, that's why I got the top job and you ended up down here." He sighed again "You have to look at things from all angles when you're the boss. If I went around telling the most successful gods how well they were doing don't you think it might just go to their heads? Next thing I know, they will be signing up giants and monsters and launching a take-over bid. It happens to Hindu deities all the time! No, he's good, but he can stay down there where I can keep an eye on him."

"Oh, come on, when did you ever hear of a giant or a dragon winning a straight one on one fight?"

"Well, it probably wouldn't be one on one, would it? I don't much fancy the thought of hopping about avoiding huge boulders and great streams of fiery breath do you. So undignified!"

"Hey, I've just had a nasty thought," said Nick. "He was always the ambitious one, wasn't he? I bet you called him "Salti" just so people would laugh at him? You did, didn't you? Right from the start you wanted him discredited?"

Uno smiled and promptly changed the subject. "I'm assuming it was Cefaboko who told you about Dreadlor? Blasted man just can't seem to keep his mouth shut. Anyway, moving on, I want to talk to you about a possible new posting…"

--/--

"So have I got this right" asked Cefaboko. "Dreadlor goes to Thunder and Lightning, because no one is going to complain about an under-active Thunder God". He sighed deeply, "what a waste of all those lovely muscles. I guess it must be Nari going to War, I mean he's clearly so hyperactive, he'll be well up for it. He'll do a lovely job?"

"No way", replied Uno firmly. "Nari goes to the Underworld".

"But he's rather fun to be with, and that means we won't see him again?" objected Cefaboko.

Uno smirked back at him "Quite, and neither will my wife!".

"Well, what happens to Nick then?"

"When I went to see him, he was droning on about the fact that everyone around him was so miserable about being dead. I could see his point. He said it was far too dark down there, too hot, and that even the demons suffered from depression – apart from the out and out sadists of course. I told him he can have the "Abundance" portfolio. Its about time he had a more popular role. It means more statues and temples, and widespread adoration. I have to recognise that hardly anyone sacrifices to the God of the Underworld! I mean it could be rather counterproductive. You know, "be careful what you wish for…" No, he's proved I can trust him so up he comes. He's bringing some of his demons with him to put a bit of life into the farming community"

"Well, I suppose he won't have to worry about Nari I grant you but what about Loki and his vexatious mice?"

"I'm just coming to that. You are going on a mission. To Odin. If his blood brother Loki knew his Boss had lent us the Valkyrie, he would have a field day with the propaganda. They are very popular up north. His people wouldn't like it one little bit, and the Norse are famously prone to speaking as they find. No, I think you will find Odin will have every reason to rein Loki in from now on, at least as far as we are concerned."

Cefaboko nodded his support. “Nice one Boss. And Plentia goes to…?”

“A new job. Goddess of Women, Moon and Hunting”. I gave it a lot of thought, and she will appreciate a job she can really get her teeth into”.

“You say you gave it a lot of thought, and I’m sure you have Boss, but, and please don’t get me wrong, she won’t much like the “Moon” bit if it means working nights. Frankly it sounds exactly like the Artemis job to me?”

“Well yes, I grant you there are precedents…”

“Well, apart from that, it all sounds great so far, but if I may say so, you seem to have forgotten one thing.”

“What’s that?”

“No God of War! We can hardly do without a God of War, can we.? The Hittites alone would have us on toast!”

Uno looked at him sadly.

“A large mouth and absolutely no imagination, perfect for this job. You start most of the wars anyway these days and you might even learn a bit of tact. Your very first task will be to find a way to beat the Hittites – oh and you had better get that spear fixed, you’re going to need it!”.

MORE TROUBLE IN PARADISE

"I've never heard of him! Is he a warrior or a sage?"

"Neither actually, he's a simple shepherd boy as far as I can tell".

"Well, what is he going to know about beauty? All he will ever see is a bunch of hairy sheep and a few even hairier farmers".

"It's not going to matter much is it Boss, the whole contest is rigged and even if it wasn't, it's pretty obvious who is going to win".

"So", said Uno pausing for effect. "You are telling me that my wife Diaphronite, Goddess of Love and Carnal Passion has arranged a beauty competition between herself; Barbie, Goddess of Wisdom; and Aroma Goddess of Health, Herbs and Healing? A contest she cannot possibly lose because not only is she, pretty much by definition, the loveliest woman in the kingdom, (and would by the way, utterly destroy anyone who had the nerve to beat her), but also because she has rigged the competition by appointing the judge herself?"

"I would say that is a pretty fair summary of the plot so far" replied Mobile, the new messenger of the gods.

"And where is this lowly shepherd boy going to get the winners golden apple from? Oh, wait, don't tell me, I think

I've guessed. My wife is providing the prize as well, isn't she? Well, what's the point of it all?"

"Apparently, she got wind of the fact that both Barbie and Aroma thought they were the most beautiful of the Goddesses and had been sharing the idea with their priestesses, acolytes and handmaidens. She wasn't happy!"

"Knowing my wife, I can well imagine that. Well Barbie is what in my younger day we used to refer to as "a cracker" and Aroma has the most gorgeous complexion, but come on? I mean Diaphronite is, well, she's gorgeous – and SO single minded. What on earth led them to take up her challenge?"

"Surely Boss, you must admit boss that Aroma has a slightly, can I say, "elevated" opinion of her attractions? And Barbie is perhaps not the sharpest arrow in the quiver?"

"True I suppose, but surely even they would have baulked at the idea of allowing one of the contestants to appoint the judge?"

"Well, somebody had to, and they could hardly ask you Boss, given that your wife was one of the candidates, could they?"

"No, I suppose not, but they could have asked Nick, or maybe Eric?"

"One of whom is her brother on law and the other infatuated with her? Anyway, they didn't. I think both took it for granted they were going to win, so it wouldn't make any difference. Anyway, by all accounts Vichy, that's the shepherds name, is some special kind of halfwit. He is completely incorruptible. Everyone says so. He **must** surely be a halfwit if he's incorruptible? That's probably why he is still a shepherd. I reckon Diaphronite chose him precisely because, knowing she must win in a fair contest, she realised the other two couldn't bribe him."

"Right, so she fixed the judge so the contest couldn't be fixed. Clever, I'll give her that. I still think Vichy is going to get himself in very hot water over this. Got to go, I understand Cefaboko, our new God of War, has important news to impart".

--/--

"Great news Boss! I bring news of a wonderous victory over the Hittites! Our brave sailors have destroyed a great Hittite fleet! We have triumphed at last and vanquished the mighty foe!"

"Ah well in that case I fear I have rather less great news for you! In actual fact we haven't!" responded Uno. I have already heard all about this so called "Great Victory". You do realise the Hittites haven't got a fleet? You do in fact know I suppose that they live in the central Anatolian uplands and haven't even got a coastline. What on earth would they want with a fleet, even a rubbish one? I think, on sober reflection, you will find that what our brave sailors so utterly destroyed was a couple of neutral Greek fishing vessels!"

"Oops" said the God of War knowing better than to argue with the Father of the Gods when he was probably hopelessly wrong. "But I was told…"

"What they knew you wanted to hear you imbecile. You wanted a victory and your hard-pressed demigods thought they had better give you one to keep you happy. Happens all the time. Trust me, the sooner you learn not to trust anyone the better!"

Cefaboko blushed, keeping to himself the question of how exactly that would work.

"In point of fact I also hear the Hittite army has now advanced into the land of the Elamites" resumed Uno.

"Well then!" Cefaboko grinned from ear to winged ear.

"Well then?"

"Well then, we are saved!"

"Well then we are saved how exactly?"

"The Elamites use huge phalanxes of defensive spearmen completely covered in plate armour to flood the middle of the battlefield. The Hittites are doomed!"

"Well, they might be doomed if they bothered contesting the midfield but I think you will find their heavy cavalry, that's basically their entire army, prefer to raid wide down the wings, thus bypassing the midfield. Their philosophy is one of outright attack".

"Oh"!

--/--

"You're kidding? What has this ridiculous beauty contest got to do with Plentia? Challenged Uno. "Don't tell me someone has asked her to take part as well, have they?"

"Boss, you appointed her Goddess of Women, Moon and Hunting and she absolutely loves the new job. She's taken women's rights to her heart and she says a contest to prove that any one goddess is inherently more attractive than another is scandalous. She says it's an obscenity. She says it's a disgrace and that women everywhere will not and should not stand for it!"

Mobile sipped his ambrosia and waited for an eruption of righteous wrath from his notoriously short-tempered Boss.

"And will they?" He hissed.

"Well, they might have done, at least some of them, but she has organised riots in the cities. Her acolytes have marched through the countryside singing songs against the contest."

He leaned forward and whispered, "some of the lesser goddesses are even said to have threatened to withdraw access rights to their partners unless they come out and openly oppose it."

"Access to what? Oh, by my divine godhead, I understand you! That's appalling. Can they do that? I suppose they can. Well either Diaphronite or Plentia will have to be made to see sense".

Mobile was uncharacteristically immobile.

Uno continued. "And I suppose you think that's my job, don't you? I suppose it has to be. You would think being a Supreme Being was easy wouldn't you…"

--/--

Uno had requested the company of his wife Diaphronite, and was waiting in the divine bedchamber sprawled across the huge mounds of cushions strewn over the divine divan sipping ambrosia and stroking his superb and lengthy grey beard reflectively when she appeared looking distinctly flushed and appropriated his goblet.

"What kept you dear? I have been waiting here for ages."

"Oh darling, I've been meaning to tell you. I found this gorgeous new handmaiden name of Felicity. Tall, slim but curvy, you would absolutely love her. She's so…how shall I put it? Well, she's so marvellously "adaptable", so "flexible" ... and inexhaustible. I simply couldn't tear myself away. I haven't felt this relaxed in months. Sorry darling, but needs must... And a girl has her reputation to think of. How can I help?"

Uno was briefly lost for words. On the one hand, the very suggestion that the company of a mere mortal could constitute a competitive attraction to his divine presence was heresy, and on the other he couldn't remember the last time he had won an argument with Diaphronite. The other hand won and he changed the subject.

"It's this competition you organised with Barbie and Aroma. It's got to stop. Plentia has got her worshippers in a frenzy of righteous indignation. Apparently, in pitting the charms of one goddess against another you are showing contempt for the divine sisterhood. She says all are equal, just in different ways, and its invidious to compare goddesses on just one criterion."

Diaphronite came closer, leaned over her reclining husband and, gently curling her long slim fingers in his enormous beard, said quietly "Change. Her. Mind!"

"Tried that. She pointed out its far too late now. If she told the people she had made a mistake no one would listen, and if I replaced her, they would assume she had been replaced for her beliefs and tear her replacement to pieces. Its not just her mind we have to change now, its everyone else's. You will just have to cancel the competition".

Diaphronite leaned even closer and whispered "My poor darling. No!"

--/--

"They were slaughtered, almost to a man. It's that plate armour, it was too heavy, they couldn't outrun the Hittite cavalry. The Hittite king Quikphitanstrong says we're next! He says they are going to burn our farms and level our homes until even the wolves in the hills can find nothing left to prey on. He has vowed to make a pyramid of our severed heads that reaches the sky and to create rivers of our flowing blood that turn the seas of the world red. He claims he will bathe in our…"

"Yes, well he does tend to go on a bit. I'm sure he's exaggerating as usual, think of the mess? But just in case my dear Cefaboko, you had better think of something quickly, hadn't you? Preventing the wholesale slaughter of our people by a horde of bloodthirsty heathens is most certainly a job for the God of War. Now go away and do your job. Oh, and send Mobile in would you, I have an errand for him".

Mobile came into the audience chamber bowing deeply with his eyes firmly glued to the floor.

"Don't creep! I'm not going to take it out on you, not yet anyway. Tell me who is our most valiant warrior since Smitus took up toga weaving?"

"That would be Tietars boss" Mobile replied.

"Fetch him now! I have an errant for him, well three actually if he comes back from the first two".

--/--

Tietars was tall and built like a Minoan bull, with a deep and loud voice like the growl of a fighting hound. On this occasion however he cowered rather uncertainly before the Father of the Gods wondering what he had done to offend.

"First off, I want you to drop in on the Scythians and have a chat about them about raiding the Hittite homelands. They will need a substantial incentive and you can offer them two".

"Two?"

"Firstly, the Hittites are not at home, they are far away sweeping up the remnants of the Elamites, and when they have quite finished with them, they are headed over here, so there won't be any opposition. Secondly, I am prepared to send them a substantial chest of gold when they finish the job"

"Sounds fair enough to me boss. Where do I find them?"

"How would I know, they're nomads. They could be almost anywhere north of the Pontus Euxinus. However, we are, as you know, in a bit of a hurry with this one, so take plenty of fine clothing and a few comely servants (male or female, I don't think it matters to them), and they will undoubtedly find you. You should be able to smell them a day or so before they turn up so you can be certain when you have the right nomads".

"No problem boss, but where are we going to get the gold from? Most of it has been pledged to one God or another and stands protected by some holy shrine. Surely, we do not wish to invoke divine wrath?"

"I think Tietars, you may possibly have forgotten who you are speaking to, but just in case…"I DO THE DIVINE WRATH ROUND HERE!" comprendi? Now I know exactly where I can find a tidy sum of gold doing absolutely nothing, pledged to no one, and just waiting to be given away to an unworthy horde of Scythian scum.

When you've finished. No, let me rephrase that, once you have been completely successful with the Scythians, let Mobile know and toddle off to Quikphitanstrong King of the Hittites. Take him this message. When he has agreed to my proposal, come back here and I will give you your final task. If he doesn't agree, let Mobile know and consider yourself banished for life beyond the Pillars of Hercules. That fair enough?"

--/--

On arrival at the audience chamber of the palace of the gods Mobile found Uno in the arms of two lovely wood nymphs who were devotedly platting his beard while a third strummed seductively on a lyre. He dismissed them all with a curl of his little finger, a trick of which he was particularly proud. He turned to his messenger and said "Well?"

"Apparently the Scythians say they are happy to take on the Hittites as long as you can assure them, they won't be in. They told Tietars they were renowned as world class raiders and pillagers but they don't do pitch battles and they want that clearly understood. They only raid when the big guys are out! Oh, and they want the gold upfront."

"That's not necessarily a problem provided Tietars makes it back from Hittite headquarters with his head at the right end of his body".

"Boss, can I ask what you wrote to Quikphitanstrong? Everyone is dying to know"

"I told him if he leaves us alone, I will make him a present of the loveliest woman in all our wide and densely populated realms for his bride."

"But boss, isn't that eh…your wife?"

"Well, apparently so, at least it is at the moment, but I very much doubt it will be for much longer, don't you?"

--/--

Tietars returned to the palace only two days behind Mobile, and Uno was eager to see him.

"Well, is Quikphitanstrong amenable to my proposition or am I talking to a ghost?"

"My lord, he said he was glad of the opportunity not to sully the blades on his chariots with our peasant blood and that his warriors had surfeited even their limitless appetites on the Elamites, but this woman had better be good or he will turn his invincible clansmen in our direction and make togas for his goats from the skins of our feeble warriors. What's the next job?"

"Splendid, So far so good. Now far away from here, in fact at the furthermost extremity of our domains, you will find an old man called Puntor. He has been collecting gold coin from our dead warriors when they pass over into the hereafter for simply ages, and at a groat a crossing he must be absolutely loaded by now. I met him once and he's a total creep. When you meet him, you will hate him as much as I did (that's an order by the way), and tell him the Supreme Being says it's high time he retired. Your job is then to personally retire him, strangulation I think would be nice, and take his gold to the Scythians. He can row himself across after you've killed him, but I want you to bring the boat back for his successor."

"But sire, if you retire the ferryman who is to convey our fallen heroes to the After world?"

"Oh, fear not, I have someone already in mind as his replacement".

At this point Mobile rushed breathlessly into the audience chamber, fell to his knees, wrung his hands in an urgent, anxious way and begged permission to speak.

"Oh, go on then if you must. On your way Tietars, the sooner the better".

"Boss" Stammered Mobile, "your wife Diaphronite is storming around the palace seething with divine fury. She has heard of your offer to the Hittite king and she is just a tiny bit upset".

"Well, that makes two of us seeing as you were the only person I told! You are getting as loose tongued as Cefaboko. I am also a little bit hurt she can think I would seriously be parted from her for even a moment, but I can see I shall have to explain this rather carefully. Bring her to me."

--/--

"Yes darling, I **have** promised the Hittite king the hand of the loveliest woman in the Kingdom. It seemed considerably more economical than losing most of the population in a hopeless massacre, but do I for one moment intend to let my beloved spouse stray far from my side? Oh, no, no of course I don't!".

Diapronite came closer to her husband and pressing her lips close to his right ear whispered "Explain please?" The lips stayed in place and began a gentle nibbling action which produced pleasurable ripples throughout his muscled torso.

"Darling, you will choose her".

"But **I** am the most beautiful…"

"Of course, you are beloved, but you must see that I have given my word. That's my word as the Father of the Gods. If you chose yourself, I will **have** to send you. Can you not, just on this one occasion, chose someone else?"

"I see. I could send Aroma I suppose. I have never forgiven her for that oil of Ramsons and Bogwort she gave you to destress your body. You stank of garlic for a week. I never understood why you thought it would work…"

"But it did…"

"Well, as you now know, it was wasted on me. Or I could nominate Barbie. We could do with a Goddess of Wisdom who could actually remember which day of the week it was..."

Uno grinned smugly. "But you surely cannot choose another goddess as the most beautiful my hearts ease. Would to do so not be to accept a public defeat in this competition between the goddesses. Perhaps in these changed circumstances it would be only prudent to call off this beauty competition altogether?"

"Oh, so that's what you are up to you sneaky old deity! Well stuff the competition, it was never going to be much of a contest anyway. But I do know who to choose now. Someone who will prove an excellent ambassadress to the Hittites, someone who cannot fail to delight, and to distract Quikphitanstrong utterly from the martial path to the marital path so to speak. Someone who is blatantly prepared to do practically anything for publicity and promotion. Its only a shame you will never get to find out what you are missing. I hereby nominate Felicity!"

"Oh, that's a bit harsh, I was looking forward to making her, ahm, acquaintance."

"Well, you are going to have a long wait darling!" huffed Diaphronite.

--/--

Announcing his presence in the audience chamber with a fanfare of divine trumpets was to be the last mistake

Cefaboko made in his brief tenure as God of War. Duly introduced he strode proudly into the divine presence and proclaimed:

"Rain! That should do it. We will make it rain. That should dampen the ardour of even the mightiest of Hittite champions. I mean a good old fashioned nine-day deluge, like we had in the good old days of Nari. A truly biblical tempest. It hasn't rained much since you sent him to the underworld has it Boss? They are bound to turn their war steeds towards somewhere sunnier, Egypt perhaps."

"Not the worst idea you have ever had" replied Uno, although do please try to remember that the word "biblical" is a "no no" around here! However, a nine-day downpour wouldn't do much for our ardour either, and I very much doubt a god of Dreadlors calibre could manage to summon up much more than a couple of hours light and intermittent drizzle.

"In fact, while you have been wrestling with the Hittite problem, I have solved it for you. At considerable cost to my personal pleasure I admit, but I think it was a rather neat solution. No more nasty Hittites for a while!

"And now I am going to solve another vexing little dilemma just as neatly. Good news, you have a new job. You are going to love it. You will get to meet lots of new people, although they will technically be dead and probably not be overjoyed about the idea. Are you good with small boats? Never mind, you soon will be! Oh, and we have a new team member, one who actually looks the part, meet Tietars the Fearless, he who does for testosterone what bees do for honey, our new God of War."

THE CHEST

Come on, surely, we have all heard it in one form or another, perhaps in several?

I see it as broadly the equivalent to the modern "urban myth", something which serves some underlying hidden function, perhaps a cautionary one about thinking first what you might be getting into. Something to help stop others from blundering into some horrible trap with no way out.

In some versions it's a little girl at a children's gathering in some old sprawling country mansion, in others it's a young teenager carried away in the excitement of a first big party gathering of all her friends, and in others again it's the wedding of a distant acquaintance. For some reason, it's always a girl, although it's the kind of foolhardy mistake I personally imagine being more attributable to a male. In any case, its invariably fatal.

They are playing Hide and Seek. It's always Hide and Seek; it has to be. The girl has waited patiently for her turn to hide and after a while it has come around. She has been thinking like crazy about a good place to hide and paying hardly any attention to finding any of the others. Now she rushes off while the others stay in the big room, close their eyes and count to a hundred. Perhaps she has already finally decided where she intends to hide, or maybe it's a sudden impulse? Either way she goes upstairs and looks around in the bedrooms. All are big open rooms with large windows and heavy curtains just inviting someone to seek seclusion behind them. They contain big high old fashioned double beds with enough space beneath them to hold a small gathering, and huge heavy dark old cupboards from floor to ceiling with long oval mirrors and double doors. These are just begging the viewer to step inside for that delicious breathless sensation of concealment amongst the long suits or dresses.

She decides these are all far too obvious for her. She briefly considers the bathroom with its baggy shower curtain, but no, too damp and chill. Then her eye spots an opening, a hatch overhead at the end of the corridor. This must surely lead into the loft, or attic. Can she reach it? Just, on tip toe. She pokes at it and is delighted when it swings open to reveal the worn end of a wooden ladder. This she jumps for and pulls down to floor level. Now she can climb up and look for the perfect hiding place.

She is inside. It's dark, with just a little pale light from a small square cobwebbed window beneath the roof on the far side. There is no obvious source of illumination inside the room which is small and low as you would expect, but as her eyes adjust to the gloom, she makes out an old chest pushed against the wall on the right-hand side.

In the "children's party" version of course, the old chest lies in the nursery, half hidden behind a pile of disused toys, dolls, teddy bears, a dolls house, a fort and an old rocking horse.

Can she get inside the chest? Will it be full of old crumbling documents she dares not damage, even in the unlikely event that she **can** open it. She tries it and, much to her surprise, it does open. There is no lock on the latch.

Short of time now, she pulls up the old ladder behind her and carefully closes the panel in the floor, or she hides the chest more thoroughly behind the pile of toys.

She hears others running up the stairs outside and has no chance to think this through. She climbs in. The chest is too small to lie full length, but wide enough to curl up in. It's a tight fit but beneath her are carefully folded old clothes rather than documents, and she finds herself more comfortable than she expects. Very gently she lets the lid down on top of her.

She hears excited cries of "she's not in here", "try that one", and "no, not there, David hid in there, try the bathroom" and for a while she is so excited, irrationally holding her breath even though no one can possibly hear her breathe. After a while of course the noises die away. Perhaps someone did look in, peered around but saw no obvious hiding place and stepped away. She stays very still, still holding her breath because to her it is amplified by the small space she occupies and the slightest sound seems very loud.

After a while she decides they must have given up and presses against the lid of the chest. It doesn't give. Of course, it doesn't, when she closed the lid, the latch flipped down over the catch at the side and although it's not locked it can't be opened again from the inside.

A sharp chill of terror flushes through her. She's trapped. She can't get out. She has to wait to be found. She is at the mercy of other people. But then she reasons it won't be long before they realise she is still missing and set out on a more thorough hunt.

But she is wrong. The game is over. Either the party has ended and everyone assumes she has gone home with someone else, or the wedding party has adjourned for dinner. If they do miss her, they assume she has wandered off on her own for a good reason. She was always moody and you just have to give her a little time and space to herself. She'll turn up eventually. Or worse, maybe they don't miss her at all?

While she waits, she begins to think about the heap of old clothes beneath her. Who did they belong to? Was it some long forgotten great uncle or some well-remembered grandmother? She can't tell, its pitch black in there. Whoever they were, the clothes smell ever so slightly of "old person". She doesn't much like it. It's a little like lying on top of a dead body, someone long forgotten – "don't go there, don't think like that".

This is the point at which she begins to scream for help. Short sentences. "Help me". "I'm in here". "I'm in the chest in the loft". "Please come quick it's scary in here". She tries to bang the sides with her arms and legs but of course there isn't enough room to achieve any momentum. You can't make much racket by flapping a few fingers and toes? She might as well be tied up for all the good it would do.

No one comes. After a while she stops making a noise and settles down for the long wait she now realises must lie ahead of her. She should be getting cramp surely, but the clothes allow her to relax her limbs and instead she feels herself getting unexpectedly drowsy. It must be dark by now anyway, no one will come until daylight, may as well get some sleep? There is little room for air in the chest but the top is slightly uneven so air can be drawn inside as she breaths. Just. It is so quiet now. As quiet as…?

When she wakes, she immediately realises how silly she was assuming that, because its dark in the chest it must be dark outside, and even if it had been, it could still be dark out there now. She has no idea of time in the chest. It just doesn't exist for an old box that has been lying there neglected for what, decades? Centuries? She cries. She cries silently and then sobs, big jerking sobs but still nobody comes.

She begins to lose the sense of being in the upper part of the house. For all she can tell she could be hundreds of feet underground. She tries so hard not to think of the heavy stone slabs that could be piled above her if she was. But maybe she is? Maybe she was dreaming about the party? Maybe she's dead?

She is hungry now all right, but even now fear predominates. She kind of forgets she is hungry much of the time, but when she remembers it's suddenly overpowering. There is a big ball of empty pain in her tummy. She would eat anything, even stuff she normally wouldn't touch.

She begins to claw irrationally at the sides of the chest. It's bound to be made of oak; old wooden chests always are. Silly girl, there is no likelihood of you clawing your way out of that even if you scratch and scratch until your fingers bleed. And they do bleed. Just as well she can't see them, because she can feel them and they throb and bleed. Of course, they feel worse in the dark. She sucks them to sooth them and is surprised by the sharp taste of her own blood. She has never felt so alone, so far from friends and family. She is quietly and utterly terrified.

She has an idea. Perhaps if she rocks the chest from side to side it will topple on to its side, the latch will come open and she can roll out. Worth a try. But its no good. The old oak chest is too broad and too heavy to be turned on its side by any pressure from within. She is too near the floor for that.

Now she begins to whimper hopelessly. "Please let me out. Oh, please don't let me die like this in the dark, alone and forgotten". She begs her family to come for her. She imagines them worrying and **knows** they will come. They will contact "the authorities" people who know how to search for missing people.

She thinks again about the old person underneath her and it's as if there are two people in the box. She begins to resent the presence of the other person. Without them there would be more room to wriggle and struggle. Who would be stupid enough to leave their clothes there for ever like that? But then who would be stupid enough to climb in with them?

Maybe somebody did search. If they did then they did what everyone does when they are searching an area they know has already been thoroughly searched for something they don't expect to find. They look in all the same places but less carefully. She couldn't be in the loft, there is no ladder. She couldn't be in the nursery; I have been playing with all the lovely toys and there was no one there.

I think someone said she was seen wandering off on her own after the party. Anyway, the Authorities are in charge now, it's their responsibility if no one can find her? If they did come, she was asleep. She spends most of her time asleep now.

When she is awake, she begins to itch, first in her lower legs, then her back and soon all over. It's a nervous reaction of course but she fears there may be tiny insects in there with her. How big are woodworms? What do death-watch beetles look like? Maybe its moths creeping out of the old clothes? There are places she can't reach to scratch. "Oh please, please, let me out!"

How long does she survive in there before death takes her? Sealed up in her own little oubliette so all alone?

How long does she survive the creeping claustrophobia, the pitch dark, the cold and the utter hopelessness of her situation? How do we define "survive" anyway? Does the time count after her mind starts to slip and she loses all rationality, trying to bite the box and breaking her teeth stuffing bits of old clothing into her mouth to fend of the gnawing starvation? Has she "gone" when she starts to talk to the imaginary insects she can now constantly feel crawling all around in her box; or when she mindlessly sings old nursery rhythms to herself over and over again, sometimes just a single line like some religious litany?

They found her in the end, surely, they must have done even if it was decades later when the house was cleared? But what did they find when they opened the chest? Could anyone remember who she was?

Of course, it's only folk law, isn't it? It's apocryphal. It never actually happened, did it? Well, probably not very often.

THE MAKING OF SIEGFRIED MCTHUG

His mother, Cherie, had been born into a wealthy family. The Greedy-Bastards owned half the county and rented the rest. They had come over with the Normans and they still holidayed together every summer. When they sneezed, the entire county said "how high". They were so rich, when they went shopping the high street was closed to the general public! Cherie was naturally raised in the expectation that she would marry into greatness, or at least royalty, but she was a strong-willed girl and had eschewed the values manifest in her privileged upbringing. In their place she embraced the certainties offered by religion; guilt, choral singing and charity work.

She had eventually left home to become a nun. Sadly, she did not make a good one. She proved to be a naughty one. Her craving for fleshly pleasure was too strong to suppress for long in the cause of religion. When her naughtiness became physically manifest, she had been asked to leave the order of Perpetual Misery. It was correctly rumoured that the father was one Hamish McThug, an ex-sailor she had met in the local village school where she taught logistics and corporate ethics.

The unruly McThug clan had originally been exiled from Scotland during the great Shortbread Riots of 1751 and their subsequent regime of cattle rustling, horse trading and dealing in stolen garden ornaments had once brought central Basingstoke to its knees.

In the years that followed, the strain of criminality ran thickly through the McThug blood like the lettering in a stick of seaside rock. In every generation one brother would be driving flash cars, another would be selling them and a third would be stealing the hub caps.

Hamish himself had been tall when he met Cherie and remained so for the rest of his life. He was dark haired and emaciated with a certain natural hauteur and a hairy chest and had been toughened by years working on freighters plying their trade from Oslo via Lagos to Montevideo, and out of sight of land for weeks at a time.

On those endless journeys fun consisted mainly in daring Hannibal the cabin boy to swallow whole the tarantulas the crew found hiding in the fo'c'sle. Shortly after his death the second mate found a couple of Norwegians stowed away hoping to find a new life selling high quality plastic food storage containers with snap close lids in the South American favella's. They were given a stark choice, entertain the crew or go overboard. Shunning this unexpected opportunity for arachnid focused good fortune they chose a brief career as shark bait. After their deaths the crew had been reduced once again to spending long hours scanning the horizon in a pathetic game of "I spy".

Then one fatal day off the coast of Senegal, a member of the crew spied pirates and when his turn came and his crew mates had guessed the word (pie was easy but they struggled for a while with rats), the captain jumped into action. Some filled their pockets with tins of corned beef, some filled pants and shoes with mild cheddar and the captain and first mate placed large blocks of pate under their caps in the hope that it would give them a head starter. It took a special kind of sailor to volunteer to hide the long chorizo sausages but the captain was heartened by the unexpectedly large number of volunteers.

The pirate captain, known to his men as "the Surgeon", was a skilled and psychopathic torturer with the proven capacity to extract brains through the nasal cavity. One sneeze could prove provocation enough and his crew dreaded the onset of hay fever or sinusitis. The crew of the freighter Nauseous now willingly complied with his every request and those who survived even offered to load the booty on board the pirate ship

Once the pirates had discovered nothing in the freight containers but brass door handles. Christmas crackers, toilet seat replacements and bicycle parts however the survivors were cast adrift. At first, after their staple fare of cooks prune kedgeree surprise and steamed rat, a diet of pate, corned beef and chorizo followed by cheese came as a welcome relief and morale was high. Optimism however turned to pessimism, pessimism to depression, depression to violence, and violence to a number of dubious creepy religious conversions. When finally rescued by a team of Namibian squid fishermen Hamish had openly declared his intention to find a new life ashore doing good.

Having done it he next considered his need to better himself. After his rejection from Harvard came through, he had forged an elaborate C.V. and moved to teach Quantum Mechanics in the little Wiltshire village school where he met Cherie.

In truth their dalliance there was but a short one, fumbling in the stationary cupboard, fumbling behind the bike sheds, or just fumbling for the fumble, fumble fun of it. There had however been that one treasured exquisite moment of transcendent cosmic oneness after which they had had sloppy sex on the stained parquet floor. Cherie would have treasured that memory forever even if she hadn't subsequently proved to have been impregnated with the zygote that was to become Siegfried.

As it was, rejected by the nuns after a pathetic attempt to plead divine intervention, she made her way reluctantly from the dormitory down to the village. She and Hamish tried at first to make a success of things as a couple but after a few hours he left her and returned to his first calling. He sought a berth on the Isle of White ferry where he subsequently became a popular bar steward, discovered a talent for joke telling and later made a modest living on the Northern club circuit.

--/-

Cherie however was alone as she had never before been alone.... only this time she was not alone.

At first, she struggled just to subsist. She would take lavender from garden borders, tie it into bunches and sell it as lucky heather outside busy supermarkets whose clientele rarely knew the difference.

Later she joined a travelling fair bagging gold fish into small plastic bags and repairing the magnetic fish in the lucky dip tank. Sometimes she absentmindedly magnetised the goldfish. Perceiving after a time that the job offered little in the way of career advancement she moved on and briefly worked as a stunt double in "The Return of the Monster of the Terribly Deep and Nasty Smelling Black Lagoon."

Her condition then began to show. She was taken in by an elderly couple in the costume department, although by that time what she most needed was to be let out. They offered her shelter and support provided she named her infant after their Dachshund Siegfried.

Siegfried the human (fortunately a boy) was born one midnight during the most terrible storm to sweep the area in decades. The old couple dressed him in a pair of theatrical swaddling clothes in the hope that he would swaddle theatrically, but cruel fate was to intervene that night. His mother barely had time for a cigarette, to note the strange marks on his behind, and write a letter recording his given name as Siegfried. The river outside rose so quickly young Siegfried was swept away in the consequent flood in the very bowl they had used to wash the new born.

He floated downstream, was found, and for the next few months, taken in by a family of friendly otters (even the brightest of new born babies are frightfully gullible!) He learnt to swim like an eel, to make silly squeaking noises, and to catch fish with his bare hands. Cruel destiny was however to intervene again when the otters were taken by a roving band of taxidermists and sold to a local museum as reconstituted roadkill. After discussion it was decided no one had the experience to cope with the challenge stuffing Siegfried presented and they left him by the roadside.... alone.

It was now that the otters' lessons proved their true value. He was found only a few hours later when his cute squeaking noises brought him to the attention of a micturating trucker by the name of Constance Surprise. Without hesitation Constance had wrapped the infant lovingly in the folds of his beard and vowed to raise him as his own. Constance was an unusual name for a man of his size and bulk but he had long born the ribaldry of his peers with calm equanimity, and now even gained their grudging respect for his parenting skills.

He converted the rear of his cab intro a nursery with en suite facilities in the form of a large bucket, and for the next few years the two travelled the open roads of Britain singing country and western ballads in discordant harmony. Once he had mastered the art of driving using only his beard while feeding the baby, only one thing remained to worry Constance and tarnish his new found happiness. He pondered those disturbing marks on the baby's buttocks. On the left cheek was a mark like a crescent moon, and on the right a large star in splendour.

Little is known of the secret life of the trucker. They travel alone, heavily tattooed, often driving through the night, beyond the pale of all other human society. Is it a surprise then that so many turn to the comfort of their secret own religion?

So, it was that one stary night Constance and the young Siegfried parked up in a large lorry park in a remote part of Manchester and made their way into the woods headed for a secret rendezvous. On arrival they joined dozens of like-minded truckers, partook silently of the prescribed libation of gin and tabasco, and line danced naked by moonlight until dawn and exhaustion ended their revels and the arcane gods of the road were appeased.

Some days later, while tucking in to a breakfast of cocoa and beans on toast Constance was approached by a close friend known as Big Jimmy Little. Big Jimmy had been at the ceremony and had been struck by the marks on Siegfried's rear – several times in fact.

"I been meanin to tell you"

"Yeah?"

"Them marks on 'is bum?"

"Yeah?"

"I reckon they mean somefing. Y'know, like a portent or somefing.

"Yeah?"

"Yeah! Like a sign or somefing."

"Yeah?"

"Yeah, or an omen."

"Yeah?"

"Yeah."

"What?"

"Avent a clue! You might wanna ask Ma Jong?"

On hearing this name Constance sucked in his breath and almost swallowed his beard, for Ma was a legendary figure in trucking circles, although she did exist. Although now living in a converted convertible camped at Campville with a band of wandering bandits, Ma was originally of Sioux extraction. She was born to an affiliated clan known as the Wham Bam. She had grown tired, when questioned by officials in regard to her ethnic origins of receiving the same tedious "thank you mam!" in reply and had forsaken her original given name of Buffalo Moon. The buffalo moon had been a common phenomenon to the Sioux, occurring whenever a buffalo got its front legs stuck in a deep snow-covered ditch, but it meant little in West Bromwich. Ma was ninety-three and on health grounds ate nothing but tinned sardines and steamed vegetables. Her breath stank like the deck of a trawler in hot sunshine. She was however widely respected for her great psychic power having successfully predicted Christmas several years in a row and averaging a one in three success rate on the toss of a coin.

Constance had briefly considered Big Jimmy's hypothesis, and Siegfried's buttocks, from all angles and decided to give her a call.

Ma Jong naturally asked that the portentous buttocks be revealed to her in person, promising to provide insights into his character and the circles in which he might one day circulate.

They had met under the doleful light of a full harvest moon, and as Ma examined the crescent moon and star in great detail Constance lay drowsily listening to the nearby strumming of gypsy guitars and the clatter as various stolen goods were stored discretely under a broken-down caravan.

At last, the seer was ready to pronounce.

"Constance and Siegfried" she intoned "you will shortly be parted. Siegfried's life will take other paths. That will be fifty pounds please. I take Visa and Mastercard, and by the way, nice bum!"

--/--

Meanwhile, distraught at losing her baby and her washing bowl in so short a time Cherie had been like a creature possessed.

She grew bitter and alienated, moving quickly from job to job, and never finding happiness until at length she chanced upon a group of partisans who went by the name of the Cotswold Liberation Front. Their aim, by increasingly trivial acts of civic incompetence, was nothing less than independence for those sleepy rural uplands. She became their most ruthless operative, missing hair and medical appointments and pretending to lose her purse when reaching the head of the queue in local supermarkets. Anything was fair game in their determined bid for freedom. New recruits were schooled to master the art of cutting corners and driving at a maximum of twenty miles an hour on all roads while remaining rooted to the centre of the highway.

There was one man among them, a loose-limbed albino named Ted of whom, in time, she grew fond. One day she joined a team Ted had put together to hit Chipping Camden. The plan was to drive in at dawn, take a leisurely breakfast in a nice café, collect signatures for their independence petition, and high tail it out of there. All was proceeding to plan until, on the other side of the main street Cherie's gaze fell upon a young boy. There was something wild about him, and just maybe, something familiar. He was standing behind a huge haulage truck and seemed to be having trouble with his trousers.

At once, Cherie crossed over and went up to him. The boy snarled and spat out his words.

"I suppose you want to look at my buttocks? Well, why not? Everyone else does, why should you be any different?

With that he flung down his trousers and revealed the hidden crescent moon and star."

"Well actually I was just going to ask for your signature, but...Oh Siegfried," she exclaimed, "I can't believe it. That tell-tale behind. It must be, it's really you!"

"Who the hell is Siegfried?" he prevaricated.

"Come with me and I'll explain everything" she entreated.

"O.K." said the boy "If you sub me a brie and chutney sandwich at the Happy Calorie".

They sat and talked for hours as the forgotten sandwich slowly grew dry and curly. At length the boy accepted his new name and the prospect of a life with Cherie. This after all was what the mystic had foreseen – or at least she hadn't specifically ruled it out.

He had the sandwich placed in a doggy bag and said a brief farewell to Constance, who had secretly been hoping for an opportunity to spring clean the facilities on his truck. Constance stroked his beard tactfully before responding. "Well kid, if it's what you want, then go with my blessing, I've taught you all I can."

"You haven't taught me anything" retorted Siegfried "except maybe the importance of regular servicing".

"I could have told you that myself" sighed Cherie rolling her eyes significantly.

Ted then drove them back to the Fronts secret H.Q. in the hills near Cheltenham.

--/--

It was not until after the Burford fiasco that Teds grip on his group really began to slip. A splinter faction based in Moreton on the Marsh argued that Cheltenham wasn't in the Cotswolds and therefore didn't need liberating. A reactionary element began pressing for minimum educational requirements and an earnings threshold for new members. Many seasoned members also pressed for the exclusion of some of the shabbier villages on the eastern Cotswold fringe from the proposed new Utopia. Before long, an anonymous informer called Ivor Story had alerted the police to Ted's long list of unpaid parking fines. One morning he awoke to find a SQUAT team resting on their haunches around the woodland clearing. That spelt "finito" for the Cotswold Liberation Group and Ted was taken away for ten years community service served in a large gated community in the centre of Windsor.

Cherie now bitterly resigned herself to resuming active membership of the fabulously wealthy Greedy-Bastard family. She had resolved that Siegfried would be home educated and in months he knew the name, function and layout of every room in Bastard Grange.

This proved to be just the beginning. Before long he had purloined the 1933 telephone directory propping up a cupboard in the spare Ballroom and withdrawn a number of classic texts from the staff Library. He worked his way laboriously through Che Guevara's "Summer term at St Ursula's"; Osama Bin Laden's "Fun with Fertiliser"; John Lennon's "Travels with my Gerbil" and Karl Heinz Stockhausen's seminal "Cooking with Goat".

His newfound literacy was kept a close secret from family members who regarded it as unbecoming in a member of the aristocracy, but Cherie faced a dilemma. Clearly Siegfried would benefit from formal structured education, but this might involve meeting poor people!

Little did she realise that matters were shortly to be taken out of her hands (again).

Siegfried's daily jog round the indoor playing field took him close to the kitchens and one day he asked the Sous Chefs for a glass of water.

It was provided by a burly giant of a man with tousled dreadlocks of jet-black hair and earrings in the form of clustered human skulls. The stranger looked at him with raised eyebrows. When he had untangled them from his dreadlocks he exclaimed "You look the spitting image of your father!"

"You knew him?" questioned Siegfried leaping to his feet. "I didn't".

"I wouldn't go that far. When I met him, he was a drifter, all at sea and headed nowhere in particular. I have no idea what became of him, and I never mutilated any of his friends, well not much anyway. Besides some of them rather enjoyed it."

"Oh, what's for dinner?" asked a saddened Siegfried peering into the bowl nearby. "Ooh, lovely, faggots."

--/--

Over the next few weeks, the two became unlikely friends and chef, now answering to his given name of Terry, began to talk openly of his former life.

"Of course, I had to play the murderous psychopath in those days, but the casual carnage, the gore and the gratuitous dismemberment took a terrible toll. I had hoped to lead my crew towards a more modern concept of piracy, one based on respect, decency and a love for one's fellow man. We would still have killed people of course, but quickly and politely, with reluctance and with fulsome apologies. Perhaps made some effort to inform the next of kin. And I would have let the parrots go. It's a terrible life for a parrot you know. No trees.

"Why did you leave piracy?" queried Siegfried.

"Had to. Crew found my poem. He closed his eyes and began to recite:

There once was a bold pirate captain
Who could make victims scream with a hatpin
He would torture and maim
To his crew's great acclaim
But the pressure to do so quite sapped him

Knowing he never could weaken
He remembered his schooldays at Eaton
Where the boys seemed addicted
To the pain they inflicted
And where he was savagely beaten

But though to the world he seemed cold
He at heart was a delicate soul
Who kept poems from home
And from men he had known
And was dreading the day he grew old

No respect for a poetic nature your average pirate. I turned to butchery instead, but even there... So, I became a cook, kept my hand in of course. Recognised for my way with offal."

"You're a good offal cook?"

"I'm an offal good cook".

Siegfried found himself moved by Terry's tales of the life he had led and began to long for his own freedom away from the suffocating luxury, wealth and good taste of Bastard Grange.

So, one night he burrowed out through the scullery to freedom taking with him, on Terry's advice, the more portable items of silverware and a large wodge of currency. He signed up defiantly for an Open University course in the History of Philanthropy. Before long he was able to pay his way through the programme by completing assignments for less gifted contemporaries. "No more Mr Nice Guy!"

These were the days of his pomp. He found sanctuary in a disused allotment shed, moved it to Wiltshire and began work on the hillside burrow he was soon to call home using the skills first taught him by his friends the otters. He quickly found work as an enforcer for a local library with a shameful record of unreturned books, and it was there one beautiful spring day that a gorgeous young woman approached him at the returns desk.

Chianti had eyes as blue as robins' eggs, shoulder length tousled blonde hair, an hourglass figure and a laugh like a hyena. He found her intoxicating.

"Do you have a copy of "Counter Cyclical Fiscal Policy initiatives and their impact on Personal Taxation Management" by Ken Dodd" she simpered?

"This is "Returns" he mumbled coyly. "You should be asking over there, but if you ask me at the Renewals desk, I'll have a look for you."

And that was the start of it. With her feral scent, that divine body, and the faint hint of linctus he had readily agreed to her marriage proposal and she had joined him in working on the new barrow. Aside from small disagreements on the respective merits of wallpaper verses tiles and the impact of the abandonment of Keynesian Macroeconomic principles on government policy, they were blissfully happy.

He soon left the library, stamping his authority on a small shoe shop catering for adult size seven and below. Here he championed an innovative discount policy for one legged customers which allowed him to make the stock go further. Chianti who had small feet was delighted and sometimes joined him on the shop floor. He then expanded the business, offering part exchange on used footwear. Sure, life as a sole trader had its disadvantages, his cardboard allergy for a start, but he had loved the smell of used boots and the shine on a new pair of brogues.

Fired by this early success and seizing the spirit of the times he opened his first Pop Up roadside Celery Café. Customers could sit in the open at cheap picnic tables, provided with a small bowl of salt, and, for just a pound a stick, chew celery with old friends or family members.

From this he extended to a range of stylish Brussels bars where customers received a cocktail stick and a small paper bag of freshly fried Brussels lightly dipped in chilli oil.

Finally, he created his greatest concept, the popular Kohl Rabi Yoga centres. Here shaven headed devotees in green leggings could sit cross legged equipped with a pencil and small notepad and meditate on possible uses for the enigmatic legume.

Chianti for her part was free to pursue her passion to open a refuge for dispossessed moles, buying a plot of land adjacent to their burrow. She also worked tirelessly to expand public awareness of weasels.

--/--

One day the following Spring, he answered a knock at the barrow door to find a middle-aged bald-headed man of middling height who bowed deeply and presented him with a small calling card.

"There is nothing written on this card" observed Siegfried cordially.

"I am here on secret business sir", responded the middle-aged man, "but we like to do things properly. I am here to invite you to join a top-secret committee which the government are in the process of establishing."

“What for?”

“I am afraid I can’t tell you sir, its top secret.”

“But if I’m on it presumably I will need to know?”

“Sir if you agree to join the committee, I feel sure you will have every opportunity to steer its work in any direction you feel appropriate.”

“Well why me?”

Sir, we have a range of specialist expertise in place already but the government now feel they also need a representative of the “common man”. They read about you and you seem to fit their exhaustive criteria.”

“But my family are stinking rich?”

His visitor looking briefly at the shabby entrance to the burrow said “Sir it would be indelicate to explain why, besides which the committee is meeting about five minutes’ walk from your abode so it will save the country on travel expenses.”

“Off to a good start then! Very well, you’ve talked me into it. When do I start?”

“In about five minutes sir, if you’re available?”

“I must say you are a very cordial fellow to do business with”

“Sir, I am a civil servant. The more amenable I am the more they pay me. I wonder if you would be so kind as to follow me?”

Pausing only to change from his slippers, Siegfried was led to a large grey armoured vehicle. It had tank tracks and a huge turret but one thing seemed to be missing. He commented on the lack of armament.

“We will not be needing that sir, it’s a think tank. The committee used to meet in a secluded location in south Devon but it kept rolling down the hill and blocking the traffic so we came here to a more horizontal location.”

The bald-headed man then opened a low door and ushered Siegfried inside before bidding him goodbye. He looked around to find six highly assorted characters sat around an oval wooden table. He sat on the only seat available next to an elderly gentleman with a florid complexion wearing a thick red robe with what looked like a dead badger round the neck who fixed him with a myopic stare.

“Good day, you must be the promised Siegfried McThug? I am Lord Elpus. He leaned in to Siegfried and whispered “I thought they said it was fancy dress, but apparently the country is in a bit of a mess”.

Next to Lord Elpus sat a tall gent with a long neck, a dense mat of red hair and eyebrows so bushy Siegfried suspected he had spotted a wren’s nest in the right one. He introduced himself as Professor Harry Tosis the distinguished anthropologist. Facing him sat a member of the clergy who Professor Tosis introduced as Pontus Malform the Bishop of Piddle Hinton, whom Siegfried knew to be a radical church reformer.

That left Dame Mary Tonsil the opera singer, and Sirius Crisis, the most senior general left in the British army. The final seat was occupied by someone he had seen on television, Ena Pickle, the shot putter. "Oh dear" he thought, she had a reputation for jumping to conclusions!"

Dame Mary addressed the meeting. "My Lord, lady, gentlemen and token plebian, we are gathered here by government decree to consider things. We have been selected as a random cross section of the British nation It is hoped that we may, after due consideration, and of course several long and well-paid holidays, come up with firm recommendations. She began to sing:

"I feel you should all be aware

I've appointed myself as the chair

Now even the meek

Can feel quite free to speak

Just by raising their hand in the air"

"Contradiction in terms" shouted Professor Tosis. "If we have been selected, we can hardly be a random cross section?" He sat back and looked smugly around him.

"Through the chair Professor, through the chair."

"I'm sorry...?"

"You speak through the chair."

"Do we?" said the general. "Which one? They all look the same to me."

"The floor is yours general."

"How kind, can I have it wrapped?"

"Breach of executive privilege, surely the member is suspended?" shouted the bishop.

"Oh dear" sighed the general, "it seemed perfectly in order when I left home this morning!"

Dame Mary Tonsil began to sing again:

"So incredibly loud is my voice.

That it leaves to you all little choice

Either sit there in awe

Or run for the door

To escape from the terrible noise."

"Well, I suggest we split up? That way we can cover several different directions at once!" suggested Lord Elpus.

"In my experience, it has never been necessary for a committee to split up to achieve that" spluttered General Crisis.

“Well, we need an agenda?” suggested Ena Pickle.

“And what would we place at the top of such an agenda?” queried Dame Mary.

“Well, we would begin with item one?” suggested Ena again.

“Oh golly! Just like being back at school!” enthused Lord Elpus

“In what way exactly? asked Siegfried

“Why, beginning with term one of course!” said the peer innocently.

“We are expected to reach firm conclusions” confided Dame Mary

“Then we need facts, lots of them” suggested Professor Tosis rubbing his hands together.

“Don’t want facts! You can prove anything with facts! We need opinions, the more outrageous, the more controversial and inflammatory the better!" ranted the bishop, jumping on the table, his eyes lolling around his head in an alarming fashion.

“Coffee?” suggested Siegfried.

“Splendid” endorsed the athletic Ena. “Better make that Item one”

"Disestablishment. That's the thing!" continued the bishop unabashed. "Get these tired old cliches out of the way. Start anew!"

"Here, here", Mary Tonsil offered her support. "But start anew with what?"

"We need a methodology!" suggested the Professor.

"Protocols" suggested General Sirius.

"Ground rules" endorsed Lord Elpus.

"We need a new direction" suggested Ena.

"That's disgusting!" gasped Lord Elpus. "Oh sorry, thought you said we needed a nude erection".

"Coffee" offered Siegfried again. "We can't have a committee without coffee? Oh, and I didn't notice any dark-skinned people among our ranks?"

"We didn't know any" several voices intoned in harmony.

"Well, I think we have covered enough ground for now" suggested Dame Mary. "I suggest we adjourn until after Christmas?"

"But that may be just what they are expecting us to do" shouted the general narrowing his eyes and scanning the room.

"Who exactly is "They?" asked Siegfried.

“They could be almost anyone” whispered the general his eyes swivelling around him “They could be here among us now. We would never know. You could well be one of them. You do look like one of them. I can always tell you know”

“Oh well. Confirmed membership plus need for coffee and a structured approach” hummed Professor Tosis. “Very positive start”. Nodding his head vigorously, he rose and led the way out of the room.

“Burn the buggers. Root ‘em out and burn ‘em to a crisp” muttered the bishop, whose thinking had clearly moved in a new direction, as he jumped from the table and followed the professor out.

It appeared the committee meeting was over. Siegfried overheard Dame Mary, whom he had realised had been under the influence of something sweet smelling, herbal and rather illicit, questioning Lord Elpus quietly about the current whereabouts of Lord Lucan as they left.

Once outside Pontus Malform asked him if he had ever woken to find himself surrounded by aliens. Siegfried replied that he had not, but presumed the bishop was familiar with the experience.

He concluded that this had not been a good time to take major decisions with potentially global implications and made his way sadly homeward musing on the advantages of his own relative obscurity. Anonymity, to be nobody, was surely a uniquely enviable status offering real freedom and a platform to be anyone you wished without fear of obligation or public ridicule. If he **had** become an exemplar of the common man, he was proud of himself.

--/--

He sat dreamily the following afternoon tucking in to his much-loved fresh curds, and drooling at the prospect of junket to follow. He was imagining himself inventing a cure for ugliness or perhaps travelling through time to the court of Moctezuma for a cup of hot chocolate. As a nobody, one could surely be anyone, at least in one's imagination.

Nothing it seemed could damp his spirits until his exotic and futile dreams were interrupted by the velvet, if penetrative voice of his wife Chianti ..."so I've decided to be off to Patagonia to raise penguins."

"Never realised they had trouble standing up" he murmured carelessly. "But we can't just be off! It would mean leaving all this behind" he added gesturing to the fetid hovel around him, to the piles of used teabags, bacon rinds and chicken bones piled against the far wall, to the rusty gas cooker camouflaged beneath by its thick, unctuous brown carapace of grease and to their faithfully humming fridge (should probably throw that fish out)."

"I could just about live with that" Chianti commented uncharitably.

Siegfried was approached by Cuddles, their pet Caiman and began playfully scratching his back. "Is Patagonia anywhere near Salisbury?" he queried.

As Cuddles casually reciprocated, Chianti patiently explained that Siegfried and Cuddles would not be coming with her and that Patagonia was many miles from Salisbury. Cuddles drooped visibly at the news. After a trapping accident he had been left with legs only on his right side and had worn a circular hole in the living room carpet. The only prey he could catch now were similarly disadvantaged mice, and they were in short supply. He had looked to Chianti for his every need, reserving Siegfried for quality back scratching.

"You surely can't blame me for the way we live?" gasped Siegfried. "I was raised as a Greedy-Bastard. I thought Bin Men were part of the ground staff."

"Well, I'm sorry. I'm sick of the smell of second-hand shoes and rotting vegetables. We hardly ever discuss post Friedman Monetarism or Central Bank policy options anymore."

"Well, if I ever hear another thing about weasels, it will be too soon" responded Siegfried. "Besides I am tired of moles appearing through the living room walls when I am trying to read. And I'm sick of watching endless episodes of Celebrity Mole Rescue!"

"Well then, it's clearly time I was watching them somewhere else!"

"Look, can we talk later? responded Siegfried. "I need time to think. I'm going for a walk."

He wiped the stray tea leaves from his old boots, selected a frayed jacket and stood up.

Cuddles looked at him intently and he realised the Caimans old comforter, a large much-chewed rubber fisherman called Tony was behind the door. He drew it out, threw it into the midden by the far wall and said affectionately "I'll help you get that later."

He went out, slammed the door behind him and walked off into the soft luminescence of early evening. At times like this, when he was uncertain or perhaps sulking, he liked to walk up through the old minefield in the adjacent army range and sit in the ruined building on the low hill in the middle. When the red flag was up and the range was in use it was the only safe place to sit.

"When had it all started to go wrong? How had they sunk to this? When had they stopped sharing? Why was she so unhappy and why had they adopted a disabled Caiman?"

In the distance in that bleak landscape, a lone blackbird resting in a dead oak tree now began to sing its mournful evening song, pausing at intervals in the vain hope of a response.

"You too huh!" he speculated as the first shell ploughed into the branch it was sitting on. "That's life all over" he thought. "One minute you're living your own life high on the adrenalin of individualism, and the next you're so not." As the bombardment gathered force and straddled the old ruin he lapsed deeply into reverie.

THE UNDOING OF SIEGFRIED MCTHUG

Siegfried sat still for a very long time thinking. His wife was leaving him; he was no longer in step with the shoe trade; he had somehow become part of a top-secret committee without having the faintest idea what it was for; and he was fed up with looking after a disabled Caiman. What exactly did life have left to offer him?

He then became aware of a small voice in his head. What was alarming was that it did not appear to be his voice, and it was apparently contradicting him. The doctors had warned him he would have days like this, so he ignored it.

"You can't just ignore me" it said.

"Go away" he replied looking at a small owl which had appeared in front of him.

"See, I won!" exclaimed the small voice. She isn't leaving you; she just feels that spending more time apart will bring you closer together. I do however agree about the Caiman. Big mistake there. Not something you can cuddle up to at night, and they don't have any "Best in Show" awards for large carnivorous reptiles, so no social status there?"

"If you are not me," challenged Siegfried, "and if you are, I shall this instant be seeking specialist medical assistance, then who the hell are you and what are you doing in my head?”

“I am your spirit owl and life counsellor.”

“I don’t want one!”

“You don’t get a choice in the matter” replied his new life counsellor from within his forehead.

“Are you in some strange way associated with the diminutive feathered presence I see before me?”

“I am, but you wouldn’t expect me to talk directly to you, would you? If anyone saw you talking to owls you would lose considerable credibility. Only red Indians and the occasional naturalist can get away with that. This way we can keep it between ourselves.”

“Oh goody!”

“I suggest a prolonged period of self-reflection. Go away and “find yourself”. Work out what’s important in your life and what you would be better off without.”

“You sound like a tacky horoscope, but you may just be right”.

“Well don’t thank me, you would have got there sooner or later on your own.”

“Will I be seeing you again or is this a one-off mental aberration?”

“Ah”, said the owl and disappeared.

--/--

Within three months Siegfried had freed himself of all business links, waved Chianti off from Southampton docks, from where she could catch a coach to Gatwick, and passed Cuddles on to a highly reluctant Animal Sanctuary. Shorn of his responsibilities, he went looking for adventure.

--/--

Lord Greedy-Bastard looked down at the graceful deer peacefully grazing in the great park below him. "Dinner" he thought. As thirty third earl of Swindon he could trace an unbroken line of descent back to the Beaker People, at which point a lot of things were broken. He had a lot to look down on in life.

Eyebrows had been raised when he bought up the bankrupt H2 project but now he was the proud owner of the longest and most exclusive executive cycle lane in Europe. Its route ran through several ancient forests, over some exquisite landscape features, and via much drained former rare wetland terrain. Well, let the eyebrows levitate if they would. Every half-completed station on its path had been developed into health spars, golf courses or wine bars. It was a goldmine in shimmering tarmac!

His laboratories now had perfected powerful new bug friendly herbicides and plant friendly pesticides which he had combined and sold to the military as a substance which could kill literally everything.

His acquisition of the National Blood Bank had enabled him to provide blood transfusions on demand to depraved rock stars at a price of his asking whenever their insatiable hedonism left them feeling out of sorts. Dubious foreheads had winkled again when he persuaded the Prime Minister to privatise the Household cavalry and, having acquired the franchise, sent them off on a lucrative perpetual tour of major North American rodeos.

In recent weeks however he had found himself thinking more and more about his legacy. His only daughter Cherie had never married. There had been that disgraceful dalliance with the appalling Hamish McThug which had generated Siegfrieg, his only partially acknowledged grandson. However, since Siegfried had absconded with much of Lord Greedy-Bastards best cutlery after subversion by Terry the cook, a broken Cherie had retired to a walled-up room at the top of one of the north towers where she lived on a punishing diet of gherkins and avocado and a cycle of repentant prayer. Prospects for a more conventional marriage appeared minimal.

To whom then should he leave his billions? Siegfried the thief had by all accounts now disappeared on an expedition to the middle of nowhere and was not expected to return. Should he, Lord Greedy-Bastard remarry at the age of 89? It was an appealing prospect, at least to him. He could begin a suitable course of injections and trawl through a list of suitable actresses and models. It was either that or reconcile himself to the adoption as heir of his cousin Cedric Foulswine-Badman. To call him the black sheep of the family was to insult the integrity of farm animals. Cedric was admittedly a card sharp, bigamist, arsonist, and cannibal but this counted for nothing against his appalling record of unpaid parking offences. No, having weighed his distaste for injections and parking cheats in the balance, Lord Greedy-Bastard decided that Siegfried had to be found and brought back to face misery as one of the nation's richest heirs. He rang for assistance and returned to his plan for franchising the Electoral Register.

--/--

Siegfried meanwhile now found himself clinging tenaciously round the neck of a large, ugly, hissing and spitting camel which smelt of the worst latrines at boyhood scout camps. His thighs were badly chaffed and his bum felt as though it had been repeatedly hit by a very large mallet.

His search for a new mission in life had led him to Ed Venture, the famous T.V. explorer. Ed was short, stocky and after so many skirmishes with rhino, bush kangaroo and angry flying squirrels had a face like an angry turnip. For all that he was a jovial, outgoing chap and had a winning way with unsophisticated peoples not unrelated to his vast supply of gaudy trinkets.

He had been the brains behind "Searching for the Elusive Snow Leopard" an ultimately fruitless TV documentary two years in the making; Flying with Flamingos, a project which never quite got off the ground;

and "The last Jaguar", a programme which had inadvertently led to the extinction of Jaguars in Columbia. Ed was now pursuing the one true passion of his life, the quest for the fabled two-legged goat of the Karakum. Others had scoffed at the legend claiming that if it did exist it had to be a man in a goatskin and therefore didn't count. Ed however had been a believer since spending his childhood roaming the bowels of the British museum where his father had worked. He was familiar with many strange beliefs and had later unearthed references to the cult in old temple scrolls found at a Luton car boot sale sandwiched between a copy of Charlton Heston's "Shooting my Way to Happiness" and a curiously well-thumbed biography of John Major.

The third member of their party sweating his way along the dusty path to nowhere was a tall slim retired tax officer named Bill Ulater, the reason for whose presence in these dry barren hills remained obscure to most of the party.

Siegfried was now trailing behind Ed's faithful manservant Andy Geezer, a dab hand with a sewing needle who could boast a mastery of sixth century Swedish runes and an extensive knowledge of Aboriginal cooking taboos amongst his many talents.

"I probably should have asked this earlier Andy, but how does Ed know where he's going?"

"No problem. He has a copy of Big Wally's guide to Asia which had a map in the back of it" replied the faithful sidekick.

"But aren't we looking for an Unexplored region?" queried Siegfried

"Exactly. It will be clearly marked on the map as an unexplored region! Unfortunately, the guvnor only has the seventh edition."

"What's wrong with the seventh edition?"

"The printers left out the Oases, apparently they ran out of yellow."

The light was now fading fast, taking the heat with it, but still Ed pressed his party on through the chill evening with his fabled tenacity and refusal to listen to reason. Finally, it was dark and their leader called time on their day's travels, permitting Andy to unfurl the large Persian carpet he kept rolled under his right arm and make camp, a performance which always had them in stiches. The intrusive stars winked down on them like an infinity of dubious salesmen.

"What's for tea?" enquired Siegfried.

"Mostly dung beetles. I think we're out of chicken nuggets" joked Andy who kept a seemingly limitless supply of the latter. He broke open a new container of disposable cigarette lighters and collected kindling for a fire.

Ed approached and squatted down beside Siegfried. "Keep your camel tethered close by you, we're in bandit country." He whispered. "They won't harm you, they are the Oolong, a people who have forsworn the use of weapons, but they are among the most sarcastic race on the planet. They'll be after your trousers. You would be surprised how much a pair of pink Ted Merry chinos can fetch in the markets of Con U or So Long Dosh.

So, this explained the mysterious heavy bags wrapped around their fifth camel! Siegfried nodded his understanding and tucked in to his chicken nuggets.

"I usually cook them first" cautioned Andy, "but don't mind me. We answer to no one out here in the desert.

Bill began strumming a plaintive nocturne on his banjo...

"Bill" called Ed, "it might be an idea to turn in now, we have a long day ahead of us tomorrow".

"O.K. Boss"

--/--

Siegfried woke as dawn spread across the sky like a set of enormous and badly inflamed tonsils. He felt an urgent need to micturate and walked off behind a large boulder which looked to be in need of refreshment.

"Oo! Look at you cheeky! No shame!" He looked down to see two swarthy but diminutive figures examining his loins.

"You're a long way from Shepherds Bush? What was it, traffic congestion on the M3 or did you take a wrong turn looking for the jacuzzi on a Saga cruise?"

Siegfried stuttered his rebuttal.

"Now hand me over those gorgeous Levi's or you'll get more of the same" commanded the leading small figure.

"You'll have to make me!" responded Siegfried whose blood was up.

"Ooh tiger! I bet your mum is SO proud of you? I haven't heard such defiance since a seagull tried to take my brothers chips. What's the problem, saggy bottom? Something you don't want to share with the group?"

The blood had reached Siegfried's face. "There is nothing wrong with my behind" he replied indignantly spinning round and dropping his trousers, an action which carried his grimy budgie smugglers with it to reveal the crescent moon and star in splendour on his modest derriere.

The bandits wrinkled faces beamed in sudden rapture. "Can it be? That which was foretold has come true? A stranger who has carried the moon and star since birth will come among us! Here, it's not a tattoo, is it?"

So saying the speaker bounded up to Siegfried and fondled his derriere before he could explain that he hadn't meant to show that much.

The bandit, satisfied with the results of his research lowered his pie crust face to the sand and began to chant. His friend followed him.

"Oh, do stop that" pleaded Siegfried, "you wouldn't believe the problems I have had over my rear end".

"Incredible" exclaimed a new voice and whirling round Siegfried discovered Ed had joined them. "The scrolls told of a talking backside but I assumed they were referring to persistent flatulence. This could be useful. We must set a course for Con U immediately."

--/--

They travelled for weeks desiccated by the dry heat beating up from the desert floor, escorted by a small party of Oolong who chanted incessantly, a word Andy had taught them for his own amusement as they appeared to find it almost impossible to pronounce.

Every time they picnicked under an immense sky whose stars spread eternally far above them, they would prepare scorpion and desert rat soup. This was new to Siegfried's culinary experience but it was either that or chicken nuggets. From time to time, the Oolong would rise and walk quietly around in a figure of eight shape. After a while Siegfried realised it was a pattern of behaviour.

At one point they awoke to find a party of villainous looking horsemen looking down upon then from a nearby ridge and waving their terrifying daggers in a swarthy and suggestive fashion but it turned out they were merely hoping for Margaret Thatchers autograph. They parted amicably after Andy had swapped one of the less useful Oolong for several of the beautiful finely engraved daggers.

The next night, with the party falling naturally into a reflective state after their indigestible soup, Siegfried had time to challenge Ed about his plans and choice of travelling companions.

"I chose Andy because I thought he said he was fluent in many exotic languages but he told me when we reached Kathmandu that what he actually said was that he had been described as effluent in a lot of exotic language. Details were never my strength."

"Isn't Kathmandu in Africa?"

"It is yes. Details were never my strength."

"And Bill, how does he fit in?"

"Simple really, he's paying for it all. He said something about recording a tax loss and needing to get away for a while. Personally, I think he was hoping to find romance."

"...and the goats, why are they so important to you?"

"Why do you even need to ask. Imagine how far they must have evolved to stand on two feet. I may even be able to communicate with them!"

Siegfried was unconvinced that standing on two feet had ever been a sign of superior intelligence.

"If there is something you need to talk about Ed, you know you can speak to me or Andy anytime, you don't need to share your personal life history with a goat you hardly know. "

--/--

At long last they approached the settlement of Con-U once one of the foremost settlements on the spice road. To Siegfried it looked like a camp site hurriedly erected by a party of drunken and negligent cowboys.

As they entered the encampment Siegfried noticed a ramshackle canvas structure away to his right. At the front were a couple of low tables offering double rows of worn hardback books. To the side was an area of ill matched chairs, benches, and tables under garish checked PVC coverings laid out for tea. From the interior beckoned the myriad offerings of a cheap hardware store.

"Perfect cover for an undercover customs and excise man" muttered Bill as he passed, though Siegfried couldn't think what possible use leisure reading, screws, nuts and bolts or tea breaks could be to a race of simple nomads?

As he pondered, a large thickset man in dark Arab dress and head covering, sporting a huge swirling moustache emerged from the shop. He looked vaguely familiar.

Andy now broke open some of the bags on the fifth camel and handed out Ted Merry chinos to the eager crowd who had immediately gathered around him.

"These are the Lapsangi" explained Ed. "It is here I believe we may obtain vital clues to the existence of the two-legged goats."

"I think you can practically guarantee it" muttered Siegfried staring at the eight-foot tall heavily bearded goatman standing behind him sporting a pair of comely pink chinos.

"Welcome to my world" boomed the goatman. I am Billy, king of the Goat people. Long have I awaited your coming."

"This is incredible" stammered Ed. "To think we are the first civilised people to meet this unique species!"

"Please, take a seat" continued the Goat king. "Actually, you are not the first. Otherwise, how would I know you might be coming. Please, keep up! Actually, a French party were here about two years ago."

"What happened to them?"

"You are sitting on what is left of them. Their gifts were rubbish! But now I have gifts I wish you to take back to your people. Follow me".

At this he led the party to a large cave behind the settlement guarded by two smaller (but still enormous) goatmen.

"This is astounding" gasped Ed "I have dreamt of this moment half my life. The race of the goatmen is not only real, it is multi lingual and clearly familiar with the basics of a barter economy! We may need to handle this situation with kid gloves."

King Billy grinned broadly. Over many years your world has in fact given us so much. These magnificent garments for a start" he said indicating his fine chino's. "Then there is the umbrella, sticky backed plastic, and, of course the baked bean! I could go on.... But in return we can offer this..." So, saying he opened one of the hundreds of sacks Siegfried could see lying around the cave. "Goats cheese. The finest available. A cheese only made possible through the flawless quality of our mountain air and the impeccable pedigree of our herds. Our goat maidens have worked tirelessly to produce this product and we wish to give it to you, yes, all of it!

Ed looked speculatively at Andy who returned his queasy expression.

"I think you misunderstand me my friend, our goat maidens have manufactured this fine product not expressed it!" returned King Billy somewhat tetchily. "But please, do not take my word for its quality, try some."

He clapped his front hooves together and a goatman came forward bearing a large wooden platter carrying portions of rich creamy yellow cheese, dry oatmeal biscuits and a pointless sprig of lettuce.

"My humble apologies," said Siegfried. "Only I'm afraid I am lactose intolerant. Do you have any jam perhaps, or honey?"

"I fear not" replied Billy looking severely disgruntled.

"But this is...this is...stuttered Andy.

"Wonderful stuff!" exulted Ed.

"Mm, mm" mumbled Bill through a mouth crammed with dairy produce.

"...and you want us to take the lot?" queried Ed. "We will need help!"

Oh, my friends the Lapsangi are at your disposal my friend" assured King Billy.

"Then it's a deal" beamed Ed.

--/--

That evening Siegfried, rendered insomniac by the nearby excited chatter of Ed and the Goatman King yearned for his faraway burrow. He was tired of vast skies of unfathomable celestial beauty, tired of chicken nuggets, and of hearing a retired tax official playing "when I'm cleaning windows" on the banjo. He would soon be returning to civilisation with an enormous cargo of exquisite cheese which he himself could not so much as sample.

He opened his eyes to see a small familiar bird with large questioning eyes on the floor before him.

"Oh, not you again!"

"That is absolutely no way to greet your spirit guide! Do it once more and I shall complain to my regulating body! I have travelled these vast barren wastelands to bring you a warning."

"Don't tell me, my car insurance has expired?"

"That too, but you need to know that now would be a very good time to leave. I know it looks good. A whole tribe who worship the very ground you sit on, a lifetime supply of goats cheese and the prospect of worldwide fame on your return, but trust me things are about to get seriously bad"

"Go away before I fetch a cat!"

"Well, you've been warned! With which the owl disappeared from view muttering its disapproval.

Suddenly he found himself staring at a large and growing tear in the canvas at the back of his tent. A split second later a familiar face emerged index finger pressed to his lips in an entreaty for silence. Shorn of his exotic head attire and dressed in khaki shorts and a Guns and Roses tee shirt the tousled dreadlocks of the tall shopkeeper were, despite his enormous moustache, instantly familiar.

"Terry" he whispered. "What a co-incidence! What are the odds in you having business in Con-U at the same time as us?"

"I think you need to brace yourself for a bit of a shock Siegfried, its not exactly a co-incidence. Has it not occurred to you to be an act of unparalleled generosity for the Goatmen to be giving all this cheese to a world they hardly know?"

"Well, ...yes..."

"Well, no actually. The cheese they gave your colleagues is indeed a thing of exquisite flavour and they are likely in thrall to it for the rest of their lives, but the cheese they have prepared for the developed world has been blended with a rare herb found only in these remote mountains. It was known to Marco Polo as Igneus furiouso. It consumes all who taste it with an all-consuming murderous wrath. It will turn the developed world against itself and leave it open for the Goatmen to take over the planet."

"Not me though, I'm lactose intolerant!"

"Don't be a fool Siegfried, in their frenzy the cheese eaters will not distinguish between their peers and those who are lactose intolerant, they will murder and destroy indiscriminately."

"Well, they do that already"

"But not on this scale!"

"How did you discover all this?"

Terry's face wore a slightly smug look as he replied "how soon you forget, I am a murdering psychopath by nature and as the Oolong have forsworn violence. It was like taking candy off a quaker!"

"We must warn Ed, Andy and Bill."

"You can't, they won't believe you. The cheese will have addled their senses. I'm afraid you need to leave with me now for Bastard Grange."

"You mean, you can't mean... are you here at my grandfathers' bequest? You loath everything he stands for, his wealth, his lack of scruple, his bestial appetites? You despise all that?"

Terry shook his head:

"I **had** turned my back on the wealth of the world

On my ways too cruel to mention

But then after careful second thoughts

I found I had need for a pension."

Siegfried was quiet for a moment. "Fair enough. Let's dump them."

Terry turned and Siegfried followed him through the tear in the tent.

Suddenly a powerful set of hooves clamped down on his shoulders rendering him helpless as he gazed disbelievingly down at the corpse of his old friend stretched out before him with a pair of enormous curved horns protruding from his back. They belonged to Billy.

"Not so fast my English friend. You think because we have hooves, we are stupid? We have been watching the activities of this fool for weeks."

"The man you call "fool" was my friend! He gave his life for me!"

"In point of fact I think you will find from his correspondence that he gave his life for an enormous bribe. I overheard everything that was said in there. Tomorrow you will join your friend. Tomorrow, you die!"

--/--

"Living in these barren hills, the Lapsangi get so little meat in their diet" chuckled Billy addressing the assembled tribesmen, his Goatmen and the small expedition. "But tonight, they will experience the retro joy of ...Fondu! Yes, you Siegfried McThug will be the first living fondu in living memory, or something on those lines anyway. My goatmen will cut and dice you and stir you into this vat of melted cheese. I imagine you will be delicious whether you like it or not. What do you say to that?"

"Siegfried unexpectedly smiled. I have lived a full and varied life. I have no intention of dying such a cliched death, boiled in a large pot for the delectation of hungry nomads."

So saying he downed his trousers and played his trump card.

For an instant the assembled Lapsangi were silent, then the air grew thin as the tribe shared an enormous intake of breath. It didn't go far and soon the familiar odours of rotting scorpion returned on the outbreath. The tribe thronged around him, turning as one to face Billy the goatman leader.

"Fair enough" he cried staring askance at the infamous birthmarks. "If I am to sacrifice a living god, even one as dubious as this, then I shall give him one last chance of escape. Release him my Goatmen. If he can bring me a willing virgin to take his place within twenty-four hours then he is free to leave." He grinned unpleasantly. "We goats are after all known for our appetites? I will even throw in a camel and a day's head start! Sound fair?"

The Lapsangi paused before nodding their assent.

To Siegfried this did not sound like much of a result. Where was he to find someone willing to sacrifice their integrity to the lusts of an eight-foot tall goatman in such empty and forbidding country. It would be hard enough to find a volunteer in even the fleshpots of Southampton for goodness' sake!

--/--

The next twenty-four hours were hell to Siegfried. Like waiting for an exam in a subject you knew you were bound to fail, perhaps German or Biology? He even found himself wishing the owl would return to offer succour. Ed came to see him with a copy of the escape clause in his contract underlined in red:

THE EMPLOYER OFFERS NO REDRESS, AND BEARS NO LIABILITY, IN THE EVENT OF A PERCIEVED NEED FOR ESCAPE. ANY SUCH ATTEMPT IS MADE ENTIRELY AT THE EXPEDITION MEMBERS PERSONAL RISK.

Andy came to visit offering a final dish of chicken nuggets in cheese sauce which he politely declined.

Then Bill arrived.

“Mine has been a life such as few would envy. Long, hard, tedious and repetitive work for little credit or reward. A lonely life without companionship or friendship, unsupported by family or friends. I worked in dull, dimly lit, overcrowded offices surrounded by silent unreflective folk lacking even an understanding of humour. HMRC – Humourless, Miserable, Repugnant Creeps. Even my parents would have preferred a poodle... ”

“Bill, if I’m honest, I think they may have had a point!” admitted Siegfried. “When did you last tune your banjo?”

“...but at last, I have a chance to do something really worthwhile!”

With this he shook a baffled Siegfried’s hand and left the tent.

--/--

The next day Billy stood once more before the crowd and gloatingly announced that twenty-four hours had almost elapsed since his generous offer. He approached the bound Siegfried brandishing an enormous carving knife which shone in the desert sun dazzling the crowd.

"Wait!"

"Who dares to interrupt me at lunchtime?"

"I do," answered a frail thin elderly voice. "You seek a willing virgin and you have one. Me"

"You're kidding?" scoffed the huge goatman. "What would I want with an elderly retired taxman? You're hardly what I had in mind."

"That's up to you kid!" responded Bill in a voice suddenly swelling with a new found confidence. I meet your criteria so you got me baby! Does that sound fair to you?" He asked the pressing crowd.

The Lapsangi paused before nodding their assent.

--/--

Siegfried pressed on under the burning desert sun sensing the remaining strength in his reluctant camel ebbing away. It was day three and there had been no pursuit. The goatmen were clearly convinced no lone westerner could survive in such a limitless inferno.

Then, suddenly, in a flurry of flailing limbs, the camel collapsed and lay inert on the burning sands.

I knew he'd given me the rubbish one thought Siegfried as he slipped slowly into a merciful unconsciousness.

What followed was a surreal tableau of familiar faces in unfamiliar contexts, Terry counting the spoons in Andy's luggage, Bill feeding chicken nuggets to a family of otters, Constance Surprise swaddling a reluctant penguin and Billy the Goatking engrossed in a copy of Che Guevara's "Summer term at St Ursula's". He was visited by the owl rebuking him for his lack of respect, by the Bishop of Piddle Hinton insisting he join a crusade against librarians and finally by Chianti complaining about a lack of personal hygiene amongst Patagonian penguins.

"Honestly darling, you have no idea how those creatures stink of fish, especially in summer, and besides, I missed all those gorgeous little shoes you used to find for me."

He found to his amazement he could open his eyes, and yet the vision seemed more powerful than ever.

"Oh, wake up darling, we haven't got all day. These little chaps charge by the hour!"

Behind the persistent image of his wife, he saw a couple of familiar piecrust faces.

One split open and said "Heaven only knows what she sees in you. I thought living gods were supposed to have at least a modicum of charisma not just swan about on dead camels while the rest of us struggle to get by?"

Siegfried tried to operate his oversized and cumbersome tongue. "You're real?"

"No dear, we're remaking "Lawrence of Arabia". You're front row of the circle at the Odeon Leicester Square."

"Behave!" chided Chianti. Here darling, have a little water and we must be going."

"How?"

"In that of course!" Dream Chianti pointed to a large green dream truck to his left.

"I booked dinner for eight o clock? Is that O.K. Do please have a bath first. The Oolong have lent me some clothes but I don't think pink is your colour. It's just as well I asked for dinner to be brought up to us?"

--/--

That night as a hungry Siegfried waited for food and drooled over the last of the courtesy biscuits, he explained to his wife that Bill Ulater had sacrificed a life of which he had grown weary to the Goatking perverted whims in the vain hope of happiness and to give him a chance of freedom. Ed and Andy however were now heedlessly transporting a huge cargo of poisoned goats' cheese which would destroy society.

"But tell me darling, why did you leave the penguins."

“Oh, my love the world is full of penguins but there is only one you.”

Siegfried was to remember this moment as the point at which divorce became inevitable. His grandfather’s money had clearly corrupted his wife’s noble environmentalist credentials as surely as it had destroyed Terry. He saw also however that he could use it as a weapon to destroy the Goatkings foul plan for world domination. He would return and take up his appointed place in the Greedy-Bastard empire **provided** his grandfather bought up a monopoly of goats’ cheese stocks worldwide. The poisoned cheese would never make it to market. That done he could sue his grandfather for making him rich and so exposing him to the profound social, chemical and moral hazards occasioned by extreme wealth.

One short phone call and the deal was done. He had drained the venomous chalice of choice, swallowed the toxic bait of the Bastard billions and shaken the poisoned hand of hedonism. He barely had room for pudding.

--/--

With the thirty third Earl of Swindon retired to a health farm the size of a small-town Siegfried found running the Greedy-Bastard empire to be something of a full-time job.

The challenge became even less welcome when the owl reappeared one bath time.

“I keep telling you, I don’t want counselling!”

"Mentoring?"

"No!"

"A little gentle encouragement?"

"No."

"Well argued second opinion?"

No. Go away!"

"O.K. By the way, you didn't hear, did you? Eds convoy only made it as far as So Long Dosh. They felt peckish and had some of the poisoned cheese. Scratched each other's eyes out! The rest was left to melt in the sun except for a little left on one of the camels that made it back to Bulukul. You have bought a world supply of perfectly good cheese you can't even eat. Great thinking, and still you don't feel you need me? Well fine, do things your own way!

By the way, you know I was lying before? I don't exist."

"Of course, I do. You are merely a manifestation arising in the left hemisphere of my medial frontal/anterior cingulate cortex and insula possibly triggered by a neurotransmitter imbalance occasioned by stress. Now go away!"

And he did.

Disposal of even the diminished repository of poisoned cheese presented a challenge until he hit on the idea of leaving it outside a Kansas gun store and letting nature take its course. Two weeks later he was able to offer a deserted USA for sale to the Swiss government.

It was time to put the second part of his plan into operation.

"Chianti? I want a divorce!"

"Darling, how kind! I will of course take you to the proverbial cleaners. I want half of everything, no, make that all of most of it."

"I am going to offer you all of everything my darling, provided that includes Cuddles. I need nothing, I will return to my simple burrow a wiser and a chastened man. This heartless, soulless world is not for a simple man like me. I shall devote my life to painting smiley faces on stones and babbling mindlessly to myself. I shall keep budgerigars. I may even redecorate the living room. I shall be happy.

"Oh darling, poor old you!"

DARKFACE

There it was, over there about twenty yards away lurking in the bushes by the park fence. Briefly he felt better for having established its location, because he was certain it had been following him for some time. He just hadn't seen it, hadn't known where it was hiding. He had felt it near him almost everywhere recently. At first it had seemed to come every week or two, and whenever it happened it was always in a crowded place. Then it came with greater regularity even when he was alone. If he was walking along the road it might pass by in a crowded bus or a car which rushed past him, usually travelling in the opposite direction. If he was on a bus himself it could be in a bus queue on the other side of the road, or perhaps peering out of a shop window or a dark alley. It might appear in a crowd on the underground only a few yards away, though he had learnt from experience he could never quite track it down, never push his way through the surging crowd in pursuit, catch it and touch it.

Even now he had never really had a single clear sighting of it. He only ever caught glimpses, perhaps out of the corner of his eye. He had no sooner spotted it, or thought he had, than it would disappear from view before he could confirm its gender or facial features. It was infuriating, this uncanny ability to blend back into its surroundings whenever he spotted it. How could it know he had spotted it? It was obviously cunning as well as malevolent. This made him wonder how often it was there unseen, he certainly felt watched almost all the time now.

He called it "Darkface". It was only ever part of the face he saw, never a torso or a protruding arm or leg. He couldn't even be sure which part of the face. It had such skill in blending into its surroundings. He couldn't be sure the face was actually physically dark, only that its presence had instantly felt very threatening, very sinister and that it meant him harm. That was how he came by its name.

But why him? He was successful of course, the youngest general manager in company history, and naturally he had paid a significant price for his business success. There would be jealousy. Successful men were never popular in the workplace, but he was unaware of having made any outright enemies during his upward trajectory over the last decade or so. He was confident he was not generally seen as a bad person at work.

He had had several romantic relationships but sooner or later these had all faded and he had never married. These too had left him unaware of any bitter spurned lovers or deadly rivals with a grudge to settle.

He had few hobbies and so little or no opportunity to pick fights or run vendettas against fellow members of golf, tennis or squash clubs, none to inspire the resentment of fellow gamblers, or to indulge in angry exchanges with teammates or opponents at hockey, football, or rugby.

He barely knew his neighbours, but there was nothing unusual in that. This was London and the population was transitory, even in the suburbs. People, even families came and went all the time. He estimated that his entire neighbourhood must have changed personnel several times during the few years he had lived in his quiet semi.

Yet Darkface now felt horribly familiar, there was nothing transitory about him. He was remorseless, and he suddenly realised he did now think if it as a "him". He had often felt on the brink of remembering exactly what this meant to him and where Darkface came from, when he would fade back into his surroundings and he would lose the trace. Until the next time.

So, if he had no obvious reason to hate him, and if he never saw the full figure, or even part of the face for more than a split second, he had surely to ask himself was he really there? Was this some kind of emerging paranoia brought on by pressure of work or some repressed anxiety. Maybe it was some childhood experience supressed for decades which had now for some strange reason emerged into his conscious to haunt his waking hours? This just didn't ring true to him. He had never been a nervous person and had surely had the happiest of childhood memories? As the eldest of four, two boys and two girls, he was the one they turned to for help and support. It was true he was perpetually busy at work, but he knew the business backwards and never felt under much real mental pressure. Or maybe he was fooling himself about that?

Whatever it was, the psychological impact of these appearances was growing. At first, he simply felt irritated to be under a stranger's frequent scrutiny, then he was angry, and eventually, when the full feeling of long familiarity emerged, somewhat fearful, well, very fearful. Did Darkface intend physical or mental harm, did his appearances portend some disaster or a profound health scare. It felt as though it could be any or all of these. It just felt bad, really bad. When he couldn't see it, he would scan his urban environment closely, anxious for a sighting, almost fearing him more in his apparent absence than during his fleeting appearances as though the phenomenon had become too clever to let itself be seen.

He had begun to see it now even in his dreams. He had no "safe place" remaining that Darkface had not invaded and sullied, even at dead of night when he lay shivering, naked and alone. He felt it watching the house while he was inside. He sensed it lurking in the bushes outside his front door, or waiting in a parked car at the far end of the road. Always out of touch yet always a threat.

For months he had kept these experiences to himself. It wouldn't look good to be telling people there was "something out there", something wanting to do harm him for no good reason and in no readily definable way. But the thing was filling his head, taking over his moments of quiet time, and even rushing up to the surface when he was in meetings or interviews. This couldn't go on much longer. The phone would ring and he would pick it up wondering if Darkface had finally gained a voice? He had to resolve the situation, encounter "Darkface" in the open or put him to rest.

Perhaps with the help of a friend he could trap the thing and have it out face to face? If of course it was flesh and blood, and amenable to rational debate. If not, he could banish it for good.

So, he rang Steve. Steve and he had been friends from the moment Steve had joined the company on his recommendation. Technically Steve worked for him, but he trusted him. The two had risen together through the company ranks. Steve had every reason to like him – and to help him if help was required.

Steve agreed to come round to his house that Thursday night at eight o'clock. He was told there was something that required his sympathetic ear, something very confidential that couldn't be put to rest without the aid of a third party. Steve had been asked to promise absolute secrecy and had readily agreed. "No problem boss. I'll be round at eight", he replied, thinking this was about a takeover, a merger or some other corporate politicking.

--/--

Steve was on time. "Thanks mate, I appreciate this. Come through, I've got to tell someone. I decided to tell you. I am going to find this difficult; I know it's going to make me sound odd, very odd, even a little bit crazy, but I have to confide in someone, and who better than you?"

He offered Steve a beer and they settled down in the lounge on two of the comfortable leather chairs he had brought the previous year. He paused and drew his breath.

"For the last few months, I have had this horrible feeling of being watched and followed. It's crept up slowly but it's got worse and worse. At first, I just thought some weirdo was watching me, then I thought maybe it was "an interested party", you know, maybe a private detective or someone with a grudge. But I always felt they wished me personal harm. It was creepy even at the start, but it's got more and more intense. Nowadays I see him even in my dreams, always at the edge of events, watching and waiting. I have no idea who or what it is, but it's got a name, I call it "Darkface".

"I need your honest opinion, Steve. Do you think a thing like that is possible or do you think there is something wrong with me? Am I going crazy, and if so, why? You know me well enough? What would drive me to imagine something like that? Have you noticed any changes in my behaviour at work lately? Do I appear to be under pressure? Do you think I've changed in some fundamental way?"

"No mate, sorry. I can't help you. To me you look and sound like the same old task driven slave driver we have all come to know and love. No change there. I kind of wish you had kept this to yourself, but don't worry, it's not going to go any further, I promise."

They chatted on for an hour or so on various other topics before Steve protested his need for an early start next day and left after a hug and a handshake. But he never forgot Steve's casual dismissal of the whole matter. It felt disloyal…and deeply suspicious.

--/--

Two days later he had gone for a swim in the municipal baths, an old Victorian place by the High Road. He felt better for the swim, as he usually did, but when he reached the showers, he started to feel the old discomfort creeping back. Could he really be the only one there? What were those noises he heard? Quiet scratching noises, and maybe a low humming to some old song he didn't remember? He couldn't face the showers. Couldn't entertain the idea of taking his shorts off and leaving himself naked and vulnerable in the face of something he didn't understand. What if something or someone crept up behind him? Instead, he dried himself, dressed quickly and drove home.

That night he recalled for the very first time the night terrors that had assailed him in his earliest childhood. He had been maybe five or six when he became convinced a tribe of hungry cannibals were living under his bed. They were cunning. Whenever he plucked up the courage to peer under the bed, they would make themselves invisible. Before long he could no longer even bring himself to look. If he were to peer under one side, surely the cannibals could creep up behind him from the other side and tear him to pieces. The very act of trying to reassure himself would sooner or later guarantee his doom.

By day it was obvious even to a very young child that the whole idea of a tribe of cannibals living under the mattress was preposterous beyond words. He couldn't tell his parents because he could imagine them laughing and telling other people how stupid he had been. But every night in bed it became horribly feasible again, and he would spend a desperate, horrible, sleepless night certain it would be his last.

Determined now that this experience and others like it must somehow lie at the heart of this new horror, he rang Steve again and asked him for a repeat of their recent meeting. Sure enough Steve arrived on time the following Wednesday evening braced for further unwelcome confidences, yet apparently happy to be helping his boss exorcize his strange obsession.

--/--

This time they were working their way through a more than acceptable bottle of claret and a delicious slate of cheeses when he opened up for the first time about his long-forgotten childhood terrors. He looked Steve straight in the eye and asked him whether he felt something like that, some long forgotten and unexplained trauma, could possibly come back in some way to haunt an otherwise sane and sensible adult so many years later? Could it possibly explain his current experiences, and if so, how could he work the thing out? In Steve's opinion should he seek the help of a trained professional, maybe take some time out, or join some kind of therapy group?

There was something unconvincing about Steve's reaction to these intimate confessions. Could Steve possibly be laughing at him? Maybe he was storing away all the juicy details to use against him in the workplace? Or just maybe it was something worse than that?

He pulled a large kitchen knife out from behind his back. It's you, isn't it?" You're him? You're Darkface. Suddenly I get it. You're the one winding me up every day, following me around, trying to catch me out, trying to push me into making mistakes. Watching me make every move from when I leave this house in the morning to when I get back at night, and even then, you don't let me sleep in peace? Well, no more! I'm going to finish this here and now. No more Darkface, no more terror!"

He thrust the knife suddenly in the direction of Steve's abdomen, but Steve quickly rolled away and stayed out of its reach leaving the knife to sink up to the hilt into the soft leather upholstery. Steve's reaction had been too quick, almost as though he had been expecting the attack.

Steve shot to his feet and yelled "Oh, I get it, great idea! Pretend you see **me** as Darkface and kill **me**. Then a little institutional incarceration, a few tablets and a few expert panel meetings later and they'll announce that you're cured and ready to take your place back in society ready and able to kill again? Well bad luck Darkface, I'm on to you. I've been on to you from the very start. You know perfectly well you are not the one under surveillance. It's **me** whose life has been a living hell. I'm the one that's been haunted. You didn't fool me for a moment, and I came here determined not to let you undermine me any longer."

Steve opened his jacket, pulled out an ugly looking clawhammer and took a vicious swipe at his friend's head….

--/--

It was a two days later before the elderly bachelor next door, his curiosity roused by the continued presence of his neighbours Golf at the end of his drive, rang the bell several times and on receiving no response, rang the local police. He had after all heard a lot of shouting and breaking of glass two nights previously, which was completely out of character for his quiet, mild-mannered neighbour.

On entry the police had found extensive bloodshed across the living room, hall, and kitchen. Splash marks covered the walls, furniture had been overturned and the TV was shattered. There was a body slumped by the kitchen table and another stretched out facing away from the kitchen in the hall. It was a nasty business and no mistake, perhaps a lover's tiff? Who could say! Report what they saw and leave the rest to forensics.

The third entity present that night during the disturbances had left straight after the second death and was never discovered. Darkface was a busy boy and had new people to see.

ON BUYING A HOUSE IN FRANCE

No one tells you what you're in for of course. The people you are going to speak to are the ones who have just bought theirs. It's the perfect house in the most perfect spot. It's either got so much room you could practically play cricket in the corridors or its so cute and "self-contained" you just couldn't find anywhere like it in the UK. It's either adorably old, has the most wonderful views over distant purple hills, or has neighbours who just can't do enough for you. Its certainly true about the land, there's just SO much of it!. France is a big country and many of its people live around the extensive coastline or in flats. As a result, houses often come with enough land for an entire estate in the UK. In fact, too much land to look after is a common reason for not buying given what you are looking for is only a second home.

What they aint gonna tell you is it took them over three years to find it.

O.K. so I started by hanging around French estate agents at lunchtimes, when I knew they were safely shut, just admiring the stock in the windows. This made me feel good, even made me feel serious about purchasing, but meant there was no risk of actually having to talk to anyone about houses (or anything else) in French.

At some point I realised I was going to have to mention the idea to my wife. We had dreamt about it often enough, who doesn't? But seriously? Who is going to look after it? Where will we buy? I mean as I said, it's a pretty big country. And apart from any other consideration, in those days you couldn't even get the beds delivered, you had to collect them from large retailers often fifty miles away and magic them home.

In the end, Liz was completely behind the idea, so telling her I was off for a bit of shopping, I sneaked round to a small Estate Agent in Roche Posay and hung around until he came back from lunch and asked if he could help me.

During holidays over the next three years, we looked into sixteen houses.

We had "Earthquake House" which had a terrace on all four sides made of paving slabs slanted at crazy angles from each other as though an army of eager zombies had pushed through from beneath and hopefully run off.

We had "Matchstick House" which had started life as a perfectly respectable bungalow before some DIY maniac decided to convert the loft into four bedrooms and a family bathroom. He must have had shares in a company making those pine slats which are so ubiquitous on French walls and ceilings (like the ones you get in sauna's). We would not have had a problem with wooden slats, but we did have a problem with the fact that as far as we could see every single slat had been broken to the required length over his knee before fitting. The upstairs was a seething mass of vicious splinters. Every wall and every ceiling was a minor safety hazard.

One particularly exciting prospect was "The Dead Man's House". The last owner had died in the large brass bed we found in the kitchen (seriously he had wanted to die in the kitchen). Upstairs there was a man-sized hole in the bedroom wall where he had risen one night thinking he had heard an owl in the loft. He had taken a sledgehammer and broken through the dividing wall to check and the family had put it up for sale like that. One added attraction here was that a distant cousin apparently owned one sixteenth of the kitchen, but we were assured he had expressed a willingness to negotiate over its sale. Thanks to the Napoleonic Code still governing inheritance in France at this time, this is actually common and probably explains many of the attractive but abandoned ruins dotted around the French countryside. No one sells unless the entire clan agree to sell.

Even more enticing was "The Cracked House". This was a beautiful old house in a beautiful situation with a lot of land including its own small wood. There were at least eight cracks wide enough to put your fingers through reaching in zigzag style from ground level all the way to the roof at intervals all around the house. Surely, we thought it can't be falling down in all four directions at the same time? Inside we found a toilet newly installed in the bend at the bottom of the main staircase. Even an idiot like me could see that the then owners had for some reason taken flight without pausing to build the room which had clearly been intended to surround it. The Agents tried the hackneyed "since you left our office just now someone has made an offer on the place, so you will need to make a decision now" scam on us. They were that desperate. We discovered months later that it had been regularly burgled during the owners' absences and that on the last occasion the burglars had brought a large lorry, secured it to the house by means of the bars on one of the downstairs windows, and simply pulled the wall down to get in.

In St Maure we found a house in which the entire garden had been converted into a giant swimming pool. You literally left the back door and plunged straight in (to an empty pool, naturally, hardly anybody ever bothers filling them up).

We seriously considered making an offer on a lovely old place in Grande Pressigny with a beautifully tiled floor in its exceptional old kitchen. Sadly, it turned out that the elderly owner had built herself a bungalow in the garden and was retiring there, fully intending to keep the entire garden. We would have been besieged, surrounded on all four sides.

And finally, I must mention "The Arsenic House". This was a gorgeous property in a lovely little village dominated by an unfinished chateau at a place called La Guerche. It had nice sized rooms, a decent garden, and a lovely kitchen. It was just a shame about all the crystalline arsenic seeping through the walls. To prevent this the interior walls had been lined with lead sheeting but nothing it appeared could stop the onward and outward march of the deadly toxicity. I swear someone told me this arose from a mass burial pit under the house but Liz says I dreamt this bit. Whatever, it was all coming from somewhere very bad under the place.

And then I saw it, my dream house.

I was lucky, I admit that. On-line I had seen a fairly promising place in an old riverside town called Descartes after the philosopher, but when I enquired, the agent, who turned out to be English, told me it had been sold. What were we looking for? I gave her a full specification. No problem, a friend of mine is selling one just right for you at a place outside Cussay (only five miles away).

After three wasted years I didn't hesitate but jumped straight on to a plane and went over.

It was pink, oldish, south facing with a large but manageable K shaped garden set mostly to lawn, well grass anyway. There was a large salon with a little kitchen in the far corner, a shower room and a loom room. A what? Yes, a large downstairs room with a large recently constructed loom in residence. Upstairs were two bedrooms and a second open lounge area which took up most of the floor area. The ceiling of this lounge was high but sloped down almost to the floor and was covered in the inevitable slim wooden slats. The original walls below it however were bare rough limestone tuffeau, the traditional characteristic old Touraine building material. Between the house and the south facing garden was a covered terrace with a low limestone sill just perfect for putting your feet up, and the house wall behind it was fully two feet thick with a window sill big enough to sit in. The door frame was several inches too small for me but I pretended not to notice.

As I went through the garden to the house, I was almost deafened by the sound of countless cicadas buzzing and clicking around me. Actually, I was told years later they are not cicadas but no one seemed to know what they were even though they were ubiquitous thereabouts. It was a beautiful spring day and the current owner had constructed a scent garden outside the terrace. The lavender, roses, honeysuckle, lilies, and other contributors were belting it out as we went indoors.

It was in fact the perfect rural idyll set in a small hamlet of six or seven old properties about a mile and a half from the main road and larger village of Cussay proper, nestling around an old disused well, hence the name, Le Puits. Best of all, the hamlet backed on to a wide agricultural drainage channel so there was no passing traffic. It was the most peaceful place I had ever been in.

Only when we sold up ten years later was it to dawn on us that the very reasons the place looked so appealing as a second home were the very reasons most French people wouldn't have touched it with a barge pole. Stuff the silence and solitude, they would be looking at proximity to jobs, schools, medical facilities, shops, family, friends and places to eat and drink. Perhaps for these reasons there were recognised to be two prices for houses in the French countryside, the French price and the price for a foreigner. Under no circumstances would a French vendor agree to sell to a foreigner for less than about a 30% premium. It was assumed another useful idiot would be along soon and they generally were.

So yes, I agreed to pay the full asking price. After all, the agent and vendor were English, I wouldn't say I was naïve enough to assume that meant they were more honest but it did mean I would understand what was going on didn't it?

I rang Liz and told her I had bought a house she had never seen, and she was, considering the circumstances, remarkable laid back about it.

If you are expecting me to say that we later regretted it, you could not be more mistaken. True it came as a surprise to find that the agent had charged both us and the vendor for her services (and at a rather higher rate than we would have expected to pay in the UK) or that she had in fact no license to sell property. When we later actually met the vendor, she expressed some surprise to find she had been described as "a friend". When we later got to know the agent well, we were introduced to other "friends" of hers, who years after when they came to sell their own place nearby got the same treatment. In fact, not only were both they and their purchaser charged handsomely for her services, but the agent had generously offered to buy up their furniture to save them the trouble of returning it to the UK. They soon discovered that the lovely chaise longue (which they had previously bought from her) and which had embellished their landing had been resold to the new owners at a mark-up of 167% and returned to the same spot. She had even charged them a commercial rate for translating all the sale documents into English. Estate Agency and antique dealing had such a wonderful synergy.

It was also a surprise to find later that the drainpipe in both front and back gardens drained into large water barrels over the fence in the adjoining property and that the house had been built without foundations, but hey, this was apparently unremarkable round there and it was too late to complain.

There was a delightful outbuilding in the "front" garden which was internally divided into two small sections with separate doors. In the furthest one there was a recently constructed ladder built onto the wall leading up into a through loft. This was lined with original old tiles (a plaque on the outside established that the building had been constructed in 1849). I had been told years earlier in the Dordogne that such tiles were extremely valuable as they were now unavailable and were much in demand for renovating old properties. Harvesting them however was impossible since the floor was visibly sagging and sky was already visible through what remained of the roof.

Why would anyone build a ladder up to a loft which it was so obviously dangerous to enter?

The "Dependence" was stuffed with old stuff, including huge glass jars for winemaking, old pieces of equipment and materials, old bottles (empty) and decayed gardening equipment. It was all charming and nearly all utterly useless. A curious incident was to occur there some years later when we arrived in the spring to find a sizeable pile of stones in the centre of the floor in both rooms. No one could suggest how these could have piled themselves up in the middle of the room when the door had been locked, or why there should be piles on both sides of a stone dividing wall. I cleared out four full wheelbarrows of stones and was never any the wiser.

Perhaps the nearest thing we had to a shock at the purchasing stage however was the discovery that we couldn't actually move from the north facing rear garden through to the large "front" garden without passing through a small patch of land at the side which belonged to the owner of a large detached house next door. This discovery however was balanced by the revelation that we in turn were to become owners of a small portion of her rear garden. Apparently, it had been everyone's intention to sort out this historical anomaly last time the house was sold but no one had ever gotten round to it. The other owner, Madame Boudin (Mrs Pudding, and yes, she **was** a restauranteur!) was fairly easily persuaded to regularise the property details. It was after all hardly in her interest that the place next door remained unsold for any length of time and it wasn't as if we were going to be there more than perhaps three months a year to disturb her peace. We even, somehow, got her to pay for it.

Then of course there were the surveys. There were seven of them. They included one on ownership, which is fair enough in a country where the inheritance laws are such that people frequently set out to sell houses which are not in fact theirs to sell; and asbestos, which again I don't feel is something you particularly want to unearth during routine maintenance. They also however included a search for termites, when the nearest known colony was seventy-five miles away south of Poitou and one for lead. My objection to a check on lead was that after some two hundred years you would think someone would have noticed lead pipes and could perhaps have been asked, in a nice tight, binding, legal way, whether they had any. It would have been cheaper. Termites I am assuming would have been a more recent innovation.

There was also a survey on septic tanks to ensure that your smelly bunker complied with current legislation. No one seemed to know what the current legislation was but ours passed with flying colours despite the two very mature birch trees growing out of it.

The next step was to raise the funds in euros. Exchange rates at the time were bouncing up and down like jet propelled yoyo's so this took a while, but the really tricky part was opening a French bank account to house the euros. You could open an account especially set up for

English speaking customers, but you had to do so while speaking in French. There was a telephone help line for the English-speaking customers, but the English spoken on it was of a kind we had never previously encountered. I imagine she had a close relative working in the local Credit Agricole branch, or perhaps she had once visited London on a school trip?

When we sold the house, had it not been for the international distain by then being expressed for Sterling, we would have realised a 37% loss on the purchase price. I was so glad I had kept such a close eye on currency markets.

We had now to become familiar with local rating systems. At first glance council taxes in France seem to be lower than in the U.K. Then you realise there are three of them. Taxe D'habitation, Taxe Fonciere, and my favourite, the Ordures tax. They come at different times, are payable to different organisations, and judging by the dire warnings which used to arrive by post even after we had paid them (by post) I think they cut your heads off if you don't cough up pretty quickly. In due course we were to discover that they kept coming even over three years after you sell up although the legal retribution threatened for not paying tax on a French house you didn't own never materialised.

We arranged to buy all the furniture in situ except funnily enough, the loom. Initially I thought the reason all French property in our area owned by actual French people was so full of hideous furniture was because it had been impossible to arrange delivery of new stuff ever since they stopped building their own. Later I realised it was because French people actually preferred hideous great lumps of dark brown furniture which would have intimidated the most traditional Victorian. These great mournful Dickensian artefacts often made a French living room look like an undertaker's parlour but perhaps they were seen as some kind of living embodiment of a highly respected family ancestor? It transpired that, at least in the countryside French people **never** throw anything away. Until only a few years earlier, even their effluent had been profitably recycled to local French farmers.

The loom incidentally was dismantled piece by piece by a wonderful English couple who had checked on the house and maintained the garden in the old owners' absence, and who agreed to do the same for us. It was then shipped back to Tyneside. The space this gave us we thought would make a wonderful large downstairs bedroom as the shower room led off it and the large window opened out into the south facing garden. We bought pots of very posh English paint and set about repainting it a tasteful light blue. Big mistake. We recognised six coats later that English paint just doesn't work with French plasterwork.

And so finally it only remained to sign the purchase documents. We were given an appointment with a local solicitor and checked out the location the week beforehand just to be sure we could find it. I still couldn't find it on the day, largely because I had driven to the wrong village, however Liz realised my mistake and got us there in the nick of time.

We were owners of a gorgeous property in France!

ON SELLING A HOUSE IN FRANCE

It was time to sell. It had only dawned on us slowly over two or three years. There were several reasons.

We had been to every chateau, garden, farmers market, nature reserve and public event for some fifty miles around three or four times – and there were over fifty chateaux alone open to the public. That wonderful freshness, the sense of discovering and exploring our part of France had gone.

The environment was slowly changing. The "cicadas" which had made such a racket when we first arrived had been wiped out by pesticides sprayed by the growing agribusinesses. We were lucky now to hear the occasional one. The decimation of insect populations was in turn beginning to have a discernible effect on higher order wildlife. There was also more (and faster) traffic on local roads. Several of our favourite restaurants and hotels had closed down, and crucially the weather was less reliable by far. One spring we had arrived to discover plant Armageddon. My diary for the fourth May 2012 reads as follows:

"On arrival, scenes of devastation. Rosemary bush dead. Forty-foot-tall Bay Tree dead. Of over thirty dahlias the few remaining in a parlous stage due to slug infestation. Buddleia looking dead. Lovely white giant

Lilies, Trumpet plant and Honeysuckle dead. All Roses severely frostbitten. Most of Lavender dead and two hundred feet of hedge along side of garden dead. Several English neighbours say winter so cold they had to sit wearing hats and coats under duvets to keep warm."

The following Spring hailstones the size of Satsumas had dented cars parked only twenty miles away and the spring and summer rains were looking more and more like our English experience.

Battling a two-hundred-foot-long garden every time we arrived was fairly exhausting and it could well take the first two or three days of every trip to wrestle my lawnmower, the mighty McCulloch, under the savage and hostile trees in the orchard; battle with huge new lengths of wild clematis and briar all over the place; weed all the flower beds; replace the dead plants; and cull the "Tree of Heaven" saplings which sprang up by the hundred around the garden.

Keeping a second house was of course a pricy undertaking and we also had the feeling that our underuse of the house was bad for it. It had after all never been built as a second home. We were righting off a washing machine almost annually through limestone scale build up during the extensive periods of disuse. One year we discovered the aftermath of flooding which of course had been neglected all through the winter months of our absence. The Septic tank had never liked us. It dried out during our frequent absences and was no longer working properly.

When it had needed emptying, we had to summon a large lorry which would struggle to gain entry to the garden round the acute angle required. Every time either a tree or the lorry itself paid the price. Once an entire metal wing mirror was ripped off. We obviously couldn't just summon these things when it suited us either. We had to wait for them. One year we were without sanitation for five hot and miserable days. When I felt the urge to poo, I had to drive off to a bar or cafe in a nearby town or village. It was embarrassing for everyone if an English stranger turned up too often, used the convenience, had a quick coffee and ran off again, so these visits had to be rotated daily. The nearest café, in Descartes promptly closed for two weeks necessitating my use of the barbaric public inconvenience with its satanic hell hole in the middle of its unspeakable floor. I still shudder to think of it!

Draining the tank would take hours and on one occasion the driver brought a very young work experience girl with him and took great pleasure in leaning over, showing her the contents and discussing them at length. We could have died of embarrassment.

Our neighbour Seth told us of the time he and his family had been enjoying lunch in a local restaurant when a septic tank company arrived and proceeded to lay their thick pipeline straight through the restaurant to the house at the back and turn it on. Apparently, the French diners didn't bat an eyelid.

Another friend had had the same experience in his own home.

Moreover, our sewerage facilities no longer complied with new legislative requirements. An act had been passed stating that local arrangements were finally to be integrated into one national sewage system. Home owners were to prepare their sanitation systems for the great day. Of course, everyone knew it was never going to happen. There were so many large areas of France where the nearest mains drainage was many miles from local settlements that it would have cost billions to connect them all. The new law however gave purchasers a hefty stick with which to beat rural house prices down and indeed there were real concerns as to whether our house would even be saleable unless we installed a new underground sewage system. Apart from the cost, this would have completely spoilt the view as the mature birch trees on top of the old one would have had to go and we would have been left looking out at a large bald mound.

Oh well, even Adam and Eve found they couldn't stay in Paradise for ever. I don't imagine their sewage arrangements were up to much either?

We played for a while with the idea of selling and tried calling up estate agents who turned out to have left the business, or who simply never turned up. In the end though, it was Yannick's death which made our minds up for us. While he lived Yannick had formed some kind of loose alliance with a ferocious and feral white cat which had terrorised the neighbourhood's wildlife A dissolute elderly alcoholic like Yannick would surely never have remembered when to feed it and the cat would never tolerate the presence of a human within fifty feet, and yet it had based its territory around his house. After his death it became apparent that the cat had lived on a diet of fresh rat. Either they now got the better of her or she just moved on, but one sad day I counted twenty-one fresh burrows along the adjoining fence. That was enough, that and the fact that the "Tree of Heaven" saplings from our garden were now marching unchecked up his garden bent on destroying his house, and so eventually ours.

They seemed to advance about two metres a year and we did once set about culling these brutes. Having decided I was too chubby to hoick up over the fence I delegated the job to Liz and lifted her over. It never occurred to either of us that she might not be able to make it back. We were watched by our other neighbour, the retired baker Hubert from the far side of the garden. He was plainly mystified by our apparent determination to weed the extensive garden for our dead neighbour.

We also had a mole problem. We were happy enough to share our extensive garden with a mole or two, but they took liberties. They built fresh mounds of soil everywhere, even in the bits I could have sworn were just old concrete. They were impinging on the main flower bed and therefore on my treasured Dahlias so they really had to go before we could sell.

I started with mouse traps. Well, I had found a lot of them in the outbuilding when we moved in (funnily enough, in ten years neither of us ever saw a mouse) and it seemed a waste not to try mouse traps first. I discovered moles don't eat cheese.

I thought about poison but it felt somehow like cheating, and anyway I didn't warm to the idea of rotting moles under the garden.

Then I read about their strong aversion to garlic. Moles of course have an amazing sense of smell so moles and garlic were held to be incompatible. One Sunday I bought a liberal supply of the largest smelliest garlic I could find and pushed one chunky clove into every mole mound I could find. I think there were over fifty. That night I fondly imagined Moley and friends disgust at the realisation that it was time to pack up and move on. When I woke next day and bounded uncharacteristically out into the garden, I was shocked to find that he or they had completely evicted every single garlic clove from their subterranean territories.

I gave up, and, robbed of their entertainment, a few months later they moved on of their own accord. A lesson was learnt.

So, we went ahead with the sale.

We started with an English agent with an English firm who quoted a price 25% lower than we (strictly speaking, I) had paid eight years earlier. This produced no viewings and it turned out she didn't even have an office in France.

My diary records that the evening after she left, I sat down with an absolutely overwhelming feeling that the house didn't want me there anymore. It had welcomed two naïve English with open arms but was now sulking over our rejection of what she ("it" had always been a "she" in my mind) had to offer.

That Autumn we tried to switch to a French agent in Descartes. She didn't turn up. Then she didn't turn up again, and again, and then when she did finally turn up, she was very late. She appeared at the same time as the dodgy English lady who had sold us the place and who was now apparently selling the one across the path. It was immediately obvious they detested each other and the encounter was, I have to admit, great fun to watch.

The new agent next produced particulars with the wrong price, for a house in the wrong place with the wrong number of bedrooms. Luckily, we had also commissioned an agent in Ligeuil.

Actually, not so luckily as when we checked on his window some weeks later, we found out he had advertised the price without details of its location or price, apparently to deter potential purchasers from coming round and trying to cut him out of the sale.

Our friend Seth mentioned someone who might be interested and he, a consulting architect, thought the place should be worth what we had first paid for it, suggesting as we thought that all the agents to date had been ripping us off. He personally however was looking for something bigger.

I tried an agent in Loche and we also advertised the place on line ourselves. Both of these approaches produced one enquiry but eventually the one in Descartes somehow claimed a grand total of twelve actual viewings. Odd that we were never in residence when any of them came round?

Finally in October 2015 we had an offer. We haggled, agreed a slight improvement in the proposed price, and returned to England only to be told by the agent not to sign the binding "Compromis de Vente" when it arrived.

For some reason we had to return to France to sign this.

When we did arrive at her office, by appointment, she wasn't there. Her non-English speaking colleague conducted the business and we signed the document one hundred and thirty-six times. Then she found another page to sign. She told us the house was now legally sold, but the new owners didn't actually have a mortgage yet. Her colleague (the one we had been expecting) then turned up to ask us if we had seen the "Diagnostique" which covers provision of services and state of the property. Hers had gone missing!

The following day the new owner turned up at "our" house bearing a tape measure.

Five days later we returned from a shopping trip to find a cavalcade of three carfuls of the owners' relatives waiting to help with the measuring up.

The following day the agent rang us to say the sale had fallen through for want of a mortgage.

We returned to the UK where in desperation I attended a French property exhibition in London sporting a tee shirt advertising our "Property for Sale" complete with rather a good picture. My spell as a human billboard produced many favourable comments and several pictures were taken, but no one expressed any interest in the house itself.

In February 2016 the estate agent rang us in England to say we had a new purchaser. On closer enquiry this turned out to be the previous purchaser – plus mortgage.

Eleven days later with huge feelings of relief we signed a new "Compromis".

Four weeks later the agent rang to say the "new" purchasers might not have a mortgage after all. This was something of a shame as we had by now sold most of the furniture.

Some of this had gone to our French neighbours, who promptly let their dog sleep on our gorgeous new John Lewis leather reclining chairs. The large, rusty and broken artifact I had proudly displayed in the garden which had apparently once been a pump for extracting water from wine cellars, but which looked as though it could easily have once been something far more grand went to English friends. It was almost the only thing I would have loved to have brought home with us, but it would probably have sunk the ferry. We kept only the kitchen clock and some very large kitchen spoons.

Some weeks later the mortgage finally materialised but there was one final hurdle to be overcome. On sale completion there was a deeply entrenched French custom that all parties would turn up at the same location, sign the necessary documents, and celebrate over more than a few drinks. We were in fact at one point told that this protocol, which would have involved us travelling back to France just to sign yet more paperwork, was enshrined in law.

It isn't. We found a Notary Public in Oxfordshire who could legally vouchsafe that the signatories were the same Mr and Mrs Warby who had been sweating over the sale for well over two years. Even then it transpired that no one on the French side had thought to give him the name and address of his French counterpart.

So that was the house sold. Now our problems could really begin. We had protracted battles with water, gas and electricity utilities, the French house money managed to get lost on its way to our bank and over a year later we were still getting threatening letters from the French council tax people threatening to take us to court if we didn't pay up.

It did have its lighter side. On the day we were finally informed that the house money had reached our U.K. bank account Brittany Ferries emailed me to inform me that I had lost a fluffy penguin, but not to worry as it had turned up in St Malo.

I am glad we decided to sell when we did. Neither of us could have gone through all of this five years later. I don't care what anyone says, as far as I can see the French **are** mad. They are certainly maddening and their institutions are grotesque, byzantine, and incompetent. However, they are also fascinating, and in many cases welcoming to strangers, warm and incredibly helpful. I am far more grateful for the opportunity to have owned a small piece of that gorgeous country for a fabulous ten-year period than I ever was furious that they wouldn't let us sell it.

THE FAERIE BOY OF LEITH

Developed from Richard Boyets "Pandaemonium or the Devils Cloister opened" 1684

His wide almost colourless pale blue eyes are staring. They are empty like the lenses of a camera, eagerly sucking in everything he sees around him, just as his ears take in the sound of every single thing that happens nearby. They reveal nothing of the intelligence stored behind them through expression or movement.

He is short with thin fine blond hair. He is only ten years old but is short even for a ten-year-old, and stick thin, wearing dark tired clothes that fit him loosely like old skin.

No one knows where he came from or when he first appeared on the streets of Leigh. He is just there, like the cobbles.

He is fed, sometimes, and often sleeps at the large house on Turf Street established by one of the big Guilds as a charitable Institution to address the needs of the urban poor, and to ensure safe passage into Paradise for the prosperous city merchants who pay for it.

Does he have a name? They call him Tom, Tom the Faerie Boy.

He is approached now by a tall, broad, stooped man in late middle age. Captain George Burton has a short but dense growth of dark beard, greying at the sides, thick accusing eyebrows and a weathered face carved from old rock. The Captain is no fool and he recognises his quarry on sight despite the crowds milling around him.

"You're the boy they call Tom, the Faerie Boy?"

Tom stares in his direction, not into his eyes but beyond them, into his soul. He says nothing.

For a moment the Captain feels uncomfortable. He had almost forgotten he had one.

"They say you drum for the Faeries?"

"Thursday nights Captain."

"What's that you say? Captain eh? And how did you know I was a captain? I hear the faeries gave you the gift of second sight, but then we both know an old sailor walks with a wide gait and rolls from side to side on dry land. I can never quite trust it not to pitch from under me. A good trick lad, but you don't fool me."

"I drum on Thursday nights. Under Carlton Hill."

"Oh, do you now? And how exactly do you get under the hill?"

"There are gates."

"Well, I've never seen 'em?"

“They’re Faerie gates. Only the chosen can see them, and only when they’re there. On Thursday nights.”

“Of course, they are.” The Captain scratches his hairy chin, a habit he follows more for the thick satisfying noise it makes inside his head than because it needs any scratching. “Well Tom, I have a bet going, several in fact, with the folk at the” Keys”. They’re a credible bunch these Scots, but I say you’re either a liar or a fool.”

The Captain has bets placed with most of the regulars of the “Keys”. If he loses, he is finished in Edinburgh. There is no way he could pay them all, but he knows he stands no risk. What kind of imbecile believes this skinny kid is of any interest to the Fairy folk, even assuming they do exist, which he is certain they do not.

He has placed the wagers in the safe hands of Bridie MacIntosh, keeper of the Poorhouse on Turf Lane. She has placed them in a pot high in a tall sideboard out of reach of the orphans. Tom has seen it.

“I’ve wagered I can keep you from these Thursday night parties under the hill. There will be no drumming next week. You are to come with me to a house on Heron Lane. The old place on the corner. It’s owned by Hamish Stewart but its empty at present. I have rented it for the evening. You will stay with us all night and in the morning, I’ll have scotched these ridiculous stories of ghosts and goblins for good.”

He will also have made enough money to give him a year away from the freezing cold and the terrifying storms on the North Atlantic runs he is accustomed to making. The older the Captain becomes the more he fears this bitter unforgiving Sea and its capricious moods.

"No ghosts, only faeries. Some nights we travel to the Low Countries or to France. I have to drum all night, faster and faster, but they feed me well. They wear wonderful things, in strange colours, sparkling like jewels in the candlelight. They are beauteous folk, but they won't be crossed. They are terrible when they are crossed." He says all this into the middle distance. The Captain even turns to see whether there is anyone there.

He scratches again at some length. "Well, I'm not afraid of your hobgoblins and banshees my boy. I daresay I have lived to see worse things than them on many a ship."

--/--

And so, it is arranged. Six evenings later the good Captain arrives before dusk on Turf Street, wishes good evening to the smiling Keeper with the greasy hair and the swaying pendulous breasts and hands over another bag of money to be added to the pot on top of the sideboard. He collects young Tom and takes him without ceremony to the house on Heron Lane.

He has two companions.

"Holy Joe" Hanson is a sailor, a stout, grey haired and god-fearing man who has sailed with Captain Burton for many years. He carries a bible with him at all times and knows it by heart. He is poor company on long cold evenings on board ship for "Holy Joe" has no sense of humour and says little. For all that he is the only crew member on board who does not drink and is as reliable and consistent a sailor as the captain has ever known. Joe speaks only the truth as he sees it and his testament on the morrow will convince all doubters.

On seeing Tom old Joe goes up to him and says solemnly "My lips shall not speak wickedness, nor my tongue utter deceit. Ye shall be kept in prison that your words may be proved whether there may be any truth in you or else by the life of Pharoah ye are a spy"

The second companion is Matty Ferguson. Matty is no sailor. No ship would be safe in his hands. Matty is a drunk who has propped up the bar at "the Keys" for at least a decade now. He drinks more at the Keys" than he can possibly earn at the printers where he works and his poor wife is glad to see the back of him. His value to the captain however is that he knows everyone in that part of town, and it is known that even with a quart of rum inside him Matty misses nothing. There is no trick or slight of cunning hand that Matty has not seen and mastered over the years. The Faerie Boy cannot hope to pull the wool over Matty's gimlet eyes.

On reaching Heron Street they ascend to the first floor. There is a broken window on the room at the back by the drainpipe and its cold inside, but the room at the front is warmer and furnished with a good table and three chairs. They settle down at the table and the captain produces the cards, but Matty bangs loudly on the table and insists they search the house first.

"The front door I ken is locked but are all the downstairs windows locked? Is there a rear entrance to secure, and there must be places indoors where a clever young lad cud hide? Captain, I must insist we search everywhere before we play to make sure this bet is secure!"

The captain can only agree and, leaving the faerie boy upstairs they search the premises. There is a large clock on the landing but not so large a boy could hide within. There is a cupboard on the landing but it is locked. The key lies on the floor so Matty places it in an inside pocket and they proceed downstairs. Here they find the downstairs windows are barred and impenetrable. There is a dusty sooty fireplace, but nowhere within to hide, and there is a kitchen door so they lock it and "Holy Joe" takes the key. There is a cellar, an evil smelling place, but it leads nowhere, contains nothing and can be searched by lantern light if needs be. The house is secure. Now let the spirits come for their drummer if they will?

For the first few hours Matty and the captain play at poker while Joe mutters to himself and buries his long-pitted nose in his Bible. Matty suggests laughing that if the boy truly has the second sight, he would be better employed at the card table than banging away at a drum all night. The Faerie Boy just curls up in a corner and makes no reply. No one has asked if he wanted to come. No one has thought to feed him. No one has said a word to him.

From time to time his ancestors scratch on a window pane or tap on the wooden furniture in the hall downstairs to remind him that even as an orphan he is still watched and remembered.

Matty finishes the last of the rum and Captain Burton sighs, scratches luxuriously, and resigns himself to going downstairs to fetch another bottle.

Matty turns to the Faerie boy. “Where do yoose keep yer drum then boy? I don’t see no sticks?”

Tom ignores him so Matty lashes out with his foot and catches him on the shin.

“It’s a Faerie drum. I can’t keep it. You couldn’t see it if I could.” He rubs his shin and stares at the wall.

“The beginning of the words of his mouth is foolishness: and the end of his talk is mischievous madness. When are yer devilish friends to come for you?” asks old Joe casting a reproachful glance at Matty.

“When they want me.”

“With your famous gift for second sight I’d have thought you’d ken exactly when they were coming” laughed Matty.

Tom stared at the empty rum bottle and then into Matty's soul.

"Three years you've got. Just three years."

Matty shudders and looks away.

The game resumes and in time the players grow weary. There is a sudden noise as a candle downstairs is knocked to the floor. Joe wakes and shoots to his feet.

"Lo, he goeth by me, and I see him not: he passeth on also, but I perceive him not. The boy is gone Cap'n!"

The captain wakes, rises and rushes from the room. He bellows over his broad shoulder. "He's here. He's down here. How the devil did we miss him. Somehow, he slipped past us, but I have him. He can't get out of the house!"

He drags young Tom back into the room by his ear. "Waste of time lad, I have the key here. You couldn't have got outside if you'd tried the door. Your beastie friends will have to party without you tonight." He laughs a rather unpleasant laugh. Perhaps it's the lack of practice?

The night wears slowly on. The old house stretches and creaks as though it has trouble sleeping. Tom just stares that unnerving stare as though only his shell is with them. But that's all the captain needs for his money.

They tire of cards and discuss the sea. "Holy Joe" has never seen a whale. The Captain has killed several. Joe asks about their next journey and the Captain confesses that he hopes it will be a while ahead of them. Joe isn't happy about that and goes to sleep at the table.

Matty looks for dawn but there is no sign. He watches the Captain absently scratching his beard and shakes his head.

"Nearly there Cap'n. What do you intend to do wi all that money? I'm hoping it will be a long time afore I have to buy another drink."

"It's been long enough since you bought the last one, scoundrel!" pronounces the Captain with a slow smile.

They set to cards again. When the Captain has lost enough, he puts the pack away and, checking that Tom over in the corner is fast asleep, rests his weary eyes. The still warm air in the room is thick with the past patiently awaiting the company of the future. The long, watching, waiting hours of darkness are only distant kin to the fleeting ones of daylight. He has long feared the dark.

--/--

Warm sunshine wakes the Captain slowly like the breath of a large animal. At first, he can't remember where he is, but then at once he is wide awake. The wagers. The money. The Faerie Boy?

He looks round but the room only holds the three companions. He groans miserably, "That's impossible!"

The others wake. No one can believe it. They rush outside the house as though the boy would be waiting on the street but of course he's gone.

Matty calculates his situation. The first to the "Keys" with this story earns a few rounds for the information and then a few more in sympathy. He's gone. Old Joe wants to search the house but the captain points out that has already been done. They check the cellar but he is now desperate to be out of Edinburgh before the news breaks. With Matty already off to the "Keys" he has minutes only before the mob come for the money he hasn't got.

Left alone Joe mutters "He disappointeth the devices of the crafty", shakes his grey head ruefully and strolls down to the harbour shaking his head, to look for work.

Back in the house Tom opens the cupboard door and listens hard, but he knows his captors too well. Fancy just accepting that the key he left on the floor underneath it was the real key to the cupboard? That drainpipe would never have taken the weight of a grown man but a slim waif like Tom? Easily. He was safe enough. If there was one thing the faeries hated it was scorn. Having checked the house for a hiding place he had to return the next evening to replace the key he had stolen but he was through the streets as silently and elusively as a feral cat. No one knew him and no one had seen him. His pretence at escape earlier last evening had persuaded his captors readily enough that he had every intention of leaving so they were never going to search the house properly. They would simply accept the story they had tried so hard to ridicule. People always did.

He heads back to Turf Street. The place is empty during the day after Bridie throws the orphans back on to the street for the day while she goes shopping. It stinks of despair. She has no intention of spending longer there than she needs to. She has a kind heart but that doesn't stop her dipping into the money they give her to feed the orphans. Her daily routine is invariable, and Tom knows he has plenty of time to fetch a stool from the kitchen and the thick branch that bars the back door from the inside. With this he gently teases the pot onto the edge of the top shelf. He watches it fall into the pile of sheets and cloths he has placed on the sideboard so it won't break. Bridie has done him no harm.

The bag of money is heavy and he will bury some of it in the pauper's corner of the churchyard where few would risk digging. There is a strong north wind blowing so he heads north. His gift tells him they are gullible folk in Aberdeen.

DRAMA IN LITTLE TRUBLING

Little Trubling is a large, prosperous village, not so much "set" in the Cotswolds as established one clumsy functional lump at a time over hundreds of years, until suddenly by some architectural alchemy a flawless set piece in glowing honey tinted stone lay revealed. It now nested cosily into the folds of the land around it like a sleepy giant, tucked beneath a mottled camouflage blanket of ancient lichens.

The source of its wealth, and that of the villages surrounding it for many miles, has been sheep, thousands of them, patiently chewing their way through the countryside, being worn, eaten and traded and slowly turning green pastures into majestic churches, elegant manor houses and quaint old village halls.

By the nineteen eighties however the sheep are no longer quiet masters of all they survey. The best and oldest properties have been sequestered by a new breed. These are typically parvenues such as venture capitalists, merchant bankers, property developers, cultists, foreigners with large and strangely unaccountable fortunes, and those curious secretive types who stay close indoors making fortunes doing incomprehensible things over the emerging internet. Most don't even live in the village, and those who do live unseen behind high fences and powerful electric gates and are therefore scarcely to be considered part of it. On a day-to-day basis therefore, the remaining residents are able to live out their fantasy of old-style village life, just as long as no one rocks the boat.

The vicar of Little Trubling, Antony Shottwell, was himself an import some fifteen years back, but has long since adapted to village ways. He is now considered an integral part of village society by Christians, atheists and agnostics alike. He is a tall thin bachelor of indeterminate age with a broad and well-worn smile, slightly stooped, and walks with the aid of an old wooden walking stick.

His essential role in the community is of course never more evident than in December when the number of believers rises exponentially as the days shorten, only to plummet inexorably come January. Moreover, in addition to church matters Antony now has to contend with the task of filling the village hall for the annual Christmas Eve Pantomime.

He has chosen the job of selling and seating. It is a simple enough job, tickets traditionally sell like mince pies, but it is time consuming and there is something particularly vexatious about the fact that customers are seemingly keen to buy but less enthusiastic about paying either promptly or in full. He has accepted this with good grace, privately questioning whether an abundance of black queens, wicked wolves, genies or “Beasts” is an entirely appropriate way of raising funds for good local causes, whilst publicly accepting that it works. It works very well indeed and having last year's takings in mind gives him something to aim at.

--/--

Antony Shottwell is not however the hero of this story. That accolade should perhaps rest on the narrow but resilient shoulders of Mrs Dorothy Poundall, producer and director of this year's pantomime and Chair of the Pantomime Committee. Dorothy has the misfortune to have been perceived locally as someone with "time to spare". Her husband Donald passed away in late middle age some ten years hence, painlessly so far as anyone could tell, in his sleep. In the years that followed Dorothy has wrestled womanfully as Chair with the various competing factions of the gardening club. She is a tireless negotiator who can somehow find common ground between those who maintain roses to be the sole legitimate basis for an English garden, and the dahlia fanatics for whom the fairground fantasia of those remarkable blooms constitute a magic world to which access can only be granted to the truly worthy. She can parley with the pro-succulent lobby and banter with the vegetable growers, even managing to pull off the annual outings without fisticuffs. On the premature death of Peregrine Fitzstanley, the previous Panto supremo, Dorothy, whose previous contributions have exclusively been backstage as seamstress, has been by unanimous consent, been snapped up as his heir apparent. It was not negotiable! No pressure, but Little Trubling has come to be defined by its Christmas Pantos. They are invariably talked about for months afterwards and this one is to be no exception.

The Committee has determined that this year's offering is to be Cinderella. It is a popular and well-known tale, with the requisite Fairly Godmother. Many of the gaudy costumes created for last year's Sleeping Beauty and lovingly preserved at Dorothy's insistence can also be recycled. This too is non-negotiable!

Casting has always been one of the most enduring problems. The waverers not infrequently decide that "yes please they would love to be involved after all" weeks after the part intended for them has been allocated elsewhere. It is also rare for autumn flu outbreaks to spare leading cast members. Someone will always have to be unexpectedly absent from the village at short notice and the substantial stock of costumes never quite seems to stretch (literally) to encompass all the new cast members.

This year had thrown up a new problem in the form of a professional actor, not well known to Dorothy, although she vaguely recognised the name. Cedric Amethyst, had moved into Little Trubling the previous March and let it be known that he would simply kill for the opportunity to help with the local Amdram production. Dorothy really could not say no to an offer like that, and the obvious part was that of Prince Charming, which, for a male, had the most lines. Her problem was that Cedric would never see forty-five again and, as she had heard it said, had for some years been "whirring his slurds"

As Cinderella Dorothy had earmarked twenty-one-year-old Jenny Puddles daughter of Dave Puddles the village Plumber. Jenny had been convincing two years earlier in a minor part of "Puss in Boots" and managed to steal the show last time out as a cute Bashful. It was no contest. Dorothy was determined that the young beauty's time had come. Despite regular bar work in the Drovers Rest, Jenny was shy in daily life although she seemed to blossom once in fancy dress. She was charming, modest, reliable and conscientious, apart from which she was by common consent, drop dead gorgeous.

Baron Hardup had virtually selected himself. George Hedges was, in more ways than one, a substantial local farmer. At six foot four with a long grey beard and a bellowing deep voice that could frighten the very wasps from his orchard, George was a natural. You just had to find the right part. He was certainly no romantic lead, nor was he "Buttons" material, but given the need for a miserable self-pitying fatherly figure, George was your man. He slightly reminded Dorothy of the actor Brian Blessed and would need to be kept well to the back of the stage. She could also foresee possible problems between him and Cedric. George was at heart a kind man, but quick to give and take offence while Cedric gave her the impression that he was more sensitive than he at first appeared.

She had no problems with the two ugly sisters either. This could have been a potentially tricky one. She had learnt the hard way that you don't pick the ugliest man in the village as "The Beast" in "Beauty and the Beast" nor did you pick the most attractive female as "Puss" in "Puss in Boots". Give a local a label and it tended to stick. She had solved the problem by casting real life sisters, thus throwing the villagers' attention back on the family relationship rather than the sisters supposed lack of personal appeal. Melanie Hughes worked part time as a stylist at "All Occasions" behind the Co-Op. Her big sister Daisy was married to George Hedges and could be relied upon to keep him under some degree of control (and at the back of the stage). Melanie, was it had to be admitted, rather too glamourous to be completely convincing as an ugly sister but as a stylist she had learnt a certain amount at close quarters about unconvincing make-up.

Her most intractable problem was "Buttons". A bland "Buttons" can be a serious irritation to the audience but no director wants a "Buttons" who acts Cinders off the stage! Nobody came to mind until she attended a production of Henry IV at the nearby Barton Secondary School and discovered a creditable Duke of Bedford whose family had recently moved back into the village. He was a tall skinny seventeen-year-old, by the unlikely name of Hereward Dangerfield. He was clearly bright and appeared to be brimming over in confidence. Although between them he and Jenny would do nothing to help a superannuated Cedric establish his credibility as the romantic lead, she would have to hope Cedric's vaunted west end experience would carry the day.

Amanda Browning had made it to mid-November before admitting to herself that this time she really was pregnant. She had been an outstanding "Puss" and a creditable Snow White, while husband Kevin, a popular village painter, was also a keen member of the amateur dramatics group playing a key backstage role for years. This year however she had decided she needed to devote all her time and attention to forthcoming family matters. "Sorry everyone!" Her withdrawal was a huge concern for the Committee in general and for Dorothy in particular.

Kate Thornton, a relative newcomer, had therefore been her second choice (from a very small pool) as Fairy Godmother and was left with a great deal of ground to make up with little time in which to do it. She had performed as "Doc" the previous year, but Dorothy had serious doubts. She could appear temperamental and was to say the least, a very private person who made little effort to socialise with the rest of the cast. She had come to the village only the previous year, lived alone and commuted to work in the tax office in Burton on the Wolds some twenty miles away. In a sense she was not yet truly a "village" person.

--/--

Inspector Max Gooding was, as was his post prandial habit, battling with the Telegraph crossword when he received a call from Superintendent Samuel Threadgold. He listened with one reluctant eye on the last half dozen unsolved clues, and when the call was over, sipped the last of his cold coffee. He picked up the phone again and rang a Little Trubling number resigning himself to getting back to work. Well, just as soon as he had finished his doughnut.

Max was originally a Londoner, initially selected for branch line duties in the sleepy Cotswolds owing to his widely perceived reluctance to spring quickly enough into action on the promptings of his higher-ups. He was shrewd enough and missed little but seemed dilatory when it came to taking action on his insights. The longer he spent in Burton on the Wolds, and the more time and effort he invested in his unhealthy gustatory preferences, the more it was assumed he no longer fitted the contemporary profile the force was seeking. There would be no return to London, and that was just the way he liked it.

He now thought carefully for a while. He needed a partner and there were few candidates in Burton. He selected young Joe Westleton. In his opinion Joe wasn't the sharpest knife in the station box, but he was tall, powerfully built and looked the part. That would be the important bit. Whatever was amiss in Little Trubling should with any luck largely monopolise their attention at least until the traditional festive mayhem on Christmas Eve. So, only about fifteen minutes after the initial call he had conscientiously downed the crossword for the last time, sucked the last vestigial grains of sugar from his fingers, and put on his overcoat. He walked through to the heavily tinselled general office, and instructed Constable

Westleton to join him outside in his shiny new red Ford Cortina.

Joe, who had joined the modest strength of Burton on the Wolds station only six months earlier straight from training college was by all accounts keen as mustard, and now, taking huge strides with his powerful rugby players legs, all but beat Max to the car. As Max drove off towards Little Trubling he brought his eager young associate up to date.

"A note, on blank cream letter paper, just saying someone expected big trouble at the Panto in Little Trubling and could we please stop it happening."

"Printed, typed or handwritten sir?" enquired Joe.

"It was printed in black and they are sending it straight over. Threadgold says there is no particular reason to take it too seriously as there hasn't been so much as a bike stolen in Little Trubling for as long as anyone can remember. Still, he wants us to be seen in the village in response. Reckons some local with a chip on his or her shoulder might be trying us out, seeing as its our busy season. You know, just checking that the local police are on the ball. God how I hate Pantomime. All that gruesome slapstick, the predictable plots and the compulsory happy ending. "He's behind you! Oh yes, he is, oh no, he isn't! Who do you think could possibly want to disrupt a village Pantomime Constable?"

"Don't know sir. Perhaps a wicked stepmother?"

"Hilarious! The plan is to turn up at the Village Hall for today's rehearsal, walk around, look menacing, you can do menacing can't you constable, ask a few general questions, and leave it at that.

"On the bright side, they do a good meat pie in the Drovers so if you like I can treat you there before we go back. I made a couple of calls and it seems the Head Pantomime Honcho is a lady called Dorothy Poundall. I asked her to let them all know why we are looking in and arranged to talk to her as soon as we arrive."

It was only a few days short of the mid-winter solstice and dusk seemed to arrive like a dilatory dessert sometime in mid-afternoon. On arrival in Little Trubling the Inspector parked in the extensive Village Hall car park. Joe commented as he did so on the extensive and colourful Christmas lights in the area. A small cottage opposite at right angles to the road showed flashing strings of coloured lights from a large shrub in the front garden while a tall pine in front of the hall showed several strings of bright white lights. The large modern house next door to the hall had corralled a sizeable herd of electric reindeer on its front lawn, while an enormous Santa Claus on the roof appeared eager to effect entry to the front room.

"I suppose I should be thankful we haven't got to try and bring him in?" thought Max.

The brightly lit hall was not of recent vintage, but it was solidly built of Cotswold stone and for many years had, if anything, been rather too large for its village hinterland. It could boast a high barn like ceiling and good acoustics although the heating was a source of grief to one and all, now including the local police. It actually felt colder inside than it had out front, a characteristic Max had noted was common to many other Cotswold village halls. On entering the two policemen drew stares from all quarters and Max felt as welcome as a Jesuit priest at a rugby club stag night. That he reflected was the obvious benefit of bringing a uniform with him.

He asked a cheerful, grey-haired lady with a tired air about her, and wearing a stained pinny, to direct him to Mrs Poundall. She sat them both down at a trellis table at the back of the hall next to a rather niggardly Christmas tree which winked spasmodically, and to Max's eyes, somewhat grudgingly. The tired lady offered tea, which both politely declined, and promised to find "our Dorothy".

Mrs Poundall when she appeared proved to be a short elderly grey haired lady wearing her glasses low over the bridge of her small nose. She joined them at the trestle table raising her eyebrows with the air of someone anticipating yet another bothersome task she really hadn't asked for.

"You said someone had sent you a letter saying there was going to be trouble at the Pantomime this year? It was anonymous I assume? Frankly there is trouble every year, but it has never yet come to blows, nor to the best of my knowledge has it ever been a matter for the police. What can I do for you?"

"Well, an obvious start would be for you to fill us in on any known animosity between cast members and whether you can think of any obvious trouble makers?" resumed the Inspector wishing he had accepted the tea as it appeared on an adjacent table accompanied by custard cream biscuits.

"Hm, well we have a new cast member, Cedric Amethyst, who simply will not keep his opinions to himself. He is, or at any rate, was, a professional actor, so he seems to think he could run the whole show single handed if anybody asked him. Mind you, nobody much listens to him and he's about as intimidating as Shepherds Pie. George Hedges is a belligerent old bugger, but I have known him for years and there is no real harm in him. If you were as fat as him and six-foot god knows what, I daresay you would come across as intimidating Inspector. Amanda Browning upset everyone when she pulled out of the Fairy Godmother role very much at the last minute, but she could hardly help being pregnant, well, I suppose she could, but you know what I mean. Kevin, her husband, is still with us though thank God, doing most of the scenery, as he has for some time. I could strangle him sometimes because he is not the most regular attender these days, but he seems to get the job done. I suppose Amanda needs him at home more these days? The rest of them are a bunch of pussycats most of the time, but I guess we all have our moments when things go wrong, and believe me, they do go wrong, regularly, with an amateur panto."

As she was speaking a tall slim elderly gentleman dressed as a vicar approached their party beaming broadly. As there was to his knowledge no part for a vicar in Cinderella, the Inspector deduced that he must be the real thing.

"I am sorry to interrupt you Dorothy but I couldn't help noticing the Constables uniform. Surely our modest efforts haven't attracted the concerns of the local constabulary? At least not before the dress rehearsal? That I know can be a little lively at times but hardly a police matter? Incidentally I was wondering when you might have a moment to discuss ticket sales. They are going splendidly and I wondered whether there might be room for an additional row of seats at the back this year?"

Amanda introduced Reverend Anthony Shottwell to her visitors and explained his role. "Anthony also played a major part in persuading Kerry, Kerry Castle, the lady you met when you first arrived, into helping us again this year. She has been running refreshments for ages. She always does in the end, but she likes to put up a heck of a fight before taking it on. She cleans for a number of houses in the village as well as Anthony's and I know she is genuinely a very busy lady. I don't know what we will do when she finally decides she has had enough.

"…and I'm sorry Vicar, Health and Safety I'm afraid. We will have to be content with the usual seating arrangements, surely you know that by now? Oh, there you are at last!"

She had broken off to address a couple who had just entered the Hall. "I don't think we will need any uglying this evening ladies. Inspector, may I introduce Melanie Hughes and Daisy Hedges to you Inspector, our Ugly Sisters, and indeed sisters of a more fetching nature in real life."

As they approached the table Joe was thinking this was a serious piece of miscasting. Melanie Hughes must have been in her early thirties, maybe too old for him, but if so it was a shame. She was of medium height, curvaceous with a small pouty mouth and short dark red hair. Daisy must have been almost ten years older, petite with a slightly cross look. He could see her doing fierce, but never ugly. And he would not have minded being on the wrong end of "fierce" from her either.

"Sorry we are so late Dorothy; we were just working through our lines at my place. Lost track of time I'm afraid". The appeasement came from the younger of the two.

"Melanie owns the luridly lit cottage opposite the Hall" explained Dorothy. "It appears she rarely feels the need to attend rehearsals unless she knows for sure we are covering her scenes. I think her proximity must offer some irresistible inducement to homeworking. Most of our cast turn up regularly to offer each other much needed moral support and encouragement. However, we make do somehow" added a frosty Dorothy with raised eyebrows fired in Melanie's direction.

Over her shoulder Joe had noticed a broad backed young man with glossy black hair and a full set of positively glowing American style teeth who had clearly noted the sister's arrival with approval. He was working on a large piece of half-finished scenery for the ballroom scene in the body of the hall and didn't appear to be one of the cast. Kevin Browning perhaps? He didn't look much like a Cedric.

"That's the indispensable Kevin Constable, Jack **and** master of all trades. Probably the most valuable member of our team."

Max had pulled back his chair and was saying "Well, I don't see any grounds for concern here, do you Constable?" when a roar from the other end of the hall interrupted him.

Slowly, a large ursine presence rumbled forward from the back of the stage eyeing a small figure on its left like a hungry grizzly spotting a juicy boy scout sunbathing. "Listen lad, you can back off our Jenny for a start. If anyone has even the slightest interest in your tedious reflections on the future of Pantomime in Little Trubling, I am sure they won't hesitate to ask for them. I have heard more "Charming" from a pig in labour than I have from you over the last couple of weeks, so shut it!"

"Well, I must say!" piped the boy scout "I was only offering young Jenny the benefits of my considerable theatrical experience! I played with Jonny Gielgud on a number of occasions you know!"

"Why doesn't that surprise me?" chipped in a thin youth clearly dressed as Buttons.

"…And what exactly do you mean by that?"

"Only that you would probably have found Helen Mirren's Miranda a little "rounded" for your personal tastes?"

"And I am supposed to take that from a preening prepubescent neophyte, am I? I don't think so!"

"That's George, Cedric and Hereford getting to know each other Inspector. The walking skeleton is Hereward Dangerfield, my great hope for the future, the bellowing bladder is George Hedges, and the voice of experience is the (self-styled) legendary Cedric Amethyst". Dorothy stood up and addressed the miscreants. "All right you lot, I can see we have done enough work for one night! Why not get changed and buy each other a nice pint in the Drovers? They don't mean anything by it I promise Inspector" she muttered turning back to her visitors.

"All the same Mrs Poundall, perhaps we will be looking in on you all again after all. In fact, Constable Westleton, could you get the home addresses for the cast from Mrs Poundall here and we'll look them up tomorrow. See if any of them have any ideas who might have written that note."

Joe perked up at these words having spent the last few minutes appraising the delightful blonde girl George Hedges had been protecting from criticism. She had smiled back. Tomorrow would be a delight.

--/--

As promised, Max then steered his Constable down the road to the Drovers Rest in the centre of the village. It was old and beamed with a low ceiling and a number of comfortable looking armchairs, but almost empty. Leaning on the polished bar he ordered two pies and chips and a couple of pints of Wadworth's from the landlord Bert McDougall.

"You know Constable, I can never understand why a strong lad like you bothers with the force these days? I mean what's the attraction? Couldn't you earn far more as a footballer with even a modest local club, or maybe use your obvious physical strength to work somewhere where you could rack up as much overtime as you fancy?

"I don't know sir, must be the uniform or the adulation we get from the public?"

"You know there actually was a time when they accepted that we were on their side. Mind you I can't help but think less of them were on the fiddle in those days. There seemed to be a lot less laws to break."

Bert McDougall returned with the sustenance which Max gleefully accepted.

"Before you go sir, do you ever get much trouble here in the village?" he was asked.

The proprietor smirked, gestured to his considerable physiognomy and replied "Never. To be honest I sometimes miss the occasional fracas. I used to help out at the Queens in Burton. Plenty of good scraps in Burton! It can be **too** quiet round here sometime. We do a fair enough trade in here round Christmas, and I could use a bit more of young Jenny's time over December, though I have to be resigned to the panto taking up a lot of her time. Good thing they only put it on Christmas Eve. Mind you, if they didn't have a bar at the Hall, Christmas Eve would probably be my best night of the year. Mel Hughes helps me out some nights when she can, but frankly the rest of the year it's a bit of a struggle to make ends meet. I know my beer is good, but I think most of those who turn up just come for a chat with Mel or young Jenny. The rest of them are all off drinking posh wine at home these days. I often wish I could move to just being the tenant not the landlord. As it is the rats downstairs seem to think it's their pub. Maybe I should have a go at running a post office eh. Mind you, I'm not really built for processing all that paperwork, am I?"

"Surely the Pantomime can't make much money for the hall in one night?" Chipped in Joe Westleton.

"You have to remember they don't get paid, and its usually a near sell out. The Village Hall also gets a fair bit of sponsorship from old Henry Wainwright."

"...and who is Henry Wainwright?" chipped in the Inspector.

"Local Entrepreneur who lives up on the green with a couple of servants. German apparently, until he changed his name. We don't ever see him in here I can tell you. In fact, you don't see him round the village at all really. Keeps himself out of village life apart from that Pantomime. What you might call a recluse? Apparently, he owns a firm that makes cast metal toys."

"Bit old school, isn't it?" asked Joe. "Aren't they all plastic these days?"

"It's what they call a "niche" market I believe. His "Classic Monsters" figures are collectors' items. They sell all over the world. You know, Godzilla, Wolfman, King Kong, Frankenstein and the like. Big mail order trade apparently, and they go down well in the big London stores. He must be worth a mint the jammy bastard. No justice, eh?"

"I don't suppose they're really toys for kids though, are they?" said the Inspector. "Oh well, can't let these pies get cold" and with that he led Joe over to a vacant table in the snug.

“It seems a perfectly normal little village to me sir, I can’t imagine anything seriously untoward happening here, can you?”

“And I’m sure that’s exactly what they were saying last year in Great Gurdie on the Water just before they found that cannabis factory behind the school bike sheds Constable.”

As they sat down, the Vicar entered the bar, looked around, went up to a couple seated nearby and handed them a collection of loose change. On seeing the police, he waved his stick courteously, stumbled slightly and came over in their direction.

“Mind if I join you? Did you have any luck at the Village Hall Inspector? Kerry told me you are expecting some kind of trouble?”

“Well, I can’t see much to worry about so far” responded Max. “I’m sure you get a few sparks flying at any theatrical production. Have you been here long?” he went on, keen to change the subject.

“Oh, about fifteen years or so. I think one or two people are almost beginning to accept me as one of the locals” he chuckled.

Max leaned forward. “If you don’t mind me asking, and I do realise its none of my business, merely professional curiosity, but how did you get that limp? Vicaring surely doesn’t involve much physical risk?”

Anthony Shotwell sighed "I didn't fall out of a pulpit if that's what you're thinking. It was the war. A ricochet from an ME Bf110 just before Dunkirk. I was no use for infantry service after that."

"You were an army chaplain then"

"Oh no, my parents were originally from Ireland and I was brought up in the country outside Angers. I used to help the local gamekeepers and became a good shot. When I was drafted, I volunteered as a sniper. That's why I ended up on one of the last boats out of France."

"So how did that take you into the church?"

"Well, I had seen the important role the clergy played in rural France. It's simply a way of life I feel suited to. One in which I feel I can make a contribution.

"I became naturalised ages ago, and yes Constable, it **is** how I chose my English name. I'm not ashamed of what I did in the war. I was a patriot, still am, just for a different country. All the same, I don't go out of my way to advertise the fact that I was originally French. You would be surprised how much feeling there is, even in this day and age, against foreigners in these parts."

As he was speaking the pub door flew open and a short dapper man in his forties strolled through. His dark hair was lightly gelled and he looked to Joe a little like a lecherous hedgehog. He rolled his large eyes speculatively around the pub and addressed the lady to whom the vicar had spoken earlier.

“Hi there Mrs Baxter. Any more trouble with your blocked pipes? If there is, just give me a ring, I’ll have ‘em fixed in no time” He chuckled suggestively. “Oh look, Constabulary! Has someone been “tapping” our phone lines? Has there been a “leak” of privileged information?”

“Oh dear” tutted the Vicar. “I’m afraid that would be joker is the infamous Mr David Puddles, plumber and heating engineer of this parish.”

“Has anyone seen my Jenny this evening?” continued the plumber. “Said I would pick her up from the Drovers when they’re done at the hall.”

“She’s still down the hall you daft bugger! Sit here and you can wait for her. I am sure she will be delighted to get you home and out of my way,” bellowed Bert McDougall who was clearly not a fan.

“To be entirely honest Inspector,” whispered the vicar, “and I say this with due consideration, if our David was any more full of himself he would have to fit an overflow pipe. If I were you, I’d go now, you won’t hear any more sense in here for a while. I’ll look after him until Jenny comes.”

--/--

Their first call the next day was to Round Top Farm. On arrival Max was frustrated to hear that George Hedges was busy in Burton that morning. Their paths had probably crossed en route. Still, he was delighted with

Daisy Hedges offer of coffee and a huge slice of Victoria Sponge Cake. Then it dawned on him that the farmer's wife and occasional ugly sister seemed happy to keep him there for what might prove to be a long session.

She was generous in her praise of Dorothy Poundall, although Joe was rapidly forming the view that whatever her skills as a director, Dorothy's casting abilities left much to be desired. Daisy felt young Hereward showed great promise and had an unusual flair for learning new lines, but she shared her husband's obvious contempt for Cedric Amethyst.

"I mean a man who so obviously can't hold his drink shouldn't be going around telling other people how to play their parts should he? No one respects him, and a man with all his stage experience should command respect, shouldn't he? I worry that George is going to deck him before too long the way things are going. Dorothy has asked me to do my best to keep them apart but every time Cedric has a go at someone George goes barging in to their defence. Especially young Jenny. He's always seen himself as her protector. It's just his way I'm afraid, bless him."

Eventually Max managed to steer the conversation round to those he had not caught sight of at the village Hall the previous evening.

"Kate Thornton is fairly new to the village. Tall, short brown hair and frankly rather a large jaw, I mean you're bound to notice! Doesn't open up to anyone much off stage, though she sees to come out of her shell in character. Here is a rumour going round the village that Kate is really a bloke! You know, one of those Transylvanians".

"I doubt very much whether she sucks blood? I think you probably mean transvestites or transexuals?" queried Max, though I can't see how that need hinder her acting career whichever one applies? What is Amanda like?"

"Amanda Browning? In a word, bossy. I've always felt sorry for Kevin tell the truth, he's lovely. She was a good actor though, got her stuff across to the audience well, and Dorothy never had to tell her to speak up like she does with some of us. I'm sorry she pulled out, but it's given Kevin a new lease of life. I know he's not there as often as Dorothy would like, but well let's just say he's taken his opportunity with both hands and to me he seems like a new man for it. Let's just hope it ends well."

"You mean the Panto?"

"Well, yes, that as well certainly".

Max was aware he was being given access to some hidden village confidence but chose to pass on the opportunity to elaborate.

After a second cup of coffee and further matching slice of sponge cake Daisy somehow wandered off on to the subject of village history which was clearly a matter of considerable pride to her.

"We were in the doomsday book" she boasted as though the village had won first prize in a major competition. "You can still find traces of the old "three field system" on our land and there was a small monastery at one time up by Bigots Wood. That disappeared in the fifteenth century of course when Sir Hugh Bartlett bought the land and I suppose things went a bit quiet after that. George can trace his relatives here back to Tudor times and there have been Hughes's and Tilers buried in the churchyard for nearly two hundred years now. There was a spot of trouble over enclosures in the eighteenth century, oh, and there was an armaments factory set up just outside the village during the second world war which they found and bombed. A lot of people lost relatives. Very tragic! Amanda lost an aunt, several of the Tilers were killed, and Bert McDougall lost both his parents. That's why he came to be brought up by his uncle Ted and inherited the Drovers."

Irrelevant as he found this digression, Joe couldn't resist asking. "Who were the Tilers? No one's mentioned any Tilers?"

"Oh, no, well they wouldn't, would they? That was Dave Puddles name before he changed it. Dear old Dave! He didn't think it was a good name for a plumber. Now he goes around telling everyone "Puddles? You get 'em, I sort 'em!" "You must admit, it does stick in the mind?"

"It certainly does!" sighed Joe wincing in his superior's direction.

Daisy continued. “He’s done well for himself has Dave. I grew up with his wife Alice that died about seven years ago. I didn’t really know Dave until then. I know he thinks a lot of himself, but he’s got a good heart and he’s good at his job.” She gestured towards the expensive modern kitchen fittings and added “he did all this for us. He has had to cope for himself since Alice died, and he knows he can’t rely on Jenny for that much longer. You can’t help but feel sorry for him really!”

When she finally paused reflectively Max made his excuses and they left.

“Well, I don’t suppose a farmer’s wife gets many visitors?” chuckled Max. ”O.k. so who’s next? Oh yes, Little Trubling’s answer to Lawrence Olivier.”

--/--

They moved on to Cedric Amethysts tiny Victorian cottage at the far end of the village. At first sight this didn’t look particularly safe to either of them. The window frames were in an advanced state of decomposition and the roof was in a poor way. The tiny front garden was badly overgrown and the doorbell didn’t work. Max banged loudly on the door and felt it shake. Why did he feel angry with the man before he had even got inside?

There was a pause before the door creaked open and Cedric’s bleary-eyed and puffy face peered round at him.

"Ooh, a visit from a man in uniform is always welcome! Two even more so. Dorothy told us you were concerned about the Panto. I'm not in any serious danger, am I? I must say I am mildly impressed that an Inspector should have come out here in person!" Cedric sniffed haughtily and stepped aside to let Max and Joe into the hallway.

It smelt damp and musty. Max resolved to be out again as soon as possible.

"No danger sir, the Super just asked us to have a quick word with the cast members to be sure they had no reason to anticipate any disruption."

"Well, sad to relate, they are not the friendliest of people in this village. You would think, wouldn't you, that such a modest collection of rustic players would be positively ecstatic to be offered the assistance of someone with my extensive West End experience? Drink gentlemen?" Cedric led the way into the living room, a low ceilinged, and even damper smelling room piled high with old magazines and full of chunky bookcases groaning under the weight of decaying and forlorn looking hardback books.

Joe noted the open whisky bottle which confirmed the hypothesis formed when the front door first opened.

"No thank you sir," replied Joe. "Bit early for me, and we never drink on duty anyway."

Max, for whom this was far from being an invariable rule huffed audibly, glanced at his watch, and found to his surprise that it was still just short of midday.

"Poor you! Luckily that's not a constraint often urged upon we poor thespians. As I was just saying, there have been occasions during this production when I have felt physically intimidated by one or more of the natives. There have even been innuendos cast concerning my sexuality! Now let me make it perfectly clear here and now Inspector, I have practiced lifelong celibacy. The supposed pleasures of the flesh remain a complete mystery to me. I've no interest whatsoever. You are both quite safe in my hands."

"Well, that's good to hear Sir." This was far too much information, "but if you feel you have been threatened in any way, you must come forward immediately and give us details."

Cedric sighed deeply "Well, when I say intimidated, I doubt they mean any real harm, I think it's just "herd instinct". You know, the instinct of the pack to protect itself when threatened by a powerful outside force. If they don't want to learn, more fool them, eh?"

They stayed long enough to establish that the "intimidation" referred to was primarily the kind of bellowing from George Hedges and sarcasm from Hereward Dangerfield that they had heard the previous evening. His intentions might fall far short of physical violence, but George Hedges had clearly taken a very personal dislike to Cedric Amethyst. To Max's mind, his aggression had surely to have some specific source, but he couldn't yet see it?

Reassured at least that the "powerful outside force" which was Cedric Amethyst was unlikely to pose a threat, whether physical or of any other kind to anyone in Little Trubling, the detectives made their excuses and with some relief left the stage.

--/--

Their next port of call was The Puddles house, a modern semi-detached building in a small modern cul de sac.

"Dads out on a call, to Round Top I think" smiled a short petite girl with curling golden hair who answered promptly when they knocked.

"No problem" Joe grinned back. "It's you we need to talk to. We are talking to all the cast" he added hastily.

Jenny walked them through to the kitchen, gestured for them to sit and replied thoughtfully: "I gathered from Bert that you met dad last night at the Drovers. He can give me a bit of a problem at times. He seems to think that with mum gone he has to take extra care over my welfare. It's a bit of a pain having him follow me about the place to be honest. I'm hoping he will eventually get used to things the way they are now. He'd better, after all, I'm hardly planning on spending the rest of my life in Little Trubling. Something to drink?"

The invitation seemed to be addressed to Joe but Max cut quickly in to remind them both who was in charge of the enquiry. “You know, I have never known a community so concerned to be filling me up with drink of one kind or another,” he laughed. Then he took in Joe’s earnest expression. “I’m fine for now thanks” he sighed.

“Perhaps you need to get someone to have a quiet word with him?” Joe observed. “I mean you must need a bit of personal freedom, especially in these parts”. He blushed, avoiding the Inspectors frown.

Jenny looked down and said quietly. “I think I can cope with my own dad thank you Constable, although I’m grateful for the offer. Anyway, you said it was me you wanted to talk to?”

“Oh, just briefly” said Max. “Dorothy Poundall will have filled you in last night. Have you felt any particular concerns during this year’s Panto? Has anyone threatened you or have you heard any threats made to anyone else?”

She looked up and smiled again. “None. Absolutely none. Even if I had, I get the strong impression George Hedges would soon see them off. I love this acting stuff. I feel I can relax into it. I wish I could do a bit more to be honest.”

There was a ring at the front door. Jenny jumped visibly “Oh my God! Tell me it’s not twelve o clock already? That’ll be Kerry. She cleans for us Thursdays and Bert lets me stay until twelve to let her in. I’m sorry, if there’s nothing else, I have to be off, I'm due at the Drovers. Do you mind if Kerry sees you out?"

And with that she was gone in a flurry, pulling on her coat, scooping up her house key from the hall table and opening the door to a short grey-haired lady in one continuous action.

Kerry Castle gave them a long appraising look before entering the kitchen. She stood with her head on one side looking not unlike a garden bird pondering whether an inviting feeding table in the middle of an open garden was worth a visit. She seemed to reach a decision and said "I don't suppose you'll be wanting a drink of anything this time of day? And if you don't mind, I need to get on. I do an hour here before the Vicarage and then on to the Drovers by mid-afternoon. Thursday is my busiest day."

"We met briefly last night Mrs Castle" Max responded, reflecting inwardly that Mrs Castle was perhaps the last person in the village he would have expected not to offer him refreshment. "As I recall you help out with refreshments at the Hall as well as providing cleaning services for about half the village. I can imagine that lot must keep you very busy but don't worry, it's the actors I really wanted to catch up with."

"Oh? I understood you had been warned about trouble at the Pantomime? What about the rest of us? What about the audience for a start?"

Max was briefly stuck for an answer. Surely the only threat to an audience would be something like a terrorist attack, or an insurers "act of God", and in Little Trubling Village Hall both appeared highly unlikely?

"Don't worry about them Mrs Castle, but thanks for the thought and I promise I will make sure I check the electrical system at the Hall is up to date before we go back to the station."

Back in the car he checked his notes. Hereford Dangerfield was still busy doing something at school that day even though term had officially ended, and he would have to bus back from Burton. Kate Thornton worked in Burton, but George Hedges was due back at the farm by late afternoon. Melanie Hughes was apparently due to finish work at "All Occasions" about 5.00pm. Best start with a spot of lunch then, check the Village Hall electrical circuitry to keep Kerry Castle happy, then visit George Hedges, and finally Melanie Hughes. Then he could anticipate going home to one of Mrs Gooding's delicious shepherds' pies.

--/--

He didn't enjoy meeting George Hedges. For one thing the large man clearly had no intention of sitting down in his huge farmhouse kitchen but kept pacing around his lair glancing at his expensive Swiss watch for good measure. That would have been off putting enough on its own, but his preferred topic of conversation seemed to be the woes of modern farming. The government were a collection of morons with less sense than his prize ram and clearly intent on choaking him to death with regulations and red tape; the weather had been uncooperative for years and was making it impossible to bring in a decent arable harvest; he was facing a bill for thousands on repairs on his barn; and there were walkers and ramblers traipsing all over his property as though it was their private back garden. Max wondered what would happen if he openly admired the watch or the new central heating which, given the drop in temperature in the yard outside, soon became his main reason for continuing with the visit.

No, George couldn't think why anyone would be bothered about the "bloody" Panto. He wished he had never got involved and could wring that Cedric's neck, but not to worry, he wasn't going to, not this year at least as he had more important things to worry about. If the police had any sense at all they would be spending their time chasing the poachers over at Drabbing on the Wold and not getting under his feet in Little Trubling.

He soon ran out of steam and insisted he had now an appointment with the local vet in his top pasture, waving the watch around as if to prove it. Max and Joe were able to escape to their final interview of the day.

--/--

It was dark again when he reached Melanie Hughes cottage opposite the Village Hall and now bitterly cold. To their surprise her vivid Christmas lights were still not in operation. Max rang the bell and waited, but not for long.

"I was beginning to wonder if you were…" said a breathy but musical voice before Melanie's neat chestnut pageboy haircut appeared round the front door.

"Oh, hello, it's you, the police. Eh, happy Christmas both. Who are you again?"

"Inspector Max Gooding and Constable Joe Westleton. We met briefly last night" Max added quickly, "if you are expecting someone, we can always call back?"

"That's o.k. Come in now you're here." Melanie frowned, bending down to switch on the lights at an electric socket in the hallway. "Come through."

As Melanie was clad only in a short dressing pink gown Max was delighted to follow and was shown to a comfortable armchair in a back room which itself leaned heavily towards pink. There were pink chairs, pink lampshades and pink curtains which were trumped only by a large, and to his eyes hideous mainly pink abstract painting over the fireplace. He was struggling to see much similarity between Melanie's garish interior and her sister's stylish kitchen at the Hedges farm. "My youngest daughter would have loved this place if she could only fit it into her dolls house" he thought.

The lady of the house now sat opposite them, slowly crossed her elegant legs and gave them her full attention.

“Something to drink gentlemen? I like to get something warm inside me this time of year.” She rose giggling and poured herself what looked like a small cognac.

Joe, to Max’s chagrin, again declined the offer (a little word was due there!). Max sat back and explained their mission.

“What kind of trouble?” she pouted “I mean a fight? Is someone going to nick the seat money? Are the parish council going to shut us down for some reason?”

Max shrugged. “I’m afraid at present your guess is as good as mine.”

“Well then?” she shrugged. “I’m afraid I can’t do your job for you.”

Melanie clearly had nothing to suggest and with some reluctance the thirsty Inspector got to his feet again.

“Well, if anything does come to mind, just give us a ring on this number. Come along Constable”.

--/--

And that was that as far as Inspector Gooding was concerned. Their questioning having unearthed no further grounds for concern he dropped any idea of a second personal visit to Little Trubling. What good could it do? The police had been seen to respond promptly and fully to a local concern and he saw no need for further action at this time.

That perspective was to last for a full week before another phone call from a rather strident Superintendent Threadgold. On this occasion, as it saved on time and shoe leather, Max summoned Joe to his office.

"There's been another one. Another letter. Same paper so no clues there. Its Basildon Bond. Sold by the ton and used by nearly every household in the country. The Super's got the original but I can read it to you:

"You don't seem to have taken me seriously. Trust me, blood will be spilt at the Pantomime on Christmas Eve if you don't do something to stop it."

"Threadgold accepts that we did all that was necessary last time, but this one is far more specific. They are talking about actual physical injury this time and it's a lot less equivocal to say it **will** be spilt rather than just "I expect there will be trouble". It's also quite clear that the incident is going to happen on Christmas Eve. At least that gives us a little time, but we've got to go back again after all".

"Who are you worried about?" asked Joe.

"Well after our visits I thought maybe that Cedric Amethyst was due a slap for sticking his beak in where it clearly wasn't wanted. I didn't think that was likely to be serious enough for our intervention. I checked by the way and his birth name is Arthur Cartwright, so you can see why he would take up a stage name. I can't seriously believe anyone is going to make trouble for the vicar just because he was once French, I mean aren't they usually on our side? After our pie at the Drovers, I thought Dave Puddles was a probable pain in the neck to many, but not to us. That was it really.

"If there is a real risk then we are missing it. We didn't catch up with Hereward Dangerfield or Kate Thornton last time round. I'll pick them up, I'll see Kate at work first thing and Hereward afterwards. School will certainly be over for the term by now. Then I think we visit the dress rehearsal tomorrow. When we get there, I want you to tackle Kevin Browning. Go through all the props and stage furniture piece by piece and make sure there isn't a weapon of some kind handy. I will go round the village hall with Dorothy Poundall and check for places you could conceal a weapon or even a whole assailant. If we don't find anything I fear we may need to put in a presence on the night in question. The problem is we still don't have a clue who or what we are supposed to be looking for."

"Why would someone take the trouble to warn us twice of a problem yet fail to tell us who is at risk, from whom, how or why?" queried Joe. "And why make it anonymous?"

"Off the top of my head I reckon either they don't know or they are afraid of the prospective perpetrator. Either way I still don't think there is anything in it. Someone may have overheard someone making vague threats, or even simply imagined someone in the village poses a threat to someone else. I do however now think the person who wrote the note genuinely believes there is an issue here and that means we have to act as if we take them seriously – more's the pity!"

--/--

Kate Thornton worked in a sad shabby looking porter cabin in at the end of a short cul de sac leading off Burton High Street. She didn't have her own office but her colleagues had found tactful reasons for going out once they heard the police were on their way.

"Not much is it? They are supposed to be looking for more permanent accommodation, but they are supposed to have been looking for nearly two years now. I would love to meet the person supposedly responsible for lumbering us with this dump. Probably sponsored by someone on the council we caught for tax evasion?"

She had a deep gruff voice and a prognathous jaw. If these together were otherwise slightly intimidating in a young woman, she otherwise seemed friendly enough.

"I was wondering when the police would get round to me. Most people seem to find me suspicious to some extent. I wonder why?" Kate grinned coyly.

"Well, I don't suppose there's not a lot of crossdressing goes on around Burton" replied Max deciding to address the elephant in the room.

"So, you've rumbled me already inspector." Kate now smiled broadly. "May I ask what gave me away?"

"When we first arrived at the village hall last week you must have been feeling overdressed and decided to take your sweater off. Many women prefer cardigans in the first place and if they don't then they certainly don't take their sweaters off by pulling them over their heads, for fairly obvious reasons!"

"Oh dear, I'm fairly new to all this. It's why I moved here in the first place. They know and accept my sartorial preferences here at work, and of course they have absolutely no bearing on anyone's tax liability, but I wanted to live somewhere where I wouldn't be stared at by people who didn't know me. I keep out of other village affairs, but I do so love costume and I couldn't resist the Pantomime."

"Look, let me come to the real point, have you ever been threatened since moving to Little Trubling?"

"No Inspector, not in the slightest. I started out in the Bristol office but there was a tiny local difficulty over the washroom arrangements. If anyone round here has a problem with the way I chose to present myself they tend to back away and keep their opinions to themselves. I did briefly wonder whether this supposed threat Dorothy mentioned was intended for me, but what harm or threat do I present to anyone here?"

"No, I agree. If you don't feel any threat, then I don't believe there is one. If someone had a strong personal objection to transvestism, I am sure you would know about it one way or another, probably anonymous letters directed to you personally."

"Well, I can reassure you Inspector, there certainly hasn't been anything remotely like that, and if there had been I think I could have coped well enough on my own".

--/--

Mr and Mrs Dangerfield were happy to leave their eldest son alone in the back room with Max and Joe provided they accepted a cup of the ubiquitous Little Trubling tea.

Hereward smiled almost smugly, leaned back in his armchair, stretched his long bony legs underneath him, and asked if he was a suspect.

"For what?"

"For anything really. I mean surely "youth" is a first suspect in most investigations?"

"What would you like me to suspect you of?"

"Gosh, what a question. Do I have a choice?"

"If it helps, I am sure a bright young man like you must be guilty of all sorts of things I know nothing about, but since I don't know about them, you are not suspected of them and I am happy to keep it that way, at least for now. So can you throw any light on these mysterious letters. Oh yes, its letters now, we had another one yesterday. Threatens bloodshed at the performance."

"Interesting. I would have said the biggest threat to the performance came from the Director/Producer. Everybody loves old Dot but she really hasn't a clue about casting. Jenny is perfect as Cinderella but Cedric? Please. Wasn't he born to play an ugly sister? George too if it comes to that. Can you imagine them playing off against each other? Dot herself would make a great Fairy Godmother and for Prince Charming I give you… Kevin Browning, he of the flashing smile. I know he hasn't acted, but he would just play himself in any pantomime I was producing.

"Are you absolutely sure these letters didn't come from a hidden critic? Someone who had been watching our rehearsals and feared the audience would riot on the night?"

Max said nothing for a while. "Oh, you are a clever boy. The second note said "You don't seem to have taken me seriously. Trust me, blood will be spilt at the Pantomime on Christmas Eve if you don't do something to stop it."
"You're thinking they mean stop the pantomime itself? **It** being the actual show? Possible I suppose. I'll admit it had never occurred to me. I can even see someone being highly amused at the idea that Little Trublings annual performance was now so bad the police had to become involved. Of course, it would have to be someone who felt it was that bad in the first place, and someone with a pretty infantile sense of humour. If I ever caught someone like that, I would have to arrest them for a serious waste of police time wouldn't I, so I very much hope I don't hear

from them again. Mind how you go Sir" he added rising to his feet. "And do thank your mum for the tea".

--/--

On their second visit to the Village Hall next day Joe was pleased to see the village Christmas lights were back at their finest. It was especially hard to imagine any real or imminent danger in the cosy setting of the old Hall and its surrounding huddle of sleepy Cotswold stone cottages.

His passenger yawned, brushed the biscuit crumbs from his lap, and reminded Joe that his mission was props and scenery while he would go round the rest of the Hall in minute detail.

Dorothy Poundall met them at the front door looking tired but determined.

"No Kerry tonight I'm afraid, a headache, so no refreshments. We've got the bar covered for tomorrow though just in case. The vicar's confirmed that we have a sell-out performance. Can't get a seat for love nor money now. It seems your cameo appearances last week haven't put anyone off. It may even have helped draw a crowd."

Max was struck by a small wooden cask on the bar. "That's the same beer they sell at the Drovers."

"Yes, Bert very kindly donated it to the Hall. It's been "settling" or something there for nearly a week now. I only hope it's made itself nice and comfortable because it won't be there much longer. He's even volunteered to close the Drovers tomorrow and help us over here, says we have already got most of his bar staff down here anyway. It's a very welcome offer in case Kerry is still poorly. Who do you want to see this time?"

"Joe here is going to go through props and scenery with Kevin if that's O.K. and I was going to ask you to show me round. For a start, I didn't see any changing rooms on our last visit?"

"That's right Inspector. The actors change at the back of the stage, although a few like Kate prefer to arrive fully made up and are happy to go home that way. There's not much room I'll admit, and Cedric in particular has been kicking up about it. Not like the Old Vic apparently where he could have looked forward to his own changing room."

Max took off on a tour of the toilets and, having remembered the relevant scene in "The Godfather" even, rather self-consciously, inspected the cisterns for concealed weaponry. There was a small committee room but the roof leaked badly and it was kept locked. No one involved with the Panto had a key except Dorothy who had access to all areas. He checked it anyway.

In his absence Joe sought out Kevin Browning, introduced himself and asked politely after his wife's health.

"She'll be fine now I expect" he mumbled looking not at Joe but at Jenny trying to change discretely into her ball gown behind him. “Baby seems to have settled down again.”

Joe was shown the Fairy Godmothers wand (wood, cardboard and glitter), Baron Hardup’s two decrepit armchairs (genuine and from Dorothy’s Living room), and the glitterball from the Ballroom scene. The latter, given the weight of the real thing, could have posed a threat had it not have been constructed from glitter covered polystyrene and aluminium foil and bereft of any electrical components.

“If you are worried about the threat from glass stiletto’s” laughed Kevin “don’t be. Jenny is using a pair of her own shoes. If they posed any kind of threat, she would have noticed months ago. And if you are thinking we have a Hollywood grade coach and four hidden somewhere on the premises forget it. For a start I can’t draw mice, and anyway we’ve got nowhere to store a thing like that. Its all “off stage” in this production. To be honest, the more you use your imagination throughout the better! Mind you, you might want to check the sweets?”

“What sweets?”

“It’s an old Panto tradition. I can see you haven’t got kids Constable. You’re expected to throw great big handfuls of sweets into the audience about halfway through. The kids love it. Can cause a near riot some years.”

Joe gulped. Was this what they were missing? Had some rural psycho nobbled all the sweets? Were they on the verge of a mass poisoning?

"I mean I guess you would have to eat the lot to be sure," laughed Kevin. "Let me know if you want any help?"

Thinking what he could do with a set of teeth and a smile like Kevin's Joe thanked him and helped himself to a brief tour of the limited scenery which was painted on harmless looking old and slightly musty cotton sheets.

Behind him he could hear the long running war between Arthur Cartwright, aka Cedric Amethyst and the rest of the cast re-igniting.

"There is simply no other way to play it! If you want to take the audience into your confidence then you have to come to the very edge of the stage" bleated a thin whining voice. "It's how they do it at the RSC".

"Well thank you Tinkerbell!" That from Hereward.

"What would we do without our handsome Prince, Little Trublings answer to King bloody Lear" that from George.

"Hm, well I suppose Philistines must come in all sizes!"

Joe and the Inspector now re-convened by the bar increasingly convinced that the pantomime trio were positively thriving on confrontation.

"Nothing? Me neither. I guess we are going to have to be here tomorrow after all. You know, I couldn't find any history of Cartwright/Amethyst ever having worked in the West End. He seems to have re-invented himself since moving down here. What little work he does seem to have had over the last two decades has been "end of the pier" stuff. I imagine he must have moved out here on cost grounds? Still, he probably is something of an expert on Panto's."

"There was just the one thing came up Inspector?"

"Eh?"

"Sweets. They throw handfuls of sweets at the audience".

"Oh no, no sweets" insisted Max. "It would be easy enough to substitute new ones at the last minute so to be on the safe side, no sweets tomorrow night". He went off to inform Dorothy of his decision leaving Joe to think "well I guess that means we've done our best to ensure there really **is** a riot tomorrow."

Max again suggested they adjourn to the Drovers to take stock. He had something he very much wanted to ask Bert McDougall.

--/--

"Last time we were in here you were telling me your pub ran on a shoestring and that the Pantomime was robbing you of one of your best nights takings. Now I'm told you have not only donated a keg of beer to the Village Hall, but you are actually prepared to serve it yourself, and close the pub into the bargain. Why would you do that. Do tell?"

Bert said nothing for a long time and then took a deep gulp of his pint. "Civic pride Inspector. I also have little to lose? I may resent the competition on Christmas Eve but I am proud of our village and all we achieve and I am as keen to see the panto succeed as anyone around here. I'll get to watch it too, and that'll be a first. The publicity probably won't hurt business either."

Max saw little point in pressing the matter further but by his count he had been given at least four reasons for the landlord's goodwill gesture.

--/--

The performance was of course a matinee. The Carol service opposite was not until six pm and was seen by many of those involved as the second part of an integrated entertainment. Max led a contingent of four and entered at two thirty, half an hour before the first act. He stationed two uniforms outside while he and Joe checked the hall thoroughly and took temporary station at the back of the Hall.

Dorothy joined them scribbling on her clipboard and raised her eyebrows to enquire if there had been any further developments.

"I still see no reason to cancel the performance, we haven't discovered a damn thing. I am sure there would be a public outcry if we stopped it going ahead for no good reason."

"And a far bigger one if someone gets hurt?" thought Joe who was feeling rather less complacent.

Kevin marched up to complain to Dorothy that Cedric had just reversed himself into the side of Hard-up House causing substantial damage to the set which he couldn't be responsible for fixing before the performance. In his view, drink was a factor.

Dorothy sighed deeply "Just do your best Kevin, that's all I can ask of any of us. Has anyone seen George or Kate yet? Why does someone always have to push it to the limit?".

Villagers were piling in now, filling up whole rows and chattering excitedly about the forthcoming show and Christmas in general. Many families had clearly been filled out with grandparents or grandchildren from outside the village, here for the next few days. Behind the bar Kerry Castle was still absent but Bert McDougall had taken charge of a small group of volunteers who were laying things out although it had been made clear nothing was to be served until after the performance. The authorities were making sure it was carols not rugby songs which would ring out around the church later that evening.

Max stepped on stage and ventured behind the curtain.

Cedric was already in costume, muttering lines to himself and looked pale and terrified. Hereford Dangerfield greeted Max with a little wave and slipped into his Buttons outfit. Melanie and Daisy were on the far side, Melanie helping Daisy who seemed to be in some discomfort, with her eye makeup. Was that a bruise she was covering up? Jenny, he knew was out front talking to Joe which just left George and Kate as the only absentee cast members.

He turned and went back into the main hall. Dorothy was approaching to inspect the damaged set and he asked if she had yet seen the missing duo.

"To be fair, Kate always gets changed at home. I am reconciled to the fact that she won't turn up until the last possible moment. George often says he feels "a pillock" when in costume. He may be hiding in the gents for all I know, but if not, I have every confidence he will appear shortly wherever he's got to."

Max looked over at the audience. The place was packed but something was wrong.

"I thought it was supposed to be a sell out?" he asked Dorothy. "There are two empty seats either side of that old man in the third row over there."

"That's Mr Wainwright. I don't know who bought the empty seats but I can check for you easy enough."

Dorothy fetched a large sheet of paper out from behind the bar. "It seems the vicar bought them. Strange, Old

Henry Wainwright isn't a churchgoer, I don't think they know each other. I wonder who the Vicar can be bringing along."

Max rushed over to Joe who was still deep in conversation with Jenny Puddles, "Get up there now and get that old man in the third row out of his seat. Be careful, but get him out of it asap. The vicar had every seat in the house to sell, why on earth would he end up with two for himself that were not even next to each other."

Joe raced across the hall, excused his way through the crush to the old man, spoke to him briefly and helped him up carefully and took him along the row to the central aisle and back to the bar area.

On instinct Max headed for the window at the side of the hall alongside the third row. What could he see? Nothing. Take your time Max. Only the church tower. But there was a light on in the second storey. Who had access to church towers on Christmas eve? There were no bellringers in the Village. They relied on recordings. It had to be the vicar surely. So why the two tickets purchased if he wasn't going to watch the show? He should be here! Max walked quickly back to the bar.

"Dorothy, I am afraid we can't let the performance start just yet. We need to check something out urgently first. Joe, with me now."

Before either of them could move however, a woman in an obvious state of pregnancy pushed through the doors and scanned the crowd.

"Jenny, you need to come quick. Its your dad, He's been involved in some kind of accident on the High Street on the way down here. I rang Burton Hospital and they are sending an ambulance. It doesn't look good love; he was by the side of the road. There's blood! You're going to need to get over there. Kevin, help her down here. Now!"

The Village Hall went silent as the implications of the woman's outburst sunk in.

Dorothy was the first to speak "Hang on, it's my decision who…oh bugger it. If Cinders isn't going to the ball neither is anyone else." She raised her voice. "I'm sorry everyone, we will have to reschedule. Bert, I think we had better open the bar now, don't you?"

"I could take her". Joe volunteered eagerly.

"I'm afraid you can't lad" interjected Max. He addressed the pregnant woman he now realised must be Amanda Browning. "You're right. You need to get Jenny over to Burton general as soon as possible. Joe, you have to stay close to me, we're going over the road to the church."

Max led the way outside and across to the dimly lit, crouching profile of the old church. Somehow it didn't feel at all festive. It proved to be unlocked and bursting in he found himself almost choking in the cold air of pious ecclesiastical rectitude that leads people to lower their voices in a church.

Peering through the thin candlelight he found Kerry Castle wringing her hands at the foot of the tower and talking to an unseen presence on the stairs.

"But you can't shoot anyone today, Vicar, they're going to have to cancel the Pantomime." She turned at their entry. "Oh, Inspector I saw Dave Puddles go down under that big green van thing, but the Vicar won't believe me. He thinks it's a trick. You've got to stop him. He's going to kill Henry Wainwright. He's got a sniper's rifle from the war. I saw it a while back when he was cleaning it thinking I had finished for the day and left the vicarage."

"Why on earth didn't you tell us?" shouted Joe.

"We were wrong" replied Max rushing over to the tower "It wasn't fear of the perpetrator, it was love. She didn't want the old fool put away!"

By now he was halfway up the narrow circular staircase and found himself facing a long thin rifle with a sight at its tip.

A gentle poke from the gun was all it took to incentivise him back down the stairs and into the body of the church.

"I have had this a long time Inspector, but I can assure you it still works perfectly well. I didn't tell you everything about my wartime experiences. After my injury, I knew I could shoot as well as ever. I volunteered to go back to work with the SOE. I was after all; a trained assassin and they had a considerable need for my services. I posed as a priest. Priests moved around a lot at the time so I could move from cell to cell. No one questioned my appearances too closely. What harm could a priest with a severe limp do?"

"But what on earth can you have against an elderly Cotswold philanthropist that would lead you to want to kill him?"

"Heinrich Wagner, aka Henry Wainwright, was the Wehrmacht commandant in my base area of South Touraine. He conveniently developed a limp himself a few weeks before the Normandy landings and was soon using a walking stick. Clever man. When his unit left the area a few weeks later he took with him a small column of very rich people.

"They were quislings, people the resistance very much wished to get their hands on. Some of them had given evidence against my colleagues. We knew they had paid for their passage in gold, but no one else could work out where he put it. It could have not been more obvious to me, walking as I had been with the aid of my stick. You could see just by watching him that his walk was wrong and the stick far too heavy. Unfortunately, he was gone before I could catch up with him.

"You never forget the face of an old foe inspector, even years later, and there he was waiting for me when I arrived in Little Trubling. He must have used the money, that quisling gold, to start his business enterprises. I had brought my old sniper's rifle back to England with me. It was like an old friend I just couldn't leave behind. I have wanted to kill him for years but I was never able to bring myself to actually pull the trigger."

He paused for breath before continuing "They want to move me next year. To a parish on the south coast. It was now or never, so I came up with the perfect plan. I created the opportunity to place him exactly where I wanted him. Seat five row three. Right in the sight line from the first floor of the church tower. I could pick him off any time in the next one-and three-quarter hours. Kerry found me cleaning the rifle weeks ago. I had to tell her why to shut her up. She wanted me to stop of course, but I was certain she wouldn't be able to bring herself to turn me in. The poor dear woman has feelings for me you see, though I swear I have never encouraged them."

"But you were never going to do it were you Vicar. That old man must have been in your sights for a good fifteen minutes before we moved him to safety. Just when do you think you were going to take a shot?"

"I… no. You're right of course Inspector. Of course, you are. I realise that now. When it came to it, I still just couldn't do it. It's been too long and I can't bring myself to hate him enough anymore."

"It's not just that Vicar. You're a good man whether you like it or not. You couldn't even bring yourself to kill a nasty old Nazi." Kerry was walking slowly towards them with her arms outstretched.

Anthony Shottwell made a strange whimpering noise, turned his rifle round and passed it to Max. "You have got your man; the show can go on."

"Except it can't" Joe explained. "Kerry was telling you the truth. They are going to have to postpone the performance for tonight at the very least. No Cinders, no play. Her dads been hit by a vehicle and they're both on their way to Burton hospital. They've opened the bar now so I don't think there's any going back and.... oh no. You told him, didn't you?" This to Kerry.

"Told who what?"

"Bert. Bert McDougall. You told him the vicars secret? And I bet you told him Henry Wainwright was a Nazi."

"Well, he is, isn't he? Bert's another good man. I was just chatting a while back while I went round the pub and it somehow slipped out that I'd been worried sick. I think I was hoping he could talk some sense into the vicar but as far as I know he never said a thing."

There was desperation in Joe's voice "Well he wouldn't would he. The Nazi's killed both Bert's parents in an air raid. I can see now why he donated that keg to the Village Hall. Being down there tonight gives him a chance to level the score. All he has to do is slip something into Wainwrights drink".

"Get over there now! Instructed his Inspector. Don't let Bert McDougall near the bar and above all don't let him serve anyone a drink. Vicar, consider yourself arrested. Stay here, both of you. We can deal with the formalities later" and with that he spun round and followed his Constable rather breathlessly out of the church.

--/--

Back at the Hall the mutinous audience and frustrated actors were gathered at the bar insistent on drawing recompense from the small team serving them. Drinks were being handed back to one another at high speed when Joe flew in and looked round urgently for Bert McDonald and the old gentleman he now knew as Henry Wainwright.

There was Wainwright, the diminutive figure at the bar talking to Kate Thornton and Kevin Browning. So where was Bert McDougall?

Ah there he was, directly across the bar drawing pints for someone.

Joe flew into the crowd spilling drinks in all directions, but he reached the group just as Wainwright accepted a half pint and tilted it towards his mouth.

"Poison" gasped Joe tilting its contents into an astonished Kevin's nether regions.

"What the…" gasped Kevin drawing back his right arm for a reflex punch at the outstretched young policeman.

"The warnings" lied a quick thinking Joe. "The drinks may be poisoned. Explain later".

There was a loud bellow from behind the bar as Bert McDougall grabbed the nearest pint glass with obvious intent. For a man soaked in beer, Kevin Browning was quick on the uptake and redirecting his punch he knocked the pint out of the publican's hand. More beer everywhere.

Bert simply reached behind him for an empty cider bottle, smashed it over the bar and swung it in the direction of Henry Wainwrights jugular.

Kate Thornton then made her presence felt, intercepting the swing with her left hand before delivering a thunderous right hook to McDougall's jaw. The man jerked backward into the wall behind, bounced forwards with a vacant expression and came to rest.

"Bert McDougall, I am arresting you for ..." Joe was out of breath and out of ideas.

"No you're not" came an older voice behind him. "Not yet anyway".

Max came closer and explained. "You have just poured any possible evidence all over the village hall floor on my instruction. There's plenty of beer down there already and we do generally need evidence before making an arrest remember?"

"Oh hell!"

"Well, have him searched. Perhaps not here though. Get them to cuff him and take him behind the stage. With any luck he will still make a confession and we'll be back in business. Tell them to wait there for me." He turned and leaned over the bar where Bert had sunk to his knees holding his jaw, shaking his head slowly and wondering when a female had last hit him as hard as that.

"Still miss the rough stuff? You're not going to run away now are you, Bert? I didn't think so. After all. you're hardly the type to have prepared a getaway plan."

He turned to the baffled looking old man next to him. "Now Mr Wainwright, you and I need to have a little chat. Could you please find a seat somewhere quiet? I need you to be patient, I'm afraid. Constable Westleton and I have to deal with another matter first. Joe, check whether George Hedges ever turned up here, I need to check the car park for his Landover. I imagine that's what Mrs Castle meant by a big green van thing, it's what he had parked outside Round Top farm last week."

"What Joe, by the look on your face you don't see George Hedges as responsible for the injury to Dave Puddles? Oh, yes, he is! Who else do you think was likely to run Dave Puddles over? Amanda said there was blood spilt so there is likely going to be some kind of evidence on the offending vehicle. With all these people coming and going he won't have had the opportunity to clean the thing up yet. After he hit him, he'll either have driven straight on to the Village Hall or else turned round and gone back to the farmhouse."

"He's not going to be that hard-to-find Sir, he's behind you!"

"I beg your pardon."

"George Hedges, he's behind you!"

Max turned round to find the woebegone figure of George Hedges standing nearby. He looked as though all the air had been sucked out of him, more bearskin than bear. Seeing Max, he came forward and loomed over the Inspector like a big grey cloud of misery.

"Have I killed him? Dave, I mean. I couldn't help myself. I came back early the day you came to the farm. I found a plumber where I wasn't expecting to find one. I've had my suspicions for weeks. You know he didn't even bother to bring so much as a spanner as cover. When I saw him outside just now crossing the road, I remembered that's what happened to Alice, his wife. She was run over. Terrible shock to all of us in the village, especially me. I loved her. Jenny was mine you know. He didn't deserve either of them. Maybe he knew. Maybe my Daisy was his idea of revenge, or maybe she just took pity on him. It would be like her that would. I couldn't resist the opportunity. I've felt sick ever since. Just take me away please. I'm not going to cause you any more trouble."

Max rolled his eyes. "If my higher ups knew all that was going on round here, they would probably declare martial law in Little Trubling! Joe, book him and take him back to Burton Station. That's one down anyway. Then you can go on to the Hospital and let me know how Dave Puddles is doing."'"

--/--

The Church was occupied by a murderous if remorseful vicar and a lovelorn cleaning lady, there was a possible killer on the way to Burton Police Station, and a wannabe poisoner in custody behind the stage in the village hall where the bar was still full of people clambering for their money back. For a moment Max was stumped and dreamt of a quick restorative pastie.

Then he decided to start with none of them. He started with Henry Wainwright.

Wainwrights not unreasonable first question was "Why would the local pub landlord want to poison me?"

"He thinks you're an old Nazi who made his money out of smuggling quislings out of Touraine. His parents were killed here in Little Trubling in a German air raid."

"Oh, for goodness' sake! Not that again. I have never been a Nazi. I'm not even German, I'm Austrian. Is this the old walking stick story again? I thought when I moved here, I had left all that nonsense behind me. Even my own men couldn't leave that idea alone! The fact is I had an infected toe before Normandy and no time to get it looked at. Very painful. Look, to a Wehrmacht officer, resistance members who targeted our men were terrorists. The people I escorted out of danger were our responsibility. If I had left them behind, they would have been strung up on the nearest lamppost. I can assure you I didn't make a penny out of securing their safety, and for what it's worth once I got them out of danger, I surrendered in Normandy first chance I got. That's how I came to be locked up over here. I have spent my life since the War trying to make amends for having had to fight on the wrong side. Isn't it a little bit harsh to be trying to kill me over twenty years later?"

"I see. I must admit I don't think I have never met such an unpopular philanthropist. You know if we explain all that to Bert, he won't be trying it again, not on you or on anyone else. You weren't hurt, were you? I thought not. Look, just at the moment we don't have any evidence. I could probably find it easily enough on Kevin's trousers, but I don't suppose you would be prepared to forget the incident, say in exchange for Bert paying to have your suit cleaned ... and perhaps offering you free beer for life in the Drovers?"

"Hm, I'll have to think very hard about that Inspector."

"Incidentally I'm afraid he's not the only person who intended to kill you this evening but I'll have to explain about that later. You are absolutely safe now."

His next stop was the church.

Anthony Shottwell and Kerry Castle looked at him bleakly as though he was about to have both of them put down. "At present no one but the four of us knows what you were thinking of doing sir. You are not going to try again, are you?

"Mrs Castle, if I waive charges and confiscate this horrible old museum piece, no, I mean the rifle not the vicar, will you promise me you will keep a close eye on this silly old man?"

Kerry vigorously nodded her assent.

"Oh, and by the way vicar, Henry Wainwright denies taking any money for the quislings escape and I doubt anyone could possibly prove anything about that after all these years. He claims he wasn't even a German. I'm going to have his story checked out as far as I can, but assuming he's telling the truth, and if I can be sure there isn't going to be any more silliness round here, then that could just be the end of it as far as we are concerned.

"And Mrs Castle, please understand that not all Germans were Nazi's. It's a very dangerous allegation to make. You could very easily have got the man killed even as you were trying to save him! I am going to suggest the two of you have a long chat with Mr Wainwright at an early opportunity."

Max then re-entered the Village Hall which, bereft of refreshment and the prospect of further physical violence was now emptying fast. He went back behind the stage.

Here he found Bert McDougall sat with his head in his hands. He glanced up at Max and muttered with evident discomfort, "I can't believe what a punch that woman throws!"

Max looked at the constable in attendance and whispered "yes, I rather think someone may have blown their cover there!"

He noticed the uniformed constable was beaming smugly.

"He had this in his left-hand pocket sir" he said holding up a small jar of white powder, "and this in his right-hand pocket" he went on holding up a small brown bottle half full of something.

"The jar is rat poison Inspector, but I never used it. It's a horrible death. In the end I used the laxative. I get it for a little problem of mine and I have been concentrating it for days. Thought that would be lesson enough for the bastard. He wouldn't have been able to stand up for at least a week."

"The only one going to learn a lesson round here is you Mr McDougall. Wainwright says he wasn't and isn't a Nazi, and I am going to check his story out as far as I can. Even if he was, he wasn't the one who bombed the village and you can't go round poisoning everyone you dislike, otherwise hardly anyone would have any neighbours left. As you didn't actually **do** anything, and provided he is happy with the idea, we need not proceed with any charges. If we borrowed Kevin's trousers, I could check your story out, and I doubt Mr Wainwright will feel he has been denied too much justice if we pass on a possible charge of attempted incontinence?

"There are of course conditions, and I can see him becoming a regular customer of yours from now on. You can use the opportunity to get to know him a bit better than you do at present. Other than that, I think a punch from Ms Thornton was probably punishment enough.

"Take the cuffs off him constable and give him a lift back to the Drovers. You know Mr McDougall you're a very lucky man. I understand what motivated you – no, please don't comment again, but it sounds as if you were very wrong about Mr Wainwright. Your job from now on is going to be making sure he falls back in love with the village."

He then rang Joe at Burton Hospital to receive the welcome news that Dave Puddles had only sustained a broken leg. Furthermore, he was refusing to press charges.

Joe explained. "He says **he** always knew Jenny wasn't his but if he goes into court, the whole village will know. Says she's worth a lot more than that. He said something about how now George Hedges knows about him and Daisy they're about even. He also said he's got more than enough action to be going on with elsewhere in the village. Oh, and he apparently noticed Mrs Castle over the road when it happened. Says he's already phoned her from the hospital and she's not so sure now what she saw. Says she agrees with him that she was "in a bit of a state" at the time. He may not be quite the prat first I took him for. What do you think sir?"

"I think, on balance that's great news, for us at least. After all our first task is always crime prevention. My last task today will be going back to Burton nick for a severe word with that Hedges idiot. Just think of all the paperwork we have saved the taxpayer and which we won't now be completing tomorrow. Instead, I can give my full attention to one of Mrs Gooding's unrivalled Christmas dinners. I am sure she could make an extra place available if you're interested? I feel I may have considerably underestimated you and I owe you an apology."

"That's very generous of you sir, and good to hear, but Jenny Puddles mentioned that she's left with a lot of Christmas food now Burton Hospital are keeping her dad in overnight. She has generously offered to share it with me".

"I remember asking you a while back why you joined the force? I'm beginning to think I now understand your thinking. Happy Christmas Constable. Oh, and it might be an idea if you were to look in at the Drovers on a regular basis for a while just to make sure they're all keeping the peace down there, assuming you have no objections?"

Joe glanced at the phone number scrawled underneath the slogan "Puddle's? No Problem!" on the card he held. "Already got that in hand sir. Oh, sir?"

“Yes Constable?”

“Jenny said she was worried about Amanda Browning. On the way over to Burton Hospital, Amanda was saying she had put up with Kevin long enough. Apparently, she knows all about Melanie Hughes and her flashing Christmas lights signals and the only present her husband is going to get tomorrow morning is a compulsory sex change.”

“Constable?”

“Yes sir?”

“Oh no he isn’t!”

Printed in Great Britain
by Amazon